The Contract

The Black Ledger Billionaires

Rebekah Sinclair

This novel contains **mature themes, explicit content, and dark romance elements** that may be **disturbing or triggering** for some readers.

This book is **intended for adult audiences** and **reader discretion is strongly advised.** If any of these topics are sensitive for you, please proceed with caution.

- Sex Work / Escorting
- Sexual Power Dynamics
- Toxic relationships & power imbalances
- Physical violence & aggression
- Emotional trauma & abandonment
- Revenge, coersion & blackmail
- Explicit sexual content & masturbation
- Explicit language & derogatory / degrading terms

- Past sexual assault (referenced)
- Past child abandonment (referenced)
- Past successful suicide (referenced)

The Black Ledger

Welcome to The Black Ledger

An elite, highly exclusive escort service where billionaires strike discreet deals, and escorts set their own terms.

~ No complications.
~ No attachments.
~ Just business.

But desire is never that simple.

Here, control turns into obsession, rules are meant to be broken, and the one risk no one dares take—falling in love—may be the most dangerous deal of all.

Because at The Black Ledger, contracts are final...

But hearts were never meant to be part of the deal.

Each book is a **standalone** with interconnected characters. ***No cheating***, ***no cliffhangers***—just powerful men, the women who bring them to their knees, and spice that will leave you breathless.

Thank you for choosing The Black Ledger and we hope you enjoy your contract.

Lucian Vale

*To the reader who use to watch
Pretty Woman and thought...*

Yeah, but make it darker. 💋

Chapter 1

Elena

"**M**iss Moreau, lovely to see you again. We have your table ready."

The hostess leads me through the softly lit restaurant, the familiar hum of conversation and clinking glasses filling the space.

"Thank you for taking me without a reservation."

"Of course."

She walks ahead of me—sleek black heels, a black form-fitting dress ending just above the knee. The air carries the rich scent of seared steak and expensive wine—comforting, in a way.

My phone buzzes in my hand just as she stops next to a small table for two.

A long-cushioned booth, wrapped in buttery-smooth leather the color of whiskey, is cool against the back of my legs as I slide in. A single, empty chair sits across from me, giving me a full view of the dining room—an old habit.

The cloth napkin glides across my lap as the heavy gaze of the man seated at the next table brushes against me.

I ignore him.

I'm accustomed to pulling the attention of powerful men.

Used to being stared at.

Sized up. Admired. Wanted.

It's my job.

And I'm damn good at it.

But I'm not working tonight.

My new contract starts tomorrow, and coming to *Ember & Ash* for my favorite steak has become my ritual. My last indulgence before I become whatever version of myself a man has paid for.

I swipe open my phone, seeing a text from my real estate agent, Nina.

> NINA: You are spot on. This little bakery is in the perfect location. I can't believe no one has scooped it up yet.

> ELENA: So, still good for Monday then?

> NINA: Still good! We'll get you in before anyone else snatches it up. This place is meant for you.

A small smile tugs at my lips.

It *is* meant for me.

I've worked and saved for four years to buy this place. And with this last contract's bonus, I'll finally have enough.

Sliding my phone onto the table just as a waiter

approaches with a glass of water, I place my order without needing to glance at the menu.

I've been here enough times to know what I want—something indulgent. Something real. A reminder of who I am before I spend the next two weeks pretending to be someone else.

"The Velvet Ash, please." I hand my menu over.

At the same time, a deep voice from the table next to me orders, "Ember Reserve."

The sound of it sends a chill running up my arm, and I can't help but glance at him.

And God—what a man.

The kind of devastatingly handsome that makes women *ruin* their lives.

Tall. Broad-shouldered beneath the tailored cut of his black button-down. His sleeves are rolled up just enough to reveal strong, tanned forearms, veins pronounced along the back of his hands.

But it's his face that really does it—strong jaw, dark hair tousled just enough to look *effortlessly expensive*, and piercing blue eyes.

Blue, like the sharp edge of a blade.

And right now, they're looking directly at me.

I feel the weight of his gaze settle over me.

Assessing. Lingering.

Not in a way that feels intrusive.

But rather... *intrigued.*

I hold his stare, raising one sharp eyebrow in silent response.

"Would you like to pair that with the Siren's Pour?"

I nearly forgot the waiter was still at my table.

"Yes, thank you."

The 2015 vintage merlot. My favorite. Along with the slow-braised short rib I ordered, it's my go-to.

"The Wolfe's Reserve."

The man gives his wine order just as bluntly as he ordered his meal.

The most expensive bottle in the collection.

Someone trying to prove something?

"And what are you celebrating tonight?"

It's him.

I barely turn my head, only enough to know he's talking to me.

"Who says I'm celebrating?"

These men of power expect everyone to dance at their feet.

Well.

I came here for my *favorite meal.*

Not to be someone's *meal.*

Two sommeliers descend the blackened steel-and-glass staircase to retrieve our wine.

It's the showpiece of the restaurant—directly behind the main dining area—a stunning glass-enclosed wine tower.

You can see it from all three levels of the restaurant.

Tall shelves, backlit and surrounded by glass walls, house rare and expensive bottles of wine, reserved for the elite wealth of New York to enjoy.

"You smiled."

Mystery Man says, half turning his body toward me.

"I didn't realize that was forbidden at *The Wolfe*."

I still don't look at him.

His chuckle is low. Smooth.

Like the deep timbre of a cello against silk.

It slides down my spine, brushing against something instinctual.

Something dangerous.

"Not forbidden," he muses, his voice laced with amusement. "Just curious."

I tilt my head, finally turning toward him.

His expression is unreadable.

But there's something in his gaze that makes my pulse slow.

Deliberate. Calculating.

Like a puzzle he wants to solve.

Or a secret he wants to unravel.

He's *studying me.*

I let him.

"So, what brings you here?"

He lifts his glass of water, his fingers wrapped around the crystal like he *owns* everything he touches.

I shrug. "The steak."

That slow smirk tugs at his mouth again.

"You don't strike me as the type to indulge in something as simple as food."

I arch a brow, feigning boredom.

"And what type do I strike you as?"

His blue eyes flicker over me. Just for a beat.

"The type that gets what she wants."

For a fraction of a second, something inside me *falters.*

It's an unsettling feeling.

To be *seen* so quickly. So precisely.

He doesn't know me.

Doesn't know how many times I've had to claw my way toward the things I want.

Doesn't know how long I've been saving for something that finally feels like *mine.*

But I don't let any of that show.

Instead, I sip my water and glance toward the wine tower, where the sommelier is returning with our bottles.

"If that's meant to be a compliment, you should work on your delivery."

His lips press together, hiding another smirk.

"Noted."

A beat of silence passes between us.

Not awkward. Not strained.

Just... *something unspoken.*

A shift in the air that makes my skin prickle with awareness.

Before I can decide whether to ignore it, the sommelier approaches, a bottle of deep merlot in his gloved hands.

"The Siren's Pour for the lady," he says smoothly, presenting the label. "A rich vintage, deep berry undertones with a warm oak finish. Shall I pour?"

"Please."

I watch as the wine slips into the crystal glass like liquid velvet.

I pick it up, bringing it to my lips, and take a slow sip.

The flavors bloom across my tongue—dark cherry, a hint of spice, and something deeper, something that lingers.

It tastes like indulgence.

Like something that belongs to me.

Out of the corner of my eye, I see him watching.

His own wine has been poured—Wolfe's Reserve, of course—but he hasn't taken a sip.

He's too busy watching *me*.

For a man with an air of effortless confidence, there's a distinct sharpness in the way he observes, as if he's used to gathering information.

Used to controlling the game before anyone else realizes they're even playing.

I set my glass down, unfazed.

"Your turn," I say, gesturing toward his untouched wine.

His fingers curl around the stem, lifting it with slow precision. He brings it to his lips, but he doesn't drink right away.

Instead, he watches me over the rim, holding my gaze.

Dragging out the moment until the tension stretches thin between us.

And then—he drinks.

My breath hitches—not that I'd ever let him see.

His throat moves, the column of his neck tightening briefly as he swallows.

The way he sets his glass back down is purposeful, as if *this*, too, is a move in the game.

"Delicious," he murmurs, voice quiet, but something in it feels like a challenge.

I set my glass down, arching a brow. "I wasn't aware I was offering a review."

His lips twitch at the edges, but he doesn't break. Doesn't falter.

Instead, he leans back slightly in the booth, rolling the stem of his glass between his fingers like he has all the time in the world.

"I imagine you have a discerning palate, Miss..."

He leaves the space open for me to fill.

Waiting for my name.

I don't give it to him.

Instead, I take another slow sip of my wine. "I imagine you like to ask for things you don't get."

His smirk deepens, and he sets his glass down with deliberate ease.

"Ah. A woman of mystery."

I give a one-shouldered shrug. "Or just a woman who doesn't hand over personal information to men who stare at her in restaurants."

He chuckles, the sound rich, amused. "That's fair."

He doesn't offer his name either.

Doesn't fill the space between us with useless pleasantries.

I like that.

"Tell me," he says, tilting his head slightly, his eyes sharper than before. "What was the news?"

I blink. "Excuse me?"

"The news," he repeats, unbothered. "Whatever it was that made you smile at your phone just before the waiter arrived."

I lean back in my booth, fingers smoothing over my napkin as I study him.

"Bold assumption, thinking a woman should share the details of her life with a stranger."

His smirk doesn't waver. If anything, it sharpens.

Like he was hoping I'd say that.

And then—he moves.

Not away.

But up.

Standing.

And—fuck, he's tall.

"Then let's fix that."

His voice carries a weight that suggests he's used to commanding a room without saying a word.

I watch, expression carefully neutral, as he steps around the small space between our tables, reaching for the chair across from me.

He doesn't sit—not yet.

Instead, he rests his hands against the back of it, tilting his head slightly.

Waiting for my permission.

"Sharing a meal means we won't be strangers anymore."

It's a line. A simple one.

But the way he says it—like he's already decided how this will go, like he *knows* I'll let him sit—that is what makes me want to say no.

But the tattoo over his right forearm makes me rethink my choice.

It's Latin:

Fortis fortuna adiuvat.

Fortune favors the bold.

A mantra I adopted during college.

I shouldn't.

But something about him...

Something about this moment...

It feels like fate is pulling us together.

And who am I to say no to fate?

Feigning irritation, I make a show of exhaling as I roll my shoulders.

"Fine."

I pretend to adjust the angle of my seat. "If only to spare my neck the strain of looking over at you since you refuse to leave me alone."

He hums, amused, as he pulls out the chair and takes his seat.

There's a distinct shift in the energy of the table.

I don't know what it is exactly, but I can *feel* it—the game changing.

And *he* can too.

I see it in the way he settles in.

The way he leans back in his chair with a confidence that feels like an unspoken declaration.

He likes this.

This push and pull.

This game between us.

And I can tell—he *wants* to win it.

The scent of seared steak and warm, whiskey-infused butter fills the space between us, decadent and heavy in the air.

My slow-braised short rib sits before me, glazed in a

deep espresso-balsamic reduction that glistens under the low, golden light. Beneath it, a truffle-infused parsnip purée spreads across the plate like silk.

Across from me, his meal is just as indulgent—a bone-in, dry-aged Wagyu ribeye, flame-seared, finished with black garlic and whiskey-infused butter, served alongside charred rosemary potatoes.

It's an *artful display of excess.*

But none of it matters the second I take my first bite.

The richness coats my tongue instantly—deep, complex, perfectly tender. I can taste every note of the reduction, the way it complements the smoky sear of the beef, the creamy truffle lingering at the edges.

A quiet sound escapes me before I can stop it—a soft, appreciative hum of pleasure.

I close my eyes, letting the flavors settle.

I don't care that he's watching me.

I don't care that I can *feel* the weight of his gaze, the quiet patience with which he observes.

This meal is mine.

And I won't let a stranger—no matter how devastatingly handsome—ruin my indulgence.

When I finally open my eyes, his smirk is waiting.

"Good?" he asks, though it's clear he already knows the answer.

I pick up my wineglass, leveling him with a cool look over the rim. "I don't waste time on anything that isn't."

His smirk widens.

"You're going to be trouble, aren't you?"

And just like that, our evening shifts.

The conversation flows effortlessly, an endless back-and-forth where neither of us holds back.

He *challenges* me.

And I push right back.

Every comment, every observation, is a test—one neither of us is willing to fail.

Somewhere between the first glass of wine and the second, I forget to be cautious.

Somewhere between his sharp wit and the deep timbre of his voice, I forget to keep my distance.

I can't recall the exact moment, but at some point—he moved next to me.

Our bodies have turned in toward each other.

The bottle he ordered, sitting between us, was another extravagant choice, the kind of expensive request he threw around without hesitation.

"Did I invite you over here?" I murmur, tilting my head slightly, suddenly aware of his close proximity.

His mouth quirks, his elbow resting on the back of the booth, his body angled more toward mine.

"No," he admits, his voice a lazy drawl, rich and smooth. "But you didn't stop me either."

He's right.

I didn't.

And I don't want to think about why.

Because the truth is, I don't want this night to end.

I don't want to admit how intoxicating he is.

The way his presence seems to fill the space.

How his cologne lingers in the air—deep, woody, with the faintest trace of spice.

The way *heat* rolls off of him, a quiet, steady thing that makes my own body respond in ways I don't care to acknowledge.

The way his strength isn't loud, isn't forced—it just *is*.

I realize the restaurant is closed, the staff is cleaning, and it's just the two of us now.

I start a new contract tomorrow.

A temporary life for the next two weeks.

I can't afford distractions—not even the kind that smell like cedar and power and trouble.

I set my glass down, ignoring the way my fingers feel slightly unsteady against the stem.

"Well, Mr. E... I should go," I say, my voice steady, controlled.

His gaze flickers over me, slow and deliberate. "Mr. E?"

"Mystery."

My small grin betrays my cleverness, but he smiles too.

"My mystery man."

There's a shift in his posture, the slight tension in his jaw—the way his hand tightens around his own glass, like he's weighing something, like he's deciding whether to say the thing that's lingering between us.

Instead, he lifts his wine to his lips, taking a slow sip before setting it down with the same unbothered ease he's carried all night.

He stands and helps me from the booth.

A perfect gentleman.

Instantly, a host appears with his suit jacket.

He gives a curt nod, taking it from him.

"Send the bill to my room."

His voice is quiet, smooth. He slides one arm into his jacket, then the other.

Buttons it.

And of course—he looks *amazing*.

Like walking sin.

My hand moves without thought, running up the silky lapel until I reach the part that is twisted, and I correct it.

"There."

My voice is a near whisper, softened by his proximity.

"Perfect."

He catches my wrist as I begin to lower my hand, stepping toward me and holding it against his chest.

"Stay with me."

Three simple words.

No elaboration. No pleading.

His voice is low, steady—but there's *weight* behind it, something that makes my pulse stutter.

I should say no.

I *need* to say no.

But he doesn't release my wrist.

Doesn't pull me closer either.

He just *holds* me there.

Against the warmth of his chest, the steady rise and fall of his breath beneath my palm.

I lift my gaze, meeting his.

And *God help me.*

The look in his eyes is *lethal.*

A deep, quiet hunger.

Like he's already *claimed* this moment.

Already decided how this will end.

But he's *waiting*.

For *me* to decide.

A slow inhale drags through my lungs.

"I don't—"

His thumb brushes against the inside of my wrist, a touch so soft, so intimate, it robs me of thought.

"No expectations," he murmurs, stopping my words in an instant. "No names," he continues, his voice silk and steel, weaving effortlessly around me.

Temptation wrapped in control.

Just like *him*.

His next words are a promise.

A damnation.

A sin spoken between us.

"Just pleasure."

I swallow hard, my resolve slipping.

One night.

Just *one*.

No strings. No messy emotions. No consequences.

I should walk away.

But then what?

I go back to my apartment.

Crawl into my cold bed.

Spend the night thinking about the way he *looks* at me.

The way his fingers *feel* against my skin.

The way his voice *curls* around his words, dark and decadent and unyielding.

I meet his gaze again.

Blue. Sharp. Unwavering.

I already *know* what he wants.

And fuck—*I want it too.*

More than I should.

A long, slow exhale shudders through me as I press my lips together.

I should say no.

My lips even part to speak it.

But then...

"Yes."

Chapter 2

Elena

Of course, he has a room here.

And not just any room—the best room.

The elevator glides to a smooth stop, the soft chime barely cutting through the thick tension stretching between us. The top floor. A private suite that likely costs more per night than most people make in a month.

The doors slide open, revealing a short hallway with only one entrance—his.

He presses a key card to the panel, the lock clicking open with quiet finality. I step inside, the lights flickering on automatically, bathing the space in a soft, golden glow.

And God help me—the suite is breathtaking.

Luxury incarnate.

Floor-to-ceiling windows showcase the glittering skyline of New York, the city stretching endlessly beneath us. The interior is sleek and modern but warm—polished marble floors, a sunken living room with deep, plush furniture, an open fireplace casting flickering shadows against the walls.

A place built for power. For men who own the world and have nothing left to prove.

I barely have a chance to take it all in before his hand presses against the small of my back.

Warm. Commanding. Just enough pressure to remind me I'm his to guide.

"This way, Trouble."

There is a slight smile in his tone, clearly enjoying this.

I let him lead me deeper inside—past the opulent living space, past the imported-whiskey collection on display at the private bar, past the heavy curtains swaying slightly from the night breeze slipping through a barely cracked window.

We reach the bedroom, and it's just as decadent. Dark. Masculine. Low lighting spills across crisp, expensive sheets —the kind soft enough to make you forget you're sleeping alone.

But neither of us will be alone tonight.

No more conversation. No more games.

We both know what we want.

Each other.

His fingertips trail up my arm—featherlight—like he's memorizing the shape of me before he takes me apart.

I shiver, but it's not from cold.

It's the way his breath ghosts against my temple. The way his body radiates heat behind me.

I close my eyes as his lips brush against my shoulder— barely a kiss. More of a test.

"You're mine for the night."

His mouth moves higher, skimming up the side of my neck, slow and deliberate, until his lips are just beneath my ear.

I exhale—a shaky breath that betrays me.

He smirks against my skin, wrapping his arms around me from behind, his hands smoothing over my stomach, pulling me flush against his chest.

The scent of whiskey, cedarwood, and something distinctly him envelops me.

"Unless you'd like to leave, Trouble," he murmurs, his voice low, a deep vibration against my back. "Now's your chance."

A part of me knows I should. I should walk away now, slip out of this opulent suite, and return to my carefully controlled world. The one where I call the shots. Where I decide who gets to touch me and under what terms.

That world is safe. Predictable.

This?

This is unknown.

He's unknown.

Men like him—sharp, unreadable, too damn powerful— always come with consequences. I've spent years perfecting the art of detachment, never letting anyone get too close.

And yet...

He doesn't feel like every other man who's looked at me like I was something to be had.

He's looking at me like he's daring me to choose him.

Just for tonight.

And God help me—I want to.

I want to forget about tomorrow. About the life I'm supposed to step back into. I want to let myself be selfish. Just this once.

I tilt my head slightly, giving him silent permission.

He takes it.

His lips find the curve of my throat, pressing deeper this time. His teeth graze, then soothe with his tongue—a slow, languid drag that sends a shiver rolling down my spine.

It's not explosive.

It's not rushed.

It's controlled.

Every touch, every breath, measured—like the slow game of chess we've been playing all night.

Like he wants to savor me.

I turn in his arms, pressing my hands against the hard planes of his chest. His pulse beats steady and strong beneath my fingers.

There's something dangerous about this.

The way I feel like I'm being worshipped.

Like he's letting himself indulge in something rare—something he doesn't usually allow himself.

The weight of that realization sinks deep into my bones.

He wraps an arm low around my back. His hand guides my head back as he pulls me against his hard body, and I don't fight it.

I lift onto my toes as he lowers his mouth to mine, our eyes closing as he kisses me.

And it's nothing like I expected.

Not greedy. Not devouring.

Just... deep.

Like he's exploring. Mapping. Learning every inch of me through the press of our mouths.

Like he knows we only have this night, and he refuses to waste a single second.

I melt into him.

His fingers slip beneath the thin straps of my dress, dragging them down with excruciating slowness. Fabric pools at my feet.

His hands skim up my bare back, tracing, memorizing.

"You're beautiful," he murmurs against my lips, his voice barely above a whisper.

His words brush over my skin like the lightest caress, sending a shiver down my spine.

I should dismiss it like I have every other compliment before this one.

But I can't.

Because there's something about the way he says it.

Not just spoken—but felt.

Like he's not telling me for my benefit, but because he needs me to know.

His lips return to mine, slow and deliberate, as if savoring the taste of me.

I sigh into him, hands tracing up the sharp lines of his shoulders, the firm muscles beneath the tailored fabric of his suit.

Too many layers.

I tug at his jacket, and he releases me just long enough to shrug it off, letting it fall somewhere behind him.

His lips drift lower, pressing against the hollow of my throat—the sensitive space beneath my ear. His breath is warm, his touch firm yet gentle, every move-ment precise.

A quiet moan escapes me when his mouth finds my collarbone, his teeth grazing before soothing the spot with his tongue.

I slide my fingers through his hair, tugging just enough to test him.

A sharp inhale is my reward, the subtle tension in his jaw the only sign that I've affected him.

I exhale shakily, my head tipping back as his lips trail a path lower—along the curve of my shoulder, the tops of my breasts.

The only barrier between us is lace.

Thin. Delicate. Inconsequential.

His hands smooth up my ribs, thumbs brushing beneath the swell of my breasts, teasing until a low growl rumbles from his chest.

He tugs the lace down.

His mouth replaces fabric with heat.

A slow, deliberate kiss to the valley between my breasts.

A teasing drag of his tongue against my nipple earns him another moan.

A deep, reverent inhale—like he's breathing me in—makes my fingers tighten in his hair as a wicked smirk ghosts against my skin.

God help me.

Because he's not just taking his time.

He's enjoying this.

Every shiver. Every quiet sound I make. Every inch of bare skin he reveals fuels him to keep going.

I don't realize he's walking me backward until my knees hit the edge of the bed, the mattress giving beneath me as I sink into it.

His lips chase mine until I'm leaning back, one hand bracing against the mattress, the other fisting the lapel of his shirt and pulling him to me.

My fingers fight against the top button until I free it—then the next, and another.

He pulls away from me, reaching behind and tugging the neck of his shirt over his head.

The hard planes of his body gleam in the moonlight. The way it kisses his tanned skin, the shadows hugging every muscle—it makes my mouth water.

I slide forward, my knees spread wide.

My palms flatten against his thighs, traveling up inch by inch as I look up at him. The heat in our shared gaze is an inferno, and we're both ready to be consumed by the fire.

I reach his cock, and—fuck—he's hard as stone.

Wrapping my arms around his pelvis, I pull him into me, my mouth working his dick through his pants.

Finally, I reach just above me, his belt only slightly arguing with me until the metal clinks as I remove it.

I keep my eyes on him as I undo the button of his pants.

His thumb rubs slowly over my bottom lip, and I know he's wondering what my mouth feels like.

The tip of my tongue darts out, making him press his lips into a thin line.

"Nothing but fucking trouble," he growls as I pull his zipper down.

And—God—he's big.

Long. Thick.

And I need him.

My grip is firm around the base of his erection, and I make a long, slow lick along the head of his cock. The salty, teasing taste of him explodes within me, and I close my eyes, moaning as I take him farther into my mouth.

My hand goes to my breast, pinching my nipple as I grind my hips against the soft mattress.

It's an impulse.

A need for friction that drives me as I suck him deeper into my mouth.

"Christ, baby," he pants, his hand holding the side of my head as he rolls his hips into me. "Oh, fuck, just like that, Trouble."

I swirl my tongue. My hand slides along his length in time with my mouth.

I have a talent for this.

And I love taking it. Owning it.

The power.

The control.

I'm owning him with just my tongue.

I could keep his cock in my mouth all day—teasing him near orgasm before slowly licking his length as it ebbs away.

Right now, I'm only thinking of what he'll taste like. His cum running down my throat as his grunts surround me.

And he wants it too—but he's fighting against the release.

He hits the back of my throat, both hands holding my head as I pump my mouth and grip his cock.

"Fuck. Thirty more seconds, and your sweet mouth would be full of me."

He pulls away from me, and I release him with a pop.

"Scoot back and spread your legs, Trouble. Let me see what belongs to me."

I smirk, one brow cocked, removing my heels and sliding myself back.

"Only for tonight," I remind him.

"Even still. Mine."

He nods once.

"But you have far too many clothes on, baby."

He holds out his hand while the other strokes his long cock, and I can't stop myself from watching.

Lifting my hips, I hook my thumbs under the thin straps and remove the black lace panties, giving them to him.

"Spread them."

His heated gaze is fixed on my pussy as I open my legs wide, my hands splayed on my thighs, rubbing myself as he looks at me.

"So fucking beautiful."

My panties move to his other hand. Then he wraps them around his cock, sliding them up his length.

He closes his eyes and drops his head back, stroking himself with my underwear.

"You're already so fucking wet, and I haven't even touched that sweet cunt yet."

He lifts them to his nose, inhaling deeply, like it's saving his life.

Holy shit.

This man is lethal.

"I can't wait another second to taste you, Trouble."

One knee hits the bed, then the other as he crawls to me, his warm mouth kissing and licking up my long legs until his nose runs up the slit of my pussy, his cock hanging out of his pants.

With a deep inhale and a growl, he looks at me.

My mouth parts, and I watch his tongue with rabid interest as he takes his time with the first lick.

Long.

Slow.

And fucking unbelievable.

"The sweetest troublemaker I've ever had."

He licks again before rubbing two fingers between the lips of my cunt, spreading me.

His eyes never leave me, memorizing every inch before he utterly destroys me.

Licking turns to sucking.

"Oh my God."

My back arches when he thrusts a finger inside me, pumping in and out.

"She's singing for me, Trouble."

The sound of my slick arousal joins the chorus of my panting.

His mouth is back on my clit, sucking me until I moan out loudly.

"That's it. You sing for me too, baby."

Another finger joins the first, curling into me.

The pace is perfect.

The pressure is–fuck.

His tongue is relentless.

Coaxing my orgasm with his "come hither" motion, I hold my legs open wide for him. My hips roll with the movements of his mouth until my nails are digging into my skin.

My hand flies to his head, threading into his hair as I come.

My clit throbs.

My hips buck.

My legs twitch.

And he doesn't stop.

"Give me another one, beautiful."

He demands another orgasm.

I imagine most of the world bends to his will, and my pleasure is apparently no different.

"Not yet,"

But my hand in his hair holds him, a willing prisoner against me.

"It's too—"

"I want you." He cuts me off adding a third finger, and spots form on the edges of my vision.

"You're going to give me everything tonight."

He sucks my clit again, swirling his tongue.

"You'll be such a good girl for me—all night."

He nips at my clit as his other hand pinches my nipple, and another orgasm crashes through me.

I'm locked in place.

The only thing I can do is grip the pillows on each side of me and hope they keep me fixed to the earth.

Crying out my release to the ceiling above me.

No sooner than it ebbs away does he pull me up by my wrist and turn me.

He's under me.

His arms wrap around my thighs, pulling my cunt down to his mouth.

My mystery man is famished for me, and the thought makes me clench.

"Oh my fucking God, yes," I breathe out, my eyes closed tight as I ride his tongue.

He fucking wants it.

And I tell him as much.

"You want me to fuck your pretty face, mystery man?"

He growls.

He wants me to say his name.

And I want it too.

I want to scream it as I start to come again.

But no names.

No expectations.

His teeth graze my pulsing clit.

"You feel so good," I cry out, each throb of my orgasm making me grunt as I work my hips against his mouth.

"I'm coming."

My hand grips the headboard, using it to keep my pace steady.

"You're making me come so hard."

I realize I'm pulling his hair, and as my pleasure fades, I release my hold and slow my strokes.

"Holy shit."

Tipping my head back, I close my eyes and pant,

catching my breath as his fervent sucking turns to tender licks and soft kisses.

"Lean forward. Get those beautiful tits on the bed and keep this ass in the air."

He pulls my hips as I drop my chest to the mattress.

He kisses my ass cheek before he smacks it.

"God, just fucking kill me so I can die a happy man."

I hear a drawer open, then the sound of a condom wrapper being ripped.

After a beat, the head of his hard cock teases my pussy, and I lean back like a cat in heat.

The dark rumble of his chest rolls over me as he chuckles.

"I'm going to take care of you, Trouble."

He slides his dick up and down my slit, making me moan.

Making me desperate to have him fill me.

"Hold still for me, baby."

One hand grips my hip as the other holds his cock at my entrance.

He pushes into me so slowly, and I swear I feel it—like a rope being pulled tight in my belly.

"Fuck, Trouble."

Both hands grip my hips as he pulls nearly all the way out, then thrusts in deep.

My back bows, and I cry out.

It feels so fucking good.

"You're so tight."

He thrusts in, pulling nearly out, then back in again. The

pacing is perfect. His long cock hitting so deep inside me every time.

I could get addicted to this.

To him.

He presses soft kisses against my spine, leaning over me and grasping a handful of my hair.

"I knew you were going to feel so fucking good, Trouble. But this?"

He fucks me faster.

Harder.

"This pussy is heaven, baby."

His grip is bruising on my hip as he slams into me.

Our flesh slaps against each other, our moans mixing together, his grunts raw and broken as he works me toward another orgasm.

"Fuck me harder," I cry out, the first wave of pleasure rolling over me.

"No, Trouble."

He quickly widens my legs and pulls my ass up more, deepening the arch in my back.

My eyes roll back in my head.

"But I'll fuck you deeper."

And Christ, he does.

I've never felt this full—never felt someone this deep inside me before.

"Fuck."

"Fuck."

It's the only word my vocal cords can form, and I say it over and over again.

"You take my fucking cock, Trouble. Every goddamn inch."

He hammers into me, my orgasm locking me in place, holding me captive as he grunts his release into the condom.

His movements slow.

The strokes of his cock still inside me become longer. His strong hands knead my ass cheeks, like he's giving them thanks and adoration.

"Oh, you beautiful troublemaker."

His words are reverent as he brings me down from the high we just climbed together.

Somehow, I want more.

My hips join his slow thrusts, and he chuckles at me from behind.

He flips me over, my hair falling in waves across the pillow as he settles between my legs.

His sinful smile is full of satisfaction, and his blue eyes instantly capture me.

Warm hands slide up my body as his weight settles on top of me. My arms wrap around his neck, and our mouths meet—both of us groaning as our tongues reunite.

Pulling back, he smooths more of my hair away, admiring the just-fucked look of satisfaction he must see on my face.

"You're perfect," he whispers, and it almost seems like he intended it for himself.

He slides off the bed, standing.

The silver light of the moon hits him perfectly, giving me a full view of his godlike body.

His pants hang low on his waist, his semi-hard cock still in his grip.

I crawl toward him, and he pinches my chin, pulling me up to him and nipping at my bottom lip with his teeth.

"I'll get you some water."

He kisses me again, his tongue demanding my mouth open for him.

"Then I'm going to fuck you again."

Chapter 3

A strand of her long, brunette hair slips between my fingers.

Soft. Silky.

It has the perfect amount of wave and bounce, making her look like a fucking goddess as she rides my cock.

Those hazel eyes, sharp and knowing, hold me captive while she moves.

Slow. Deliberate.

Like she's in control.

Like she *owns* me.

And her mouth—

God, *her fucking mouth.*

Lips swollen from my kisses. From the way she took me deep, her tongue flicking against the head before she swallowed me whole.

I groan, gripping her hips, my fingers digging in as I thrust up to meet her movements.

She feels fucking amazing.

Tight. Hot. Like she was made for me.

She's close—so close. I can feel her body tightening around me, her breath turning into soft, desperate gasps.

Her head falls back, her spine arching, and her mouth parts—

A sound slips from her lips.

It's muffled. Unintelligible.

My brow furrows, but I keep my hold on her hips.

She's coming, her body trembling, but that sound—

What the fuck was that?

Then it happens again—louder this time.

It's sharp. Persistent.

It doesn't belong here.

BZZZT. BZZZT.

The sound drags me under, distorts everything—

BZZZT. BZZZT.

I jolt awake, jarred by the too-bright room.

Blinking, I exhale sharply, my pulse still *fucking pounding* in my ears.

What the fuck—

BZZZT. BZZZT.

My phone vibrates on the nightstand, rattling against the crystal glass.

The *culprit* that disturbed what was about to be an *amazing fucking dream.*

Christ.

I drag a hand down my face, forcing myself to sit up.

My muscles are tight.

My cock is *rock fucking hard* from the dream I just had—about *her.*

Turning around, I look at the barely disturbed bed next to me.

I can see the divot on the pillow where she laid her head.

The gentle scent of her perfume still lingers in the air, like a ghost of our night together.

Only *my* clothes litter the floor.

Hers are gone.

I exhale slowly, clenching my jaw.

Of course, she's gone.

One night.

No names.

No expectations.

It was *exactly* what we agreed on.

So why the fuck does it *piss me off?*

I shake it off when my phone vibrates again.

I grab it—

And immediately swear under my breath.

Lucian Vale.

Shit.

I *overslept.*

I *never* oversleep.

"You're late."

Lucian's voice drips with amusement, and I already want to hang up.

I pinch the bridge of my nose, exhaling sharply.

"I'm aware."

"Shit, did hell freeze over? Damien Wolfe *oversleeping?* I thought you didn't do things like sleep in, take days off, or— God forbid—have fun."

I grunt, looking toward the window, drapes thrown back, letting the bright sunlight fill the room.

The city sprawls below, glittering with morning light, but I'm not seeing any of it.

"Didn't oversleep," I mutter, rubbing the heel of my hand against my temple. "Just got behind this morning."

Lucian's chuckle is way too entertained for my liking.

"Morning? Try again, lover boy. It's almost *noon*."

Noon.

I *never* sleep this late.

The tension pulls tight in my chest, and I swing my legs over the side of the bed, pressing my forearms to my knees.

Lucian hums, *way* too entertained. "Uh-huh. And what was her name?"

"What's the point of your call?"

Dead silence.

Then—a bark of laughter. "Holy shit. That good?"

"Lucian." *Warning.*

"Do I know her?"

Lucian's still talking, oblivious to the fact that I'm *one comment away* from throwing my phone across the room.

"I assume she was spectacular, considering you went full Sleeping Beauty over there."

I pinch the bridge of my nose.

"Drop it."

"Oh, come on. You expect me to just *ignore* this? Damien Wolfe, sleeping past sunrise? Canceling meetings?"

A pause. Then, with mock concern—

"Do I need to send your assistant with an emergency espresso?"

I exhale sharply, already *done* with this conversation.

Lucian gasps in all seriousness this time.

"Wait, was it *Vanessa?*"**

His voice pitches on the end of her name before he starts whispering like someone is eavesdropping on our goddamn phone call.

"Did you fuck your assistant?"

"Christ, Luc. I'm not even going to dignify that with a response."

Speaking of which—

I pull my phone away from my ear, texting Vanessa.

> DAMIEN: Clear my calendar today.

> VANESSA: Everything? Are you sure? Is everything okay?

> DAMIEN: I don't pay you to be my therapist.

> VANESSA: Yes, sir. I'll take care of it.

"I swear I'm interviewing for new assistants as soon as this fucking merger is done."

I mutter it more to myself than Lucian.

Lucian snickers.

"Poor girl."

"She's fine."

"You *say* that, but I'm pretty sure she cries into her designer notebooks after every conversation with you."

I don't respond.

Because the crystal glass—half full of water with a red lipstick smear on the edge—has me *frozen.*

One more *remnant* left behind of the woman I should stop thinking about.

I *shouldn't* think about the way she fit against me—

Soft and warm.

The way her lips parted under mine.

The way she looked at me like she *knew* exactly what she was doing—like she was playing the game and *winning.*

But I *do.*

And I *fucking hate it.*

The call goes quiet for a second.

Then—

"You still there?"

I drag my gaze across the room, searching for anything else she left behind.

Nothing.

No forgotten earrings.

Not even a *fucking note.*

It's like she was never here.

Except she was.

I *feel* her absence, and it's *irritating as hell.*

"Yeah," I say, voice flat. "I'm here."

Lucian is too perceptive for his own good.

"Alright, Moody Judy. You coming in, or should I start sending out condolence letters for your tragic demise?"

"I'll be there in an hour."

"Good. I hand-picked this contract for you myself. She's sharp, elegant, knows how to play the game. She'll be perfect."

I drag a hand down my face.

"She better be."

Lucian chuckles.

"See you soon, lover boy."

The call ends before I can tell him to go *fuck himself.*

I slam the phone down a little too hard.

My chest is tight with something I *refuse* to name.

I step inside the shower, hands braced against the marble wall, head bowed beneath the scalding spray.

She left.

Like we *said.*

So why the *fuck* does that bother me?

Why do I feel like I *lost* something I never even had?

I get some food in my stomach and caffeine in my system as I check my emails and fire off a few more orders for my assistant.

I've been staying at the Wolfe Grand more often than my own fucking penthouse, so I pull a black suit with a crisp white shirt from the closet.

I'm straightening my black tie and spritzing my cologne when my phone chimes.

> LUCIAN: Tick-tock… you know… since you're having a hard time with your punctuality today.

Asshole.

Snatching last night's pants from the floor, I fish

through the pockets while using voice assistant to order a car. I shove my money clip and other contents into my pockets while checking my watch one more time.

Fuck. I needed to leave five minutes ago.

In no time, my driver is pulling away, heading to The Black Ledger's sleek high-rise about thirty minutes from my hotel.

I ring the concierge at Ember & Ash.

The steakhouse is reservation only, so my little mystery woman can't hide for long.

"Hey, Cal." I greet the general manager, knowing they're getting ready to open for dinner. "Can you check the reservation log for me from last night?"

"Of course, Mr. Wolfe. Anyone in particular you're looking for?"

"Yeah. A woman, table for one around eight."

I wait, knowing he's sliding his finger along the tablet, eyes scanning for my request.

I pretend like there's no reason I'm holding my breath.

"Doesn't look like there was one." He sounds confused. "Was there a complaint last night? The staff didn't—"

I cut him off. "No. Nothing of that sort." The words trail off. "If there was a walk-in?"

"Ah, likely it. We don't add the walk-ins typically since they're usually regular guests, Mr. Wolfe."

A regular.

Could this get any easier for me?

I almost grin in early celebration.

I'll know her name before dinnertime.

"Can you ask around? See who sat her last night?"

"I'll be happy to, Mr. Wolfe. Anything else I can do for you?"

"That's it, Cal. Thanks."

I end the call before he answers.

Cal's a great guy, but I'm in no mood for pleasantries today.

God help this poor contract Lucian set up for me.

Only days ago, I called him needing one of his girls for a two-week contract.

My multi-billion-dollar merger is on the line, and the CEO's wife wants a *family man* to take over her husband's business.

Well... I can't buy a family, but I can buy a fiancée.

Especially when my good friend owns the world's most prestigious escort agency.

The Black Ledger

Fifteen minutes later, the elevator doors open, and I'm greeted by The Black Ledger's marble entrance.

"Welcome to The Ledger, Mr. Wolfe."

The receptionist is clearly a pro, greeting me by name instead of asking who I am.

Only the best from Lucian.

"Right this way."

She stands, leading me through a set of heavy, opaque doors where my old friend is already walking toward us.

"Ah, Mr. Vale for you. Enjoy your contract, Mr. Wolfe."

I nod at her, then give Lucian my best eat-shit expression.

Lucian—tattoos covering his forearms and neck, slate-blue eyes that match his dress shirt, three days' stubble—

looks every part the man who has connections everywhere.

He's a hard businessman and a damn good friend.

Self-made, just like me.

And we're both at the top of the pyramid in our respective fields.

"'Bout time, Moody Judy."

"I'll throw you out the window of your own high-rise."

He throws his head back, laughing loudly, drawing a look or two from a few women in red—the signature color of a Black Ledger companion.

"Okay, okay. I'll stop busting your balls now." He greets me with a familiar handshake and one-armed hug.

"You're getting old."

I gesture to his tight cut.

His salt-and-pepper hair seems to have more salt than pepper these days.

He's only thirty-eight, six years older than me, but I need something to toss back at him with all the jokes he's been spouting today.

"Speak for yourself."

He turns, and I follow him toward his office at the end of the hall.

He holds out a closed folder. "I'll be young forever."

He nods at one of his girls—another wearing the signature red ensemble, signaling she's meeting her new contract today.

They're all beautiful, pampered, and perfectly poised for the billionaires they're contracted to.

The women set the terms of the contract, and God help the person who tries to break it.

Lucian came up hard, and he won't hesitate to spill blood over the safety of his enterprise.

I peek inside the envelope, seeing printed papers I'll look at later. "My contract is clear? No physical needs. Only public appearances? Big fucking bonus at the end."

"Hey, who are you talking to here?"

Lucian holds his hands out in mock offense. "The contract is perfect. I've got my top girl for you. Background checks on your CEO cleared. Your romantic backstory is in that envelope. She'll handle the rest."

We pause at his door, his hand gripping the matte-gold handle.

"She'll treat you so nice, you'll never want to let her go."

He winks at me, pulling the handle and holding the door open wide.

"It's two weeks, and trust me, I will let her go."

I turn from Lucian to the woman in red before me—and instantly swallow my words.

Fuck me sideways.

It's her.

It's *Trouble*.

My heart surges in my chest like a stampede of galloping horses, and I feel the blood drain from my face.

Long brown hair with the perfect amount of wave and bounce.

A figure that makes my cock twitch.

And hazel eyes that look just as surprised as I feel right now.

I see it—the flicker of recognition.

The way she hesitates, just for a second.

But then—nothing.

She smooths her expression into polite indifference.

Poised. Professional.

Like she doesn't fucking know me.

Like she didn't have my cock down her throat last night.

Like she wasn't in my bed, moaning my name, looking at me with those same hazel eyes that are now pretending I'm just another client.

Lucian, oblivious, gestures to her like this isn't a fucking disaster.

"Damien, meet Elena Moreau. Your fiancée."

Chapter 4
Elena

His voice.

Deep, smooth—commanding.

Even before I look up, my stomach clenches.

No.

It *can't* be.

I lift my gaze, and *everything* stops.

It's him.

Standing in the doorway, broad-shouldered, composed —the very picture of power and control.

The man I spent the night with.

The man whose touch is still burned into my skin.

The man whose name I don't even know.

But I'm about to.

Because for the next two weeks, I'll be playing the convincing role of his fiancée.

A slow, suffocating beat stretches between us, thick with recognition.

His sharp blue eyes lock onto mine, unreadable, but I see the flicker of realization. The shock he doesn't want to show.

Lucian, oblivious to the sheer catastrophe unfolding between us, gestures toward him with an easy grin.

"Elena Moreau—meet Damien Wolfe."

The name hits like a freight train.

Damien Wolfe.

A man I should have left behind in that hotel room, nothing more than a fleeting memory of heat and indulgence.

But no—he's here, standing in front of me, threatening to unravel everything I've worked for.

I built my life on rules. Boundaries. Contracts that keep things clean, controlled.

And last night?

Last night was the opposite of that.

I need distance. I need separation.

I need him to be just another client I can pretend to love.

But how the fuck am I supposed to pretend when I already know exactly how he feels between my legs?

Oh. My. Fucking. God.

The Wolfe Grand.

The luxury hotel The Ledger frequently books for its highest-tier clients.

The same hotel where I spent last night with him.

Lucian has an account there—a standing arrangement for his most exclusive companions.

I hear his voice in my memory, casual over drinks one night.

"An old friend owns it. We go way back."

An old friend.

Damien Wolfe.

The man whose name I wanted to moan into a pillow just hours ago.

I grip the contract folder a little tighter, my nails pressing into the glossy surface, my pulse hammering against my ribs.

This is a joke.

A fucking disaster.

But I've spent years mastering the art of composure.

So I don't react.

Not visibly.

I tilt my chin, keeping my expression carefully neutral—even as my pulse jackhammers in my throat.

I can't let him see it. Can't let him know just how badly this is throwing me off balance.

I've spent years ensuring men like Damien Wolfe don't get to me.

That they see only what I want them to see.

But this man?

He's already seen too much.

Touched too much.

He's in dangerous territory, and I need to put him back where he belongs.

As a job.

As a contract.

As nothing more than another temporary illusion.

I lift my chin, my voice steady, my mask perfectly in place.

Lucian is watching me, waiting.

"Mr. Wolfe."

Damien, to his credit, doesn't let anything slip.

But his jaw tightens, his fingers flex slightly around the folder in his grip—like he's seconds from crushing it.

He exhales sharply through his nose, shifting his weight slightly.

Then—his voice.

Clipped. Controlled.

"Miss Moreau."

Lucian clasps his hands together. "Perfect. Now that you two have met, let's go over the contract details."

Oh, I have no doubt Damien already knows every detail.

Just like I do.

We're supposed to be engaged.

A deeply in love, can't-keep-our-hands-off-each-other engagement.

My stomach clenches.

Lucian flips through the contract with ease, barely glancing up as he lists our obligations.

"Public appearances together, charity events, dinners, meetings with Wolfe Industries' board."

Damien stays silent.

But I can still feel his fucking eyes on me.

"Of course," Lucian continues, flipping a page, "the engagement must appear convincing, which means there will be physical expectations in public—hand-holding, the occasional affectionate moment."

My throat tightens.

Affectionate moment.

I already know exactly how his hands feel on my body.

How his lips feel against mine.

I feel the shift in Damien—so small, so subtle, but I sense it.

He's thinking about it, too.

"Elena has a strict 'No Intimacy' rule behind closed doors. This arrangement is strictly for appearances..."

His voice, when he finally speaks, is even. Emotionless.

"That won't be necessary."

I swallow hard.

And I swear it echoes around the entire office.

Lucian doesn't catch the tension snapping between us like a live wire.

"And at the completion of the contract, there is a generous ten-million-dollar payout."

I nearly choke.

I try to play it off with a cough, reaching for one of the crystal glasses and the pitcher of water—but Damien is closer.

I feel his presence as he lifts the pitcher and pours the water.

His fingers brush mine when he hands me the glass.

I barely breathe. "Thank you."

I force myself to look at him. A flick of my gaze—then away.

Lucian leans back in his chair, grinning. "And that's it. Everything is settled."

Settled.

Sure.

If pretending I don't know how Damien Wolfe tastes counts as settled.

Then okay, we're settled.

Lucian clasps Damien's shoulder. "You two are a match made in heaven." His grin is sharp. "Elena here will give you a run for your money, old friend."

I almost laugh.

Oh, Lucian.

You have no fucking idea.

***

The Blackstone

A name synonymous with prestige and power.

A high-rise that looms over Fifth Avenue like a silent, watchful king.

I read about it earlier.

Damien owns the entire damn building.

It was a side note in one of the articles I skimmed—an almost casual mention in a long list of properties under Wolfe Industries.

The Wolfe of Fifth Avenue.

And now, I'm stepping directly into his den.

After meeting my walking disaster, I excused myself while Lucian explained the final logistics to Damien.

I felt every bit of his heavy gaze on me with each step I took out of Lucian's office.

"Elena is leading orientation for the newest companions joining The Ledger family," Lucian had said. "She'll meet you at your penthouse tonight. And since your first outing is tomorrow, I suggest you use the evening to get better acquainted."

I wanted to say:

I don't think that will be necessary.

Instead, I let the heavy door close behind me.

The doorman immediately opens the door as I step out of the car, my heels clicking against the smooth black marble of the entrance.

Inside, everything is sleek, modern—cold in its perfection.

No personal touches. No warmth.

Just power.

The elevator ride is smooth, quiet—too quiet.

I shouldn't be nervous.

But I am.

Not because of the contract.

Because of him.

Because the moment I step inside that penthouse, there will be no distractions.

No polite small talk.

No audience.

We will be alone.

And we'll have to talk about last night.

I swallow hard as the elevator reaches the top floor, the doors sliding open with a soft *ding*.

The penthouse is beautiful—sleek, expensive, immaculate.

Floor-to-ceiling windows stretch across the living room, the glittering skyline spread before me like something out of a dream.

It's rich and warm, instantly comforting.

Until I find him.

Standing near the window, one hand in his pocket, his broad, powerful frame silhouetted against the city lights.

His head turns slightly, pausing—as if still deciding how this second meeting will go.

His phone is pressed to his ear, likely listening to the caller on the other end.

"Thanks for checking on it, Cal."

He ends the call.

Then finally, his piercing blue gaze settles on me.

The air charges between us.

And then—he speaks.

"Didn't think I'd be seeing you again so soon."

His voice is deep, the timbre smooth and low, dripping down my spine like warm silk.

I tilt my chin. "Neither did I."

And just like that—the game begins.

Chapter 5

Damien

I could kick my own ass for setting up this dinner.

At the time, it had seemed like a logical move—a necessary step to break the ice before introducing her as my fiancée at tomorrow night's formal dinner with the executives involved in the merger.

A simple, controlled environment where I could gauge her approach and ensure we were on the same page before stepping into the spotlight together.

But now?

Now I know exactly how Elena Moreau operates.

I know the way her body moves, the way she sounds when she's coming apart in my hands, the way she takes me so deep that my vision goes white at the edges.

I groan, dragging a rough hand down my face before reaching for the crystal tumbler beside me. The whiskey burns on the way down, but not nearly enough to erase the memory of her.

I should be focused on the contract—on ensuring this

arrangement plays out exactly as intended: with precision, without complication. Instead, I can't seem to get the taste of her out of my goddamn head.

My phone vibrates in my pocket, and I set my glass down before glancing at the screen.

Cal.

I nearly forgot about the request I made earlier today—the one that now seems so fucking irrelevant.

I swipe to answer. "Hey, Cal."

The familiar hum of Ember & Ash fills the background—muted conversation, the subtle clink of fine crystal against white linen.

"I looked into that reservation you asked about," Cal says, his voice smooth and professional.

My other hand slips into my pocket, my fingers brushing against something soft and delicate. It takes me a second to realize what I'm holding.

A small scrap of black silk and lace.

I go still.

Her panties.

My chest tightens as I drag my thumb over the delicate fabric, remembering exactly how they ended up in my pocket.

She had slipped them off last night, her dress and bra on the floor behind me as I told her to spread her legs for me—all soft sighs and creamy skin. And I—like a fucking deviant—had tucked them away after rubbing them against my cock.

Did she run out so quickly she forgot them?

No.

Not a chance.

That dress she wore last night was barely enough to cover her perfect ass. She left them on purpose.

A slow smirk pulls at the corner of my mouth. My little mystery woman wanted to leave a parting gift to remember her by.

Well, who would I be to refuse her offering?

I bring the lace up to my nose, inhaling the faintest trace of her scent—warm, sweet, decadent.

Cal clears his throat on the other end of the line, oblivious to my distraction. "The hostess confirmed the young woman dined alone. Her name is Elena Moreau. She's a frequent guest under The Ledger's account."

I stiffen.

For a moment, I don't move.

Of course, I learned earlier today that she was a Companion. It's another thing to hear it spoken aloud.

Elena Moreau.

A Ledger girl.

A professional.

This is what she does.

What she's been doing for years.

I should have known—the way she carried herself, the way she met every challenge I threw at her last night with effortless ease. She wasn't just some beautiful woman out for a casual dinner. She was trained for this.

The realization shouldn't bother me.

And yet, something about it does.

Was she supposed to meet a client there? Or had she already been with one?

I need to check into her stays at the Wolfe and lock that reminder away for tomorrow.

I slide the lace back into my pocket, clenching my jaw as I hear the soft chime of the elevator behind me.

Fuck. She's here.

I take a slow breath, willing my body to behave before turning my head just slightly, catching a glimpse of her out of my periphery.

She's standing in the entryway, poised and elegant as ever. The same woman who had been pressed against me just hours ago is now standing in my home—not as my mystery lover, but as my contracted fiancée.

And just like that, the rules have changed.

I tighten my grip on my phone, forcing my voice into something smooth and unbothered. "Thanks for checking on it, Cal."

Then, finally, I turn to face her.

For a moment, I just take her in.

She looks the same as she did last night, but somehow completely different.

Last night, she was undone—flushed, breathless, wild beneath my hands. Now, she is the picture of control. The perfect Ledger Companion.

The part of me that thrives on control should appreciate that.

But all I can think about is the way she unraveled for me.

I let a slow smirk tug at my lips, my voice low. "Didn't think I'd be seeing you again so soon."

Something flickers across her expression—just for a

second—before she smooths it over, her posture remaining composed.

"Neither did I," she admits, stepping fully into the space.

A charged silence stretches between us, thick with unspoken words.

Then, her lips part, as if she's about to say something. "Mr. Wolfe, about last—"

"Damien."

The word leaves my mouth before I can stop it, firmer than I intended.

She hesitates. I see it—the brief uncertainty, the way she almost steps back, like she can sense the shift in the air between us.

But she recovers quickly, pressing her lips together before continuing, her voice calm and measured.

"I just wanted to say... if I had known you were my contract—"

I already know where she's going with this.

And I don't want to hear it.

That she wouldn't have slept with me.

That last night was a mistake.

That she regrets it.

I step toward her, cutting her off before she can say another fucking word. "It doesn't matter."

Her hazel eyes flick to mine, sharp and assessing. "I just meant—"

I tilt my head slightly, keeping my expression unreadable. "You don't need to explain anything, Elena. We were two strangers enjoying the night. It's irrelevant now."

She studies me carefully, as if trying to see if I really mean that.

I give her nothing.

Because if she sees how much her leaving pissed me off, I lose.

And I don't lose.

Eventually, she exhales, nodding once.

Something about the way she does it feels too much like relief, and that only irritates me more.

She straightens her shoulders, all business now. "Then let's be clear on the terms of our arrangement." She sets her purse down deliberately.

"No intimacy," she states. "No kissing. My contracts have never included that aspect, and I see no reason to change my terms now."

My eyes glance at her mouth on instinct.

No kissing.

It shouldn't bother me.

Hell, I specifically requested no intimacy as well—that this remain professional.

So why does it feel like a challenge?

Like she's daring me to see how long I can last before breaking that rule?

I keep my expression easy as I pour two glasses of wine, handing one to her.

She's careful not to let our fingers brush as she takes it.

A moment of silence passes.

Then, I lift my glass, smirking slightly. "Understood. This should be an easy two weeks," I murmur, my voice dripping with irony, "with a big payout at the end for both of us."

Elena meets my gaze, tilting her glass in return.

But we both know the truth.

This won't be easy.

And it sure as hell won't be clean.

The scent of fresh coffee drifts through the penthouse, mixing with the faint remnants of her perfume—vanilla and something warmer, something I still can't place.

Outside, the city is already alive, the distant hum of traffic bleeding through the floor-to-ceiling windows, but in here, it's quiet. Controlled.

I shrug on a black compression shirt, rolling my shoulders as I make my way toward the gym. It's not part of my usual morning routine to check who's using it. No one else lives here. No one else has ever used it.

But now, I have a guest.

Not just any guest.

Elena.

A steady, rhythmic sound filters into the hallway as I get closer. The low whir of a treadmill. The soft exhale of measured breaths.

I step into the doorway and spot her instantly.

She's running—focused, precise, entirely in control. There's nothing casual about the way she moves. Every shift of her body, every stride, every roll of her shoulders is deliberate. Purposeful.

She's not just working out.

She's training.

A faint sheen of sweat clings to her skin, making the smooth plane of her stomach glisten under the recessed lighting. Her fitted leggings move with her, emphasizing the strength in her legs, the flex of toned muscle. The thin straps of her sports bra leave her back bare, her shoulder blades tensing subtly with every controlled movement.

She's strong. Disciplined. Built for endurance.

Just like me.

I lean against the doorframe, arms crossing over my chest as I watch her.

Her brow is slightly furrowed, her lips parted as she keeps her pace, oblivious to my presence. For someone trained in performance, she's not putting on a show right now. There's no pretense. No carefully crafted persona.

Just her.

And fuck if I don't find that interesting.

The treadmill slows, winding down from a run to a steady walk before stopping completely. Elena steps off smoothly, grabbing a towel as she dabs the sweat from her brow.

She still hasn't noticed me.

That small detail twists something deep in my gut.

Not many people overlook me.

I wait another second, my gaze tracking the curve of her waist, the effortless way she moves.

And then, finally, I step forward.

The moment my foot hits the mat, she turns.

Her hazel eyes land on mine, and for just a breath, something shifts into something I can't pinpoint.

She smooths it over, her expression turning neutral.

If she's surprised to see me, she doesn't show it.

Instead, she tosses a towel toward me, her voice even. "I hope I didn't take your gym time." She wipes the back of her neck before continuing. "It wasn't on the schedule, so I figured it was open."

Ah, The Ledger schedule I had to fill out. I should be at the office by now.

I catch the towel easily, my grip tightening around the fabric for a beat longer than necessary. "It's fine."

She nods, making no move to leave right away.

Her gaze flickers—almost imperceptibly—over my arms, my chest, the snug fit of my shirt where it stretches across my shoulders.

She lingers there for just a second too long before pulling her focus back up.

She's not as indifferent as she's pretending to be.

And that knowledge settles low in my stomach.

Elena exhales, rolling her shoulders back. "All right then. I'll leave you to it."

She turns, walking out of the gym, her posture composed, confident.

I shouldn't push this line.

I should start my workout, push last night—and every thought of her—out of my fucking head.

But fuck it.

Just before she passes by me, I reach for the hem of my

shirt and pull it over my head, tossing it onto the nearby bench.

Her steps slow—just slightly.

Her cheeks flush, and she cuts her eyes at me.

I watch her walk away in the gym's floor-to-ceiling mirrors.

Just before she disappears around the corner—she glances back.

A split-second flick of her gaze. But I see it.

And she sees me.

She looks away too quickly, as if realizing her mistake.

I smirk, slow and knowing.

Did you like what you saw, Trouble?

I know she did.

Exhaling, I roll my shoulders before reaching for a set of weights.

Two easy weeks. That's what I told her last night.

But if she keeps looking at me like that...

I already know how this is going to end.

Chapter 6
Elena

The quiet hum of the city filters through the expansive windows of the penthouse, softened by the sound of light rain tapping against the glass. The morning is slow, unhurried. Exactly the kind I need.

I sit at the marble breakfast counter, a sleek tablet propped up in front of me, along with a black leather-bound ledger neatly placed to the side. My stylus rests between my fingers, but I haven't started working yet.

Instead, I focus on my breakfast—a simple plate of sliced fruit, eggs, and toast, something light to fuel the rest of my day. Across from me, on the counter, there's another plate, untouched.

I don't know why I made extra. Habit, maybe. I usually cook breakfast for my roommate and best friend, Eve.

She'd probably burn our place down if she tried to use the stove.

Or maybe I made it for the ridiculous notion that good manners should extend even to fake engagements.

I don't expect company.

The penthouse is so large, Damien could go about his day without crossing my path once if he wanted to. And based on the quiet atmosphere, I guess he's already at his office.

That assumption is shattered when I hear the sound of dress shoes approaching.

I glance up just as Damien enters the kitchen.

I ignore that stab in the pit of my stomach.

He's dressed in a tailored deep-blue suit, the crisp white shirt beneath it open at the collar, his tie hanging loose around his neck like he hasn't quite decided whether to finish the job. The controlled energy he exudes is effortless —a man who is used to commanding a room the moment he steps into it.

I expect him to grab a coffee and go.

Instead, he hesitates.

His blue eyes flick to the extra plate sitting untouched on the counter, and suddenly I wish I hadn't made it. His expression remains unreadable, but I don't miss the way his fingers brush against the marble surface, as if debating something.

And then—he makes a decision.

Rather than leaving, he changes course, stepping closer and planting himself across from me on the other side of the counter.

I blink, caught off guard.

He doesn't sit, doesn't make himself comfortable—just stands there, all sharp edges and intensity, the weight of his presence impossible to ignore.

I say nothing, waiting.

He exhales, rolling his shoulders slightly before speaking.

"It was really no problem, you using the gym this morning."

I pause, my fork halfway to my mouth. *That's what he came in here for?*

Before I can respond, he continues. "You don't have to check the schedule for things like that. You're welcome to use anything in the penthouse." A small pause, then, "The building, too, actually."

I tilt my head, intrigued. "The building?"

He nods, picking up a stray piece of toast from the extra plate—bold, considering he didn't even ask if it was for him.

"Yeah. Anything you need. The gym, the spa, the indoor pool, the concierge service. Hell, there are shops and plenty of restaurants."

A flicker of amusement tugs at the corner of my mouth. *Is he... rambling?*

Damien Wolfe. *The Wolfe of Fifth Avenue.* Rambling.

He doesn't seem to notice. Or maybe he does, but he keeps going anyway.

"There's a car service on standby, too. If you ever need to go anywhere, just tell them, and they'll take care of it." He shifts his weight slightly, breaking off a piece of toast and popping it into his mouth.

I narrow my eyes, watching him carefully.

Is he trying to impress me?

The thought is ridiculous.

Damien Wolfe is the last man on earth who needs to

impress anyone. He has wealth, power, and an entire city at his feet.

But still...

I study him for another second, trying to piece it together. His tone is too even, like he's trying too hard to sound indifferent. And now that I think about it, there's something almost unnatural about the way he's lingering here—like he doesn't actually want to leave but doesn't have a reason to stay.

The realization is... surprising.

And strangely endearing.

I let a slow, amused smile pull at my lips before responding lightly. "Good to know. I appreciate your hospitality." My coffee cup clinks softly against the marble counter. "We have Ledger resources, so we don't impose, but thank you all the same."

For a second, I think the conversation will move along, easy and effortless. But something shifts in his expression, subtle yet distinct, like my words land in a way he wasn't expecting.

His jaw tightens slightly before he speaks. "You wouldn't be an imposition."

Then, as if realizing he's given something away, he adjusts.

"It." A quiet correction. "It would be no imposition."

I recognize what just happened. A small slip. A moment of unconscious honesty before catching himself.

It's not what I expected from him, and that alone makes it stand out.

The silence between us lingers a beat too long, and the

weight of it makes something twist in my stomach. I don't know what it is—discomfort? Curiosity? Either way, I do what I do best.

I smooth it over.

"Busy day at the office?" I ask, tilting my head slightly. "Before tonight's event?"

The change in topic is exactly what he needs. His shoulders ease just the slightest bit, and the tension that had begun to settle between us lifts.

"Always," he says, the edge of a smirk playing at his lips. "But nothing I can't handle."

I don't push for details. Men like Damien don't discuss business over breakfast. That's reserved for boardrooms, for closed-door meetings over top-shelf whiskey, for negotiations worth billions.

But I've done my own research.

Wolfe Industries is in the middle of acquiring a major competitor. This merger is high-profile—the kind that cements power, the kind that makes headlines.

Tonight's event will be a crucial moment in securing that deal.

Damien doesn't offer more, and I don't ask. Instead, I simply nod, taking another sip of coffee, letting the conversation settle.

And then, just as I think he's about to leave, he surprises me.

Instead of walking away, instead of disappearing into his empire as I expected, he pulls out a chair.

And sits down.

His movements are unhurried, deliberate, but there's

something almost uncertain about them—like he hadn't quite planned on staying.

I say nothing as he reaches for the extra plate of food, sliding it toward himself.

A silent decision.

I recognize this moment for what it is.

He's choosing to stay.

And for reasons I don't fully understand, that realization sends a quiet shiver down my spine.

For a moment, we eat in silence, the only sounds the occasional clink of silverware against porcelain, the hum of the city stretching high beyond the penthouse windows.

Then, after another bite, Damien speaks again, his voice even.

"I'll usually be gone before you wake up."

It's not an apology. Just a statement of fact—a warning of sorts.

I nod, unbothered. "That will be no problem. I keep busy."

His gaze flicks up, studying me over the rim of his coffee cup. "Doing what?"

There's something about the way he asks—not just the words, but the hesitation before them.

Like he's debating how to phrase it.

I already know what he's really asking.

What do you do all day until I need you?

I set my fork down, leveling my gaze with his. "You mean until my contract requires me?"

I don't miss the way his grip tightens slightly around his coffee mug.

He doesn't correct me, doesn't clarify.

Instead, he just watches me. "Yeah." He nods once.

I hold his gaze, my voice smooth. "I do have my own affairs to manage." A small pause, letting it settle. "I don't need to be entertained, Mr. Wolfe."

Something flickers across his face. It's so small, so quick, but I see it.

"Damien." He corrects me, and I nod.

Something switches in him in an instant. For just a moment, it's as if the polished, controlled version of Damien Wolfe slips, and what's left behind is something quieter. Something simpler.

Not a billionaire. Not the infamous Wolf of Fifth Avenue.

Just a man.

A man sitting at his own kitchen counter, eating breakfast with someone else.

And for the briefest moment, I wonder if anyone has ever actually seen him like this.

He takes a breath as if to say something—holds it—then wars with some decision in his mind before releasing it.

I see the *fuck it* moment happen, and he snaps his eyes to mine.

"If I ask you a question, will you answer honestly?" His voice is steady, but there's a quiet intensity behind it.

"I've answered every question honestly."

Even at Ember & Ash. I want to add, but I don't.

"What made you smile?" His voice deepens, like we're sharing a secret. Like he's daring me to answer.

A fraction of a grin spreads across my face, and he looks at my mouth before returning to my eyes.

"I smile often. Be specific."

It's a game, and he wants to meet the challenge.

"At the restaurant. On your phone."

Ah, *that.*

Still bothering him, I see.

"What was it that made you smile?"

It's like he *needs* to know. Like the rest of these two weeks will hang on my answer.

I hesitate, fingers resting lightly on the rim of my coffee cup.

Sharing personal details isn't something I do.

Not with clients. Not with contracts. Barely with my friends.

It's a line I've always kept firmly in place—one of the few things in this job that has always been within my control. I offer exactly what's required, nothing more. My clients get what they pay for: charm, poise, companionship. But my real thoughts, my real dreams?

Those belong to me.

But with Damien...

We crossed so many lines before this even began.

Maybe that's why I decide to answer honestly.

I take a slow sip of coffee, gathering my thoughts before setting the cup down carefully.

"I want to open a high-end cheesecakery and café."

Damien's brows lift slightly, his head tilting just enough to show his interest. "You're serious?"

A soft smile tugs at the corner of my lips. "Why wouldn't I be?"

He doesn't answer right away, but his gaze sharpens, studying me like he's trying to piece something together.

I shift slightly in my seat, tracing the rim of my cup with my fingertip as I continue.

"There's a specific location I have my eye on. Not just any storefront—it's personal."

I don't explain right away, and he doesn't press. He just waits, silent and patient, as if he knows there's more.

And for the first time in a long time, I let myself remember.

My early adult years were difficult, and I made hard choices.

Some of those were painful. Horrible, even.

The darkest days of my life. And that's really saying something.

But the bakery, my job there—those are some of the happiest memories I have.

I don't tell Damien all of this. Some things are still mine to keep.

"My realtor went and checked it out. And we're meeting soon to look at it."

I stare at my coffee, light brown and still steaming, about to lose myself in the memories before I snap them shut again.

"That's what made me smile."

His expression shifts slightly, something flickering behind those blue eyes, something unreadable.

"You don't plan on staying at The Ledger?" he asks, his voice measured. "Lucian says you're one of the best."

I let out a soft breath, shaking my head. "Women in my line of work have a shelf life."

The words hang between us, stretching out the silence.

After a moment, quieter now, I add, "I don't want to be a hired companion forever, Damien."

His gaze lingers on mine, and for a brief moment, I see it again—the man beneath the billionaire, the one who's been sitting with me, eating breakfast like it was something he wasn't used to sharing.

Like maybe, in some ways, he's just as unfamiliar with real companionship as I am. When it's not bought.

He exhales slowly, almost like he's considering my words, turning them over in his mind.

But then, the shift happens. Seamless and almost imperceptible, but it's there.

"Dinner tonight." His voice is back to business, clipped and professional. "I'll pick you up at eight. Mr. and Mrs. Calloway will be there."

I nod, the mask slipping back into place as easily as breathing. "Mrs. Calloway is the key."

His gaze flicks to mine. "Exactly. Mrs. Calloway is the key."

I don't need him to elaborate. If he's bringing her up specifically, it means she's the one with the final say in this merger. She'll be scrutinizing every detail, looking for any cracks in our relationship. If I can win her over, this entire deal becomes a sure thing.

I offer him a confident smile, smoothing my hands over my lap. "Leave Mrs. Calloway to me."

A beat of silence stretches between us before Damien raps his knuckles against the counter twice and stands.

"All right then." He pulls up a contact in his phone, heading toward the elevator. "Hey, Marcus, can you pull something up for me?"

No goodbye. No pleasantries. No lingering hesitation.

And why would there be?

This is a contract.

I don't need small talk. I don't need warmth.

I don't need *anything* from him.

But as he walks away without another word, I find myself wishing he'd said something else.

Chapter 7

Damien

Offers are being made as I get into the backseat of my SUV.

By the time I make it to the office, they're done and signed.

My assistant, Vanessa, is up my ass as soon as I step foot in the lobby.

Contracts to review.

Schedules to confirm.

Pushing off a day and a half of meetings is catching up to me. But fine.

The day rushes by in a blur, and I'm thankful for the distraction. Though, as the afternoon wears on, I can't stop looking at the time every ten fucking minutes.

Finally, I can't handle it anymore, and I bark at my assistant to reschedule the rest of the evening and leave early. She rattles off something about her birthday, but I'm already moving to the SUV.

Within two minutes, I'm headed back to the Blackstone.

On a typical day, I'd just work at the office, change, and head to my event from there. But I have a fiancée now, and we need to arrive together.

It's not a bother. I'll just work in the car and take a quick shower when I get to the penthouse.

Elena is nowhere to be found, and I assume she's putting the finishing touches on her outfit for the night.

Dinner is at The Scallop, another five-star restaurant in one of the world's most top-rated hotels. Mine, of course.

Marcus, my best friend and business partner, will be there with his husband.

Mr. and Mrs. Calloway, our newest multibillion-dollar business takeover.

And me, with my blushing bride-to-be in tow.

Marcus and I both know tonight is a test—a big one. Which means Elena's role will be that much more important.

I adjust the black-and-silver cufflinks and inspect my tux once more. Black on black. A spritz of cologne, and I head out of my bedroom to wait for Elena.

Elena doesn't hear me approach, and when I step into view, she startles so hard she nearly jumps out of her heels.

Her hand flies to her chest, eyes wide. "Jesus, Damien," she exhales, pressing a palm over her heart. "You scared me half to death."

I arch a brow. "You didn't hear me come up?"

She shakes her head, still catching her breath. "I thought I'd just meet you downstairs."

I don't answer right away, my attention snagging on

something else—her hand. More specifically, the ring on her left finger.

My eyes narrow as I take it in. A simple, uninspired band with a modest stone. It barely catches the light, let alone commands it.

I frown. "What's this?" I ask, reaching for her hand, lifting it between us.

Elena barely glances at it. "A prop," she says, shrugging. "It'll pass for real. I have others if you prefer something else."

A prop. A placeholder. Something temporary and meaningless.

The thought irritates me more than it should.

Before she can react, I slide the ring off her finger, tossing it onto the counter behind me. Her brows pull together in confusion, but I'm already reaching into my pocket, pulling out a sleek black velvet box.

She notices, and her eyes narrow. "What are you doing?"

I flick the box open with a sharp snap, revealing a real ring. One I purchased the moment I left the office after meeting her.

I hadn't thought much of it at the time—just that my fiancée, fake or not, would wear nothing but the best. The idea of her walking around with a cheap imitation is unacceptable.

Ignoring the way the word *fake* sits like ash in my mouth, I say simply, "Making sure my fiancée looks the part."

She blinks. "Damien—"

She's about to argue, but I cut her off. "I won't have my fiancée walking around with a fake diamond."

Her lips part slightly, like she's weighing her next move, like she's considering fighting me on this.

I don't give her the chance.

"It's only on loan, Elena."

I take her left hand in mine, my thumb brushing over the delicate bones of her fingers. Her skin is warm, soft. *Too* soft. I shouldn't be noticing that.

I slide the ring onto her finger.

Cool metal. Heavy. *Perfect.*

The moment it's in place, I catch the way her breath hitches. Just slightly. Just enough for me to notice.

I should let go. I should step back.

Should.

I hold her hand for a second longer than necessary. My thumb moves without thinking, tracing along the band, as if testing how it feels there.

My gaze flicks up.

Not on the ring. On *her.*

"Perfect fit," I murmur.

I release her hand and turn away, adjusting my cufflinks —again—ignoring the tension coiled in my gut.

"Let's go," I say, my voice steady.

I don't look back.

Because if I do, I might start wondering why it matters so much that the ring fits.

The Scallop is as polished and exclusive as it gets, a beacon of fine dining nestled in one of my top-rated hotels. Every detail, from the ambient lighting to the private sommelier service, is designed to impress. To remind people of their place in the hierarchy of power.

Elena fits here like she was carved for it.

She moves beside me with effortless grace, her posture impeccable, her presence impossible to ignore. Her gown—black silk—clings in all the right places, drapes in others. Just enough bare skin to tempt but never offer.

Elegant. Dangerous.

A walking contradiction of allure and restraint.

And every single man in this room notices.

The realization grates more than it should.

It's instinctive, the way my hand settles low on her back as we're led toward the private suite. A light touch. Possessive, but not obvious. Just enough to remind those watching who she belongs to.

She doesn't react, doesn't lean in, doesn't cling like so many women before her.

She simply walks at my side, like she *belongs* there.

Inside, Marcus and his husband, James, are already waiting.

Marcus looks up first, standing as we enter. Not just my business partner—but my longest, most trusted friend.

He masks his amusement well, but I know him too well to miss it. The slight arch of his brow, the flicker of sharp curiosity in his eyes. He's waiting to see how we play this.

I feel Elena's inhale, feel the way she shifts slightly

beside me before stepping forward—not waiting to be introduced.

She turns to James first, offering a warm smile.

"Elena," she says, extending a hand with easy confidence. "I was looking forward to meeting you. Your photography portfolio is absolutely stunning."

James blinks, momentarily thrown before his expression shifts into something surprised—genuinely pleased.

"You've seen my work?"

Elena nods. "Of course. The exhibit you did in Paris? *Breathtaking.*"

Marcus steps closer to me, watching the two of them fall into effortless conversation.

"Oh, she's good," Marcus exhales a quiet laugh, shaking his head.

"Only the best," I answer thoughtlessly.

He lifts a brow. "Careful, Wolfe. Sounds like you almost believe it."

I don't answer.

Because Mr. and Mrs. Calloway enter the room, and everything shifts.

Elena slips her hand into the crook of my elbow, her posture straightening, her expression poised and polished.

She's *ready*.

She takes Mrs. Calloway's hand and smiles.

"It's such a pleasure to finally meet you."

The older woman studies her for a second longer, then glances at her ring.

"What a stunning ring."

Elena glances at me, eyes softening with a look so devoted, so seamless, it *should* be illegal.

"It is," she agrees smoothly. "Damien spoils me."

I don't correct her.

Because right now, in this moment, it *doesn't* feel like a lie.

And that should fucking terrify me.

Mrs. Calloway studies Elena for a beat longer, her sharp gaze flicking between us as if weighing every detail.

Then, finally, she smiles.

Warm. Approving.

A critical win.

Dinner flows seamlessly, and Elena is flawless. Her conversation is effortless, her responses precise. She engages in just the right places—knowing when to be inquisitive, when to flatter, when to let a moment sit in silence.

She never overplays it. Never forces it. And it's *working*.

Mr. Calloway watches her with appreciation, his demeanor warming.

His wife? She's *enthralled*.

It should impress me. It *does* impress me.

But it also unsettles me.

Because for the first time tonight, I realize something.

She's done this before.

She knows *exactly* what she's doing.

Some other fuckers before me paid for her time, for her to sell whatever fantasy they wanted, and all that practice is helping her deliver tonight's performance.

I have to remind myself—again—who she is.

She's an escort. A professional. This is what she does.

So why the fuck does it feel like she was *mine* first?

I shake the thought, forcing my focus back to the room.

Elena is deep in conversation with Mrs. Calloway, her tone warm, genuine, as they discuss charity work. It's a stroke of fucking genius.

"I knew I recognized you from somewhere," Elena says, tilting her head as if just placing it. "You were featured in a piece about the Global Future Fund's Gala for Children's Education."

Mrs. Calloway visibly *glows* at the mention. "You read that article?"

Elena nods. "Of course. Your work with at-risk children is incredible. I volunteer often at St. James Orphanage, so I hope you know how far your reach extends."

Marcus and I exchange a look. Neither of us uncovered this in our research.

Mrs. Calloway places her hand over Elena's in a compassionate squeeze. She looks at her like she's found a *kindred spirit*.

Then she turns to me, her smile warm, her voice weighted. "Damien, you are one lucky man. A woman like this is one in a million. I hope you realize you've got quite a catch here."

Elena's hand rests on my thigh. A light touch. Measured. Controlled.

She tilts her head toward me slightly, her eyes holding mine just a beat too long.

My response is delayed.

I force myself to move, to react—my arm settling along

the back of her chair, my fingers grazing the bare skin of her shoulder in a slow, deliberate stroke.

It's for *them.*

For the audience.

For the performance.

But that doesn't explain why my fucking heart is hammering in my chest.

I clear my throat, offering Mrs. Calloway a smooth smile. "Nonsense. She's worth it a hundred times over."

The older woman beams, her approval locked in.

Elena shifts closer, just enough that I catch the faint scent of vanilla and something *warmer.* Something I still can't place.

Then—the question I've been waiting for.

"So, how did you two meet?"

Elena doesn't hesitate.

She dives smoothly into our fabricated story, painting it in perfect strokes—how we met at an event, how I pursued her with single-minded determination, how she resisted at first—she smirks at this, the perfect touch of teasing—but I wouldn't take no for an answer.

Mrs. Calloway *loves* it.

"Elena, you must join me Thursday for doubles at the club," she says warmly. "My old friend Sandra is bringing her daughter. I won't take no for an answer."

I fight the urge to smirk. *Perfect.*

"Thank you so much. I would love to." Elena answers with a bright gleam in her eye.

It's a masterpiece of deception, even Marcus was watching, impressed.

But something twists in my stomach.

Like she's too good at this.

Like she's done it before.

I school my reaction fast, smoothing my expression before anyone notices.

Because for the first time tonight, I realize something unsettling.

She *has* done this before.

Some other fuckers before me purchased her time to sell whatever fantasy they wanted, and all that practice helps her deliver tonight's performance.

What the fuck is wrong with me?

I have to repeat something I realized yesterday when we met at The Ledger.

She's an escort. A professional.

This is what she does.

So why the fuck does it feel like she was mine first?

The limo ride back to the Blackstone is quiet.

I reflect on the evening—every question asked, every answer I gave—making sure my stories remain consistent with the write-up prepared for our contract.

Things went *perfectly* with Mrs. Calloway, and securing a tennis outing in two days was unexpected. Something that bodes well.

Inside the penthouse, Damien moves toward his room without hesitation, his jacket draped over his arm, his bow tie undone at the collar. He looks composed. Unbothered.

But I caught the way his jaw clenched when Mrs. Calloway praised our match.

The flicker of something unreadable when I recited the engagement story.

And now, he keeps his back to me, offering nothing.

I should let it go.

Instead, I take a step forward. *"Wait."*

He stops but doesn't turn right away. When he does, his expression is unreadable, a single brow lifting in question.

Smoothing my hands over the silk of my dress, I keep my voice even. Professional.

"I just wanted your impression on how things went. Anything you'd like me to adjust going forward?"

His jaw tightens. So faint I might have missed it if I weren't *looking*.

A second passes before he answers. "Things went well." His tone is clipped. Final.

That should be the end of it.

But I hesitate, and he *notices*.

His attention sharpens, waiting, sensing there's something else I want to say.

"It's just..." I pause. "You made a face. After the engagement story."

The words settle between us, quiet but not unnoticed.

Damien doesn't answer right away, and when he does, his voice is unreadable. "You're a very good liar."

A statement, not a compliment.

His eyes stay on mine, searching, as if trying to find something beneath the surface. But I hold his gaze, steady, unwilling to give him anything more than what I already have.

After a long moment, I reply, "Everything about these next two weeks will be a lie."

The space between us *shifts*.

Charged with something neither of us is willing to acknowledge.

"It's important you remember that."

For a moment, he doesn't move, his exhale slow and controlled, as if resetting.

"Noted."

He sets his jacket on the kitchen counter. "Any—*adjustments*—for me?"

I take in a breath, releasing it carefully.

"Well..."

My eyes lower, weighing how to phrase this. With any other contract, it would be *clinical*. But not with Damien.

"It's fine, Elena. I can take criticism." His tone is calmer now. More patient.

"You should be more affectionate with me when we're out in public."

I try to keep my tone neutral, but I *feel* my cheeks heat because we both know what his affections look like.

What they *feel* like.

He looks out at the city, swallowing hard before turning back to me.

"I touched you plenty tonight."

"Not like a fiancé would."

He takes a deep breath, releasing it hard and slow. "Anything *specific*?"

The tension in the room *shifts*.

I step toward the living room, glancing back just enough to let him know I expect him to follow.

Damien hesitates, watching me for a beat longer than necessary, then moves. The quiet sound of his footfalls behind me is unnerving in a way I can't quite name.

I sink onto the couch, smoothing my dress over my thighs before patting the cushion beside me.

His brows lift slightly. Surprise. Amusement.

But he doesn't argue.

He moves, slow and deliberate, taking the seat beside me.

And suddenly, the penthouse feels *too small.*

He's *close*, the heat of him bleeding into my skin, the scent of his cologne lingering from the long evening. His thigh brushes against mine as he settles, and I keep my expression composed, even as the awareness between us *sparks hotter.*

Stay professional. Stay in control.

"It's not just a touch—it's the *feeling* that needs to be sold along with it."

Not just holding hands, but stroking mine.

Like *this.*

I trail my fingers lightly over his skin, demonstrating the motion.

The first touch of my skin on his is *electric.*

"Your hand on my back as we move through a space was perfect."

"Well, thank you for the good marks, *teacher.*" His lips curve, the ghost of a smirk teasing the edge of his mouth.

I ignore it.

"When we sit close together, your arm should be around the back of my chair."

I move his arm around my shoulders.

"Or on my knee. The thoughtless caress as we enjoy the evening."

He doesn't need instruction here.

His fingers trail gently along my arm as I speak, and my stomach *flips* in response.

I reach for his other hand, holding his gaze as I guide it down, pressing his palm against my thigh, covered in the rich silk gown.

His fingers flex slightly—the only indication that he *feels this* just as much as I do.

Good.

I move his hand slightly higher.

"This," I murmur, smoothing his palm over my skin, encouraging the motion. "A casual touch. Comfortable. Familiar."

We're *too close.*

I *should* move away.

Damien hums low in his throat, watching me carefully, his fingers moving in slow, measured strokes.

My voice is quieter when I speak again, the atmosphere *shifting*, darkening.

"And if I tell you a secret..."

I lean in slightly, my breath warm against his jaw, watching the way his own deepens—slow and measured.

His hand slides *higher* up my thigh.

His touch is *firmer*. More confident.

I exhale, dragging my fingertips along his jawline, the stubble sharp beneath my touch.

"It should be the most captivating secret you've ever heard."

Damien turns into me as if we're sharing a sacred moment. His cologne is an overload I'm already *struggling* to temper.

His dark gaze locks onto mine. Searching. *Challenging.*

"People notice the small things."

I don't look away.

Neither does he.

A slow, unbearable beat passes between us.

We're *still too close.*

With a deep breath, I pull back, putting inches between us that feel like miles before standing.

"And when dancing—"

I hold my arms out expectantly.

Waiting for my dance partner.

Waiting for the controlled, practiced steps of our arrangement.

Damien stands, smooth and deliberate, but there's something *different* now.

Something in the way his features sharpen.

The faintest shift in his expression.

A glimpse of the man people call the Wolfe of Fifth Avenue.

I *don't* expect him to take control.

I *don't* expect him to pull me into his body like he owns me.

Like he *knows* my body.

Even though he *does.*

His hand settles *low* against my back, pressing me flush against him, his grip firm but unhurried. The other closes over mine, his thumb brushing the inside of my palm, his touch sending a slow pulse of heat up my arm.

My breath *hitches* as he moves.

His steps are precise. Dominant.

A *push and pull*. Effortless. Seamless.

Except it isn't a lesson anymore.

Before I can register it, he dips me back, the world *tilting*, his body molded to mine.

His breath warms my skin as his nose drags along my collarbone, then up my neck.

Slow. Unhurried.

Like he's *memorizing* me.

His voice is a whisper, dark and rough.

"I didn't need a map of your body two nights ago, Trouble."

The nickname rolls off his tongue *effortlessly.*

Like he's been saying it for *years.*

Like he didn't mean to say it at all.

My breath catches. His does too.

For a fraction of a second, something *passes* between us.

And I don't know what the hell to do with it.

I don't move.

Neither does he.

The room is too quiet.

Or maybe it's just *us*.

Trapped in this moment, in this *tension* that coils so tight I can feel it like a tangible thing between us.

Damien's grip on my waist is firm, his fingers pressing into the silk of my gown like he's considering *something.*

Like he's debating whether to let go.

Or to hold on tighter.

He doesn't blink.

Neither do I.

I feel his breath, warm against my skin. His body, impossibly close.

I should step back.

I *need* to step back.

But I don't.

And neither does he.

Not until his gaze drops—to my mouth.

A slow, calculated flick of his eyes.

A single second.

But I *feel* it.

Like a brand.

And suddenly, I can't breathe.

I open my mouth—to say something, to force distance, to *fix* this—

But his fingers tighten, just slightly, his grip shifting at my waist.

His thumb brushes against my ribs, the contact featherlight but devastating.

My stomach clenches.

A *warning* flares in my brain, sharp and insistent.

This is too close.

Too *dangerous*.

I should break away.

But his hold is *anchoring*, like he's waiting for something.

Like he's testing how long I'll stay *right here*.

Too close. Too deep. Too much.

A sharp exhale leaves my lips, and that's all it takes.

Damien blinks, then releases me.

Abrupt. Controlled.

Like the moment never happened at all.

I stumble a half step back, my breath uneven.

His expression is unreadable.

And then—he walks away.

Just turns, grabs his jacket, and leaves the room without another glance.

Without hesitation.

Without giving me a chance to catch up.

The only sign that something just happened—the tension still crackling in the air.

The way my body *aches* from the ghost of his touch.

I don't move for a long time.

Not until I hear the door to his bedroom shut with a quiet *click.*

Not until I realize my fingers are still curled into the fabric of my dress, gripping it like an anchor.

Not until I exhale and force my shoulders back, schooling my expression into something smooth.

Something *untouched.*

Because *that*—whatever just happened—was nothing.

It *had* to be nothing.

And I refuse to let it become anything else.

Chapter 9
Damien

I storm down the hall, tension rolling off me in waves, my pulse a violent drumbeat in my ears.

My hands flex at my sides, aching to grab something.

To *touch* her.

To *pull* her back into my arms and finish what she started in the living room.

Behind me, I hear her—soft footfalls, the click of her heels as she finally retreats to her own room.

I exhale hard, shoving a hand through my hair as I step into my bedroom and slam the door shut behind me.

A whisper of ambient light intrudes on the darkness.

It's quiet.

But it does *nothing* to ease the storm in my chest.

My jacket is the first to go, hurled at the closet wall. It slides down in a heap. I don't care.

Next is my tie. I yank it loose with a sharp pull, the silk sliding over my fingers before I fling it aside.

But it doesn't help.

I can still *feel* her—the warmth of her skin against mine, the way her scent wrapped around me, heady and sweet.

I rip open the buttons of my shirt, my breath heavy, my chest rising and falling as cool air finally touches my overheated skin.

I sit down hard on the edge of the bed, my head dropping into my hands as I drag in a breath that does nothing to steady me.

How the fuck am I supposed to survive two weeks of this?

Her *proximity.*

Her body wrapped in fine silks that were made to *worship* her.

Those little gasps she makes when I catch her off guard.

The way her pulse flutters in her throat when I get too close.

She's intoxicating.

Infuriating.

And my cock is hard as *fucking marble.*

I drag my palms down my face and groan.

I should have never agreed to this contract.

I should have told Lucian to *fuck off.*

Should have carried Elena out of his office like a goddamn caveman, thrown her over my shoulder, and taken her straight to my penthouse—contract be damned.

I grit my teeth, my jaw clenching so tight it aches.

Instead, I agreed to *this.*

This *charade.*

This *torture.*

I think of her in that tight, short red dress at The Ledger. The way it clung to her like a second skin, teasing with every step, every shift of her hips.

How her lips were painted a deep crimson, that perfect red just *begging* to be smeared along my cock.

I exhale hard, my pulse pounding as the fantasy unspools behind my closed eyelids.

She would have let me push that dress up the second we got in the limo.

Would have *gasped* when my hands parted her thighs, baring the softest part of her to me.

Would have *shivered* when my tongue dragged along the silk of her panties, my breath hot, my hunger impossible to miss.

She would have been wet for me.

I *know* it.

I *remember* it.

My steps are slow, deliberate, as I move to my dresser.

The top drawer slides open with barely a sound, and my fingers find what they're looking for.

A delicate scrap of black lace.

The panties my little troublemaker left in my pants pocket as a token of her goodbye.

Unwashed. Untouched. Still carrying her sweet scent.

I bring them to my face, inhaling deeply, and my cock throbs so hard it's *painful*.

Fuck.

My free hand moves to my belt, unbuckling, unzipping, shoving my pants just low enough to free my aching length.

I fist my cock, the soft lace brushing against my skin as I stroke from base to tip, a slow, torturous drag.

She was *soaked* for me that night.

I imagine that wet heat against my tongue, imagine pressing my face between her thighs and licking her through this lace, teasing her with the promise of my mouth.

I tighten my grip, sliding my hand down my shaft, slow and firm, a growl rumbling in my chest.

In my mind, she's in my lap in the limo, *straddling* me, those soft moans spilling from her lips as I shove her panties aside and slide into her—deep, raw, *bare*.

I groan, my pace quickening, my other hand holding the lace, pressing it against my nose as my body tenses, my release so fucking close.

I tighten my grip, stroking harder, faster, as my mind drowns in the fantasy.

I could *rip* that fucking dress open.

Spill her *perfect* tits into my hands. Into my mouth.

I'd suck one deep, my tongue flicking against her hardened nipple while she rode me, her thighs gripping my hips as the limo carried us through *my* city.

Driving her to orgasm. *Pleasuring* her like no one else ever could.

She'd arch for me. Whimper for me. Her fingers fisting in my hair, holding me to her breast as I *bit down* just enough —just enough to pinch and send her *spiraling*.

And she would sound so *fucking beautiful* as she called out my name.

My name.

Her body clenching around me, pulsing, tightening, *milking* every last drop of pleasure from me as she shattered in my arms.

The thought alone is enough to send me *over the edge.*

A guttural groan rips through me as my orgasm crashes over me, my cock jerking, pleasure rolling through every muscle, the scent of her thick in my lungs.

I barely manage to grab a handkerchief from my dresser before I spill into it, my strokes slowing, dragging out every last wave of bliss.

Her name slips from my lips.

Quiet.

Reverent.

Wrecked.

"Elena."

She has *no idea.*

No *fucking* idea what she does to me.

If she knew—if she even *suspected* how deep she's sinking into me—

Would she use it against me?

Would she push me just to see how far I'd let her go?

Would she press her lips to my ear, whisper my name in that same breathless way I remember, just to watch me unravel?

Or worse—

Would she *exploit* it?

Would she look at me the way so many have before—calculating instead of captivated?

Would she realize that my desire—this *obsession* clawing under my skin—makes me just as vulnerable as the men who have spent their fortunes trying to claim her?

Would she test how far she could bend me?

How much deeper she could sink her nails into me?

Not just for the contract.

Not just for the *ten-million-dollar payout.*

But for *more.*

More access. More power. *More of me.*

Just like all the others who have wanted to use my name to cement their place in this city.

To take what they could before I *inevitably* cut them loose.

That thought—that *fucking* thought—is what kills me the most.

Because if she tried—if she looked at me and saw nothing but another mark to conquer—

I don't think I'd let her.

Not without *proving* exactly who holds the leash in this game.

And that?

That would be *dangerous* for both of us.

The second it's over—disgust claws up my throat.

I exhale harshly, my grip tightening around the lace in my hand.

What the fuck is wrong with me?

She's just a contract. Just a *means to an end.*

And yet here I am—fisting my cock to the thought of her like a *fucking obsessed man.*

Like I have any fucking *claim.*

I yank open the drawer and shove the lace inside, slamming it shut so hard the wood rattles.

Two weeks.

I drag a rough hand down my face, my chest still heaving.

How the fuck am I supposed to survive two weeks of this?

Chapter 10
Elena

The sleek black town car glides up the winding drive of the Westbury Country Club, its pristine grounds sprawling in all directions, bathed in the golden morning light.

It's the kind of place where old money is inherited, not earned, and where women like Mrs. Calloway—graceful, poised, and influential—hold court like modern-day aristocracy.

As the car rolls to a stop beneath the covered entryway, I exhale, smoothing my hands down the white pleated tennis skirt I chose for today.

Classic. Elegant.

The kind of attire that blends in effortlessly among the ranks of country-club wives while still making an impression.

A crisp-uniformed valet opens my door, offering a polite smile as I step out, my white sneakers barely making a sound against the smooth pavement.

I nod in acknowledgment, offering a small smile before stepping forward into the club's grand entrance.

The air is cool, scented with expensive cologne and freshly brewed coffee, the quiet murmur of moneyed conversations echoing against the vaulted ceiling.

Confidence, I remind myself. This isn't just a game of appearances—it's a battle of positioning.

My positioning.

If this deal goes through, it won't just solidify Damien's merger—it will be my success, too.

My payout. My future.

The ten million dollars at the end of this contract is the key to my freedom. The key to finally owning something of my own. To finally walking away from the Black Ledger with enough to never look back.

I'm so close I can feel it.

And I'll be damned if I let anything—or anyone—get in the way.

Stepping past the entrance, I follow the concierge's direction toward the club's private courts. The sound of tennis balls hitting taut strings echoes through the mani-cured hedges, the distant chatter of the morning social crowd humming in the air.

I spot Mrs. Calloway immediately.

Dressed in a crisp white tennis dress, she's the picture of effortless wealth, her sleek blonde ponytail pulled high, her diamond tennis bracelet catching the sunlight as she gestures animatedly to one of her friends.

She's exactly the kind of woman who holds the power to make or break men like Damien Wolfe.

And today, I need to ensure that power works in our favor.

Straightening my posture, I push my shoulders back and stride toward her, a warm, confident smile curving my lips.

"Mrs. Calloway," I greet smoothly as I approach. "I hope I'm not too late."

She turns, her sharp eyes sweeping over me with appraisal before softening into a pleased smile.

"Not at all, dear. And call me Margo," she says, reaching out to clasp my hand in a delicate but firm grip. "I was just telling Sandra about you. She's absolutely dying to hear more about your work with St. James."

I smile at the mention—perfectly timed, perfectly placed.

The game begins.

Sandra's daughter arrives—another blushing bride planning a lavish spring wedding next year.

Mrs. Calloway—Margo—wants to know my plans. She hasn't read anything about our engagement in any of the papers.

Ah, she's been looking.

"Damien has paid a pretty penny to keep our relationship private." I take a sip of cool water. "Sometimes I feel like there's nothing he can't do."

I find myself staring off for a moment, the weight of that statement settling deep inside me.

"Young love," Sandra teases, nudging Margo with her elbow and a smirk.

"It looks beautiful on you, Elena." Margo's eyes gleam with something almost maternal. "So, tell us—where do you plan to marry? Richard and I couldn't have children, so allow me to live vicariously through you and pretend I'm the mother of the bride."

We chuckle, but I hide the burn in my chest that comment causes.

"I bet your parents are just thrilled—"

She's cut off, noticing someone behind us. Margo smiles and raises her hand.

"Over here, dear." With her hands on each side of her chair, she stands. "My nephew."

Sandra falls into a quiet chat with her daughter, and I rise as well, turning around to make a polite greeting to the newcomer.

My breath stalls mid-inhale. A cold grip seizes my spine, locking me in place as my eyes meet his.

Familiar. Unmistakable.

A ghost I thought I'd buried for good.

Adrian Kingston.

He's every inch the same spoiled rich boy he was back then—tailored sportswear, designer sunglasses perched atop his head, that same lazy, self-satisfied smirk that used to make my skin crawl.

It still does.

My hands curl into the fabric of my skirt before I force them to relax.

Breathe. Stay calm.

"What a surprise, Adrian." Margo beams as she hugs him.

He watches me over her shoulder, never looking away.

The shock barely has time to register before his lips stretch into a slow, sinister smile. It's the same arrogant, entitled smirk I remember—one that once made me feel small, insignificant.

Powerless.

Not anymore.

I smooth my expression, shuttering the moment of recognition, slipping into the role I've perfected over the years. The woman I am now doesn't flinch. She doesn't cower.

Margo beams, blissfully unaware of the storm brewing beneath my skin. "Elena, dear, this is my nephew, Adrian. Adrian, meet Elena—Damien Wolfe's fiancée."

The amusement in his gaze sharpens.

I extend my hand as if I've never seen him before, as if the touch of his skin on mine wouldn't make me want to scrub it raw.

"A pleasure to meet you."

Adrian takes it. Holds it a second too long.

His grip is firm, his thumb brushing over my wrist—subtle, intentional. Testing me.

"Haven't we met before?" His voice is smooth, laced with mock curiosity.

My stomach twists, but I don't blink.

I keep a polite smile on my face, slipping my fingers from his grasp. "No, I don't believe so."

His smirk deepens.

"Hmm." He tilts his head like he's picking apart a puzzle. "I never forget a pretty face, and someone as beautiful as you would leave an impression."

The words slither through the space between us, wrapping around my ribs like a slow constriction.

Before I have to reply, Margo calls for the server.

"Oh, let's have some iced teas brought over, please." She waves a hand, distracted, her warm attention still blissfully unaware of the tension radiating from me.

I rip my hand away from him.

His eyes gleam with something wicked. Calculating.

And suddenly, the stakes of this entire charade feel so much higher.

Because Adrian isn't just some old flame.

He's the kind of problem that doesn't go away quietly.

And he's just found his favorite plaything again.

Sandra and her daughter are already moving back toward the court, rackets in hand, chatting about their last set.

Perfect. A distraction.

I move to join them, eager to put as much space between myself and Adrian as possible. My grip tightens around my racket as I exhale slowly, resetting.

I can do this. Just one more round, then lunch, and I can leave.

But fate—or rather, Margo—has other plans.

"Oh, one second, dear." She frowns, glancing at her phone as it rings on the side table. "It's Richard. I need to take this." She stands, already answering. "Adrian, you go ahead and play in my place."

Shit.

I school my expression, even as dread lurches in my stomach.

Adrian smirks, already stepping onto the court. "Love to."

Sandra and her daughter are oblivious to the sudden shift in energy, already positioning themselves for play. I force my feet forward, gripping my racket so hard it creaks.

The game is tense.

I keep to my side, moving quickly, efficiently, avoiding him at every opportunity. But Adrian is determined to do the opposite.

He lingers too close. Moves into my space under the guise of gameplay.

When I call a shot and move to return it, he's suddenly there, right behind me.

"Nice reflexes, baby," he murmurs, just low enough for only me to hear.

My spine stiffens.

I don't respond. I won't give him the satisfaction.

Instead, I focus on the game—on anything but the dark, simmering satisfaction in his voice.

The round is over quickly—too quickly.

Margo, now off the phone, calls out from the sidelines, "Lunchtime, ladies! Sorry, Adrian—girls only!"

Adrian feigns offense at his aunt, who chuckles. Sandra and her daughter are already walking toward the umbrella-covered table, distracted as they chat.

Margo turns, heading in the same direction, leaving Adrian and me a few paces behind.

Too close.

"We should get coffee sometime," he says smoothly.

"No."

I raise my hand just enough for the sunlight to catch the glint of my engagement ring. "I'm engaged, remember."

His smirk doesn't falter. If anything, it widens, dark amusement flashing in his eyes.

His fingers tighten around my wrist, pressing against my pulse—a slow, deliberate squeeze. My stomach turns, a cold sweat prickling at the back of my neck as he tugs me just close enough for his breath to ghost my cheek.

My eyes dart to Margo, but she's not looking.

No one is.

"We both know you're not."

A chill slithers down my spine.

Not because he's guessing. Because he's certain.

His tone isn't curiosity. It's a threat.

"Get your hands off me," I say, my voice cold, steady as I rip myself away from him.

He lets go, but his smirk stays, tilting his head slightly, like he's toying with a puzzle he already knows the answer to.

I don't wait for another word.

I turn sharply, walking away toward the safety of Margo and the others, already slipping my mask back on.

"I'll be in touch," Adrian calls after me.

I don't stop.

But my heart pounds so hard against my ribs I swear the entire country club can hear it.

This doesn't happen. The Ledger does exhaustive background checks—on clients, on anyone in their orbit.

Especially for a high-stakes contract like this.

A Ledger Companion faking an engagement to a prior client?

Impossible.

So how the fuck did Lucian miss this?

I need to get a moment away so I can text him. Because this may very well bring this contract, this merger, and my dreams crashing down around us.

Chapter 11
Damien

I should be reviewing the latest reports. Should be preparing for my next meeting. Should be doing anything other than sitting at my desk, phone in hand, staring at Elena's name on the screen.

I have her number. I'm allowed to use it.

I've started a text at least twenty times today. Typed out the words, stared at them, then deleted them.

How's tennis?

Did you make a good impression?

Do you need anything?

That last one makes my jaw tighten. *Do you need me?*

I release a slow, frustrated exhale, setting my phone facedown on the desk like that'll stop me from picking it up again.

I feel fucking pathetic.

This isn't a problem I have. *Ever.*

Women don't make me second-guess myself. They don't make me hesitate. If anything, I'm the one pushing them off when they start clinging too tightly, expecting something more than what I'm willing to give.

They always want something.

My money. My power. A headline.

Fifteen minutes of fame being photographed with one of the city's most eligible bachelors.

I learned that the hard way.

Once.

Before I was this man. Before Wolfe Industries became an empire. Before I understood exactly how people worked.

Her name was Genevieve Mercer—daughter of one of my first business partners. Beautiful, poised, effortlessly charming. The kind of woman bred for high society. And I was fucking stupid enough to believe she loved me.

I was on the cover of every business and finance magazine that existed. Quickly rising to the top of every list, and she was on my arm. Brought her into a world most could only dream of. Introduced her to people who could shape any future she wanted. And in return?

She fucked her ex in my own bed.

One of those *ran into each other at a bar* situations.

And *one thing led to another.*

I walked into my own home, found my girlfriend in my bed with another man, and she didn't even have the decency to feel sorry about it.

She didn't cry. Didn't beg. Didn't even look guilty.

Just wrapped herself in my shirt like she still had the right and gave me a long, pitying look.

"People like us don't do love matches, Damien. We do power. Position. What we can offer each other. And when we need some-

thing else?" She had the audacity to shrug, like it was the simplest thing in the world. *"We find it where we can."*

And that's when I knew relationships weren't for me.

People don't want love. They want leverage.

So, when Marcus brought up my problem—when he suggested I needed a fiancée to close this deal—there was only one solution that made sense.

A contract. A business exchange. Something professional. Mutual.

And The Ledger was exactly that.

No emotions. No risk. Just a perfectly packaged arrangement where everyone gets what they want.

That's what I know. That's what I'm good at.

But not once have I felt that with Elena.

I rake a hand through my hair, jaw clenching.

Is that part of the act? A carefully calculated move?

Or is that the real her?

And why the fuck do I care so much?

Why the fuck am I staring at a text like a man who doesn't know better?

My assistant, Vanessa, steps into my office, tablet in hand, her usual polished smile firmly in place. She moves with ease, setting the schedule down in front of me like she does every week.

"Your schedule for next week, sir," she says smoothly.

I cringe at the way the word *sir* grates against me. I think it's the way she says it that makes me want to fire her.

I barely glance at it before nodding. "Fine." Then, without looking up, I add, "Clear my schedule Monday after four."

There's a slight pause—a hesitation that doesn't belong.

"That's... unusual," she notes, keeping her voice light, casual. "Is it for an event?"

I flip a page in my contract notes, my attention already elsewhere. "No."

The silence that follows is longer this time, like she's waiting for me to elaborate. When I don't, she shifts her stance, clearly searching for another angle.

"If it's an event, I could come along. Be close by."

Her implication is obvious, but I don't take the bait. My focus remains on the documents in front of me. "I won't need anything."

Still, she lingers. And it's grating on my fucking nerves.

"Noted," she finally says, though something in her tone suggests otherwise. "Should I mark it as personal, then?"

When I don't respond right away, she presses a little further. "I am happy to make myself available to you, Mr. Wolfe... anytime you need... anything. Even outside of work."

I finally look up, my patience nearly eviscerated. My voice is flat, final.

"Noted," I correct. "Should my fiancée suddenly be unavailable, of course."

Her reaction is subtle, but I don't miss it—the way her eyes flicker, the brief hesitation like she's recalibrating.

"Oh," she says after a beat. "I... didn't realize you were seeing someone."

There's something almost expectant in the way she says it. Like she's waiting for me to clarify. To correct her.

I don't.

The door behind her opens before she can come up with another excuse to stay. Marcus steps inside, his presence a welcome distraction.

Vanessa hesitates, clearly debating whether to press her luck. I don't give her the chance.

"That's all," I say dismissively, already shifting my attention to Marcus.

She lingers just long enough to toss out one final remark. "Let me know if anything changes."

Marcus waits for the door to click shut before shaking his head, amusement lacing his voice. "You know your assistant wants to fuck you, right?"

I exhale sharply, irritation simmering just beneath my skin. "No," I correct, leaning back in my chair, fingers tapping once against the armrest before I let out a slow breath. "She wants *me* to fuck *her*. There's a difference."

Marcus smirks, amusement flickering in his gaze. "Either way…"

"She's gone as soon as this merger is over."

My phone buzzes twice in quick succession, the vibration rattling against my desk. Across from me, Marcus's phone lights up as well.

I glance down, eyes catching on the name flashing across my screen.

Elena.

There's a flicker of something I don't want to name—a tightening in my chest that shouldn't be there.

She's texting me.

I ignore the feeling and open the message.

ELENA: Back at the penthouse. Tennis went great. On a first-name basis with Mrs. Calloway. Margo, as I call her. My new bestie.

A grin tugs at the corner of my mouth before I can stop it.

Fingers hovering over the keyboard, I hesitate for a second before finally typing out a response.

DAMIEN: Aw. Did you two make friendship bracelets on the tennis courts?

It's dry, neutral—at least, that's what I tell myself. It's not flirtation, just conversation.

Her reply comes back almost instantly.

ELENA: She said that's next time. We're up for a mani-pedi on Sunday.

I huff out a quiet breath, shaking my head, a smirk creeping in despite my best efforts.

My thumb taps idly against the edge of the phone—one tap, then two—like I can't quite let go of the moment.

Across from me, Marcus shifts, and when I glance up, he's watching me with an arched brow, phone in hand.

"Please tell me you're not smiling at the email we just got from Calloway."

"What?" My brows furrow as I click into my inbox.

Marcus lifts his phone, shaking it once as he exhales. "Check your damn email, Wolfe."

My fingers move, quick and efficient, navigating to my

inbox. The moment I see the subject line, my focus sharpens, all thoughts of Elena momentarily shoved aside.

From: *Richard Calloway*
Subject: *Weekend Itinerary – Hamptons Retreat*

I scan the contents, reading once, then again.

A slow, creeping realization settles in.

My jaw tightens.

"What the fuck?"

Marcus lets out a low whistle, still staring at his screen in disbelief. "Tell me I'm seeing things."

I don't answer right away. I read the email again, slower this time, hoping I've misread something—that some detail will shift into place and make this all make sense.

It doesn't.

It's the usual bullshit—finalizing details, wrapping up negotiations in a relaxed setting—except for one line that sticks out like a fucking landmine.

Bringing in his nephew to consult on a few things.

My grip tightens on my phone as I lean back in my chair, exhaling sharply through my nose. My jaw ticks once, then again.

"What the fuck do we know about his nephew?" My voice is sharp, cutting through the quiet hum of the office.

Marcus shakes his head, already typing something on his phone. "Not a damn thing. I ran checks on the immediate family, but the nephew never came up in anything relevant."

I mutter a curse, scanning the email again, irritation bleeding into something darker.

This just got complicated.

"We're on high alert," Marcus says, mirroring my thoughts. "This could bring trouble."

"No shit."

I don't like trouble. I don't like surprises. And I sure as hell don't like unknown variables fucking up my plans.

With a slow exhale, I open my text thread with Elena.

> DAMIEN: You up for that spa day to happen at the Hamptons?

Her response, once again, comes almost instantly.

> ELENA: 🐿 I'm your beck-and-call girl. At your service, sir.

My lips twitch before I can stop them.

I stare at that last word longer than I should.

Sir.

It sinks into me, warm and slow, curling low in my stomach in a way I don't have time to fucking analyze.

I force myself to close the text thread before I do something stupid.

Like text her again just to see what else she'd call me.

Chapter 12
Elena

Damien is dressed down this morning—well, as dressed down as I've seen him so far.

His slate-blue linen suit fits him with effortless perfection, the lightweight fabric a clear nod to the sun-drenched weekend ahead.

The crisp white button-down underneath is open at the top, the deep V revealing defined muscle beneath. It's sexy—just enough of a glimpse to remind me exactly how hard he works in that private gym of his.

The blue suit makes his eyes so vibrant it's hard to look away.

I smooth my hands down my darker-blue summer dress, its flowy silhouette a perfect complement to his suit.

It hadn't been intentional, but when Damien's eyes drag over me in that sharp, assessing way of his, something flickers in them. Approval, maybe.

The thought shouldn't thrill me the way it does, so I push it down.

A black metal tumbler of coffee is waiting for me on the kitchen counter, lid already on.

I lift a brow. "Breakfast on the go?"

"Seemed efficient," he replies simply, taking a sip from his own.

There's a blanket folded neatly beside it.

Before I can stop myself, I nod toward it. "And that?"

"It can get chilly onboard."

I narrow my eyes slightly. *Onboard what?*

It's early—the city still wrapped in that muted, pre-dawn quiet—and I curl my fingers around the warm tumbler, savoring the rich, perfectly made coffee.

Of course, he got it right.

Of course, he knows exactly how I take it.

"Time to go."

He leads the way, and I follow him to a door just off the kitchen. I hadn't even noticed it before.

We exit into a long hallway. Stairs that lead down. A service elevator for the staff. Then, at the end of the hall, another elevator. Damien steps inside, pulling a small silver key from his pocket.

He inserts it, twisting smoothly, and I catch sight of the illuminated *H* with a circle around it just as the elevator doors shut.

A helicopter.

My stomach dips slightly.

"We're flying?" I ask, perking up despite myself.

Beside me, Damien's mouth pulls into something resembling a real smile—relaxed, effortless.

"We are."

It's only a few floors up, but when the doors glide open, I realize exactly what that means.

An impressive black-and-gold helicopter sits waiting for us, its polished exterior gleaming under the soft glow of the rooftop lights. The Wolfe Industries emblem is emblazoned on the side—sleek and powerful.

I let out a low whistle. "Very fancy."

Damien doesn't acknowledge the compliment right away, but I don't miss the way his lips twitch slightly at the corner.

"I'm glad you like it."

I can tell he really does—that he enjoys this more than he's letting on.

A flight attendant greets us, handing over two headsets as Damien moves ahead, opening the door and gesturing for me to climb in.

Not the side door, where the guest seats are situated.

The front. *As in, next to the pilot's seat.*

I step inside, settling into the buttery leather seat, but before I can reach for the harness, his hands are there first, buckling me in with calm efficiency.

"Comfortable?"

I lift my chin slightly. "I was before I climbed into the front."

His lips quirk, and I expect him to shut the door and walk away. Only, he doesn't.

Instead, he reaches for the blanket, spreading it over my lap, his movements smooth and attentive.

I glance up at him, brows lifting slightly. "I didn't peg you as the doting type."

He scoffs, adjusting the fabric with a little more attention than necessary.

"I'm not. Just making sure you don't freeze to death and give me a poor satisfaction rating with Lucian."

A laugh bubbles up before I can stop it, but I smother it with a sip of coffee. "Consider your rating safe—for now."

He shuts my door, walking around the front of the helicopter to the other side.

And that's when I realize—all the attendants are stepping back. Their positions close to the wall, near the door. They're waiting for us to take off.

I blink. "Wait... *you're* flying us?"

Damien chuckles, the sound deep, boyish, and entirely too self-satisfied.

"I am."

I stare at him, half expecting him to admit he's joking. But instead, he rounds the aircraft, climbing into the pilot's seat, completely at ease as he adjusts the controls.

"Just picked up the license yesterday," he adds smoothly, cutting me a quick side glance laced with amusement.

I narrow my eyes. "Funny."

"Only if you doubt my abilities."

He winks—*actually winks*—before shifting into full focus, his confidence almost maddening as he maneuvers the controls.

I fumble slightly with my headset, settling it over my ears just as his voice comes through the connection.

"I've flown for several years now," he says, flipping a few switches. "You're in good hands with me."

Oh, I know exactly how good those hands are.

But instead of saying that, I take a slow sip of my coffee and check out the rest of the cabin.

There are two seats behind us, then a bench seat at the very back. It's lavish.

Made for comfort on short jumps when the *Wolfe of Fifth Avenue* needs to arrive and make an impression.

The blades whir louder, a steady rhythm slicing through the quiet morning air.

"Ready?" He quirks a brow at me, and I nod, smiling.

Damien maneuvers the controls, and my stomach drops to the ground as we rise.

My hand flies to the armrest of my seat on instinct.

I take a deep breath, watching the city shrink below us as we ascend, my eyes flickering to the horizon just as the first sliver of sun crests over the skyline.

It's breathtaking.

Stunning in a way that makes my chest tighten, something warm settling beneath my ribs as I take it all in.

I feel the weight of Damien's gaze and turn my head just slightly.

Damien isn't watching the view.

He's watching *me*.

The atmosphere crackles in the small space, thick and dangerous.

Then, just as quickly as it happens, he turns away.

Focuses on the controls.

And I turn back to the sky, pretending I don't feel his gaze still lingering on me anyway.

Forty-five minutes later, we land smoothly at the private airfield near the Hamptons.

Damien is a wonderful pilot. Without question, he puts his every effort into the excellence of flying, and it's impressive.

Part of me thinks it was a show on my behalf. The logical side of me—the business side that knows this is a temporary arrangement—reminds me it's simply the fastest way to travel.

With powerful men like Damien, time is money.

The transition from his helicopter to the sleek, waiting town car is seamless, and by the time we pull through the gated entrance of the Calloway estate, my shoulders have finally relaxed.

I'm in Ledger mode, the perfect Companion, ready for whatever the weekend ahead will demand of me.

It seems Marcus arrived just before us, *sans* James.

I think he's going to open my car door, but Damien beats him to the handle, and I don't miss the teasing look Marcus gives him or the look of warning Damien returns.

"No James this weekend?" I ask, genuinely disappointed.

"Photoshoot in L.A., unfortunately."

Marcus tenderly touches my upper arm, pressing a false kiss to my cheek as if we're old friends.

It looks convincing to the observing Calloways, who are making their way toward us.

The estate is stunning—floor-to-ceiling windows open to a sweeping ocean view, sheer curtains billowing softly in the salty breeze. The air is thick with the scent of sun-warmed wood and sea spray, and for a fleeting second, I let myself take it in.

If this were any other weekend, any other situation, I might have actually enjoyed it.

But then, just as quickly, the moment sours.

Because over Damien's shoulder, lounging on a sun-drenched chair like he owns the place, is Adrian Kingston.

His drink swirls lazily in his hand, dark eyes locked on me with a smirk that makes my stomach twist.

Fuck.

I was hoping the weekend away—him remaining back in New York—would give Lucian time to figure out what's going on and throw me a lifeline.

He was my first call as soon as I left the country club, just before I texted Damien.

Hold tight, he told me.

Well, with the grip I have on my purse, I can't hold any tighter than I am right now.

This is bad.

Really fucking bad.

An attendant walks ahead of us, showing us to the private bungalow we'll be staying in for the weekend. Damien refuses the man's help with our bags, carrying them both with one hand while his other holds mine.

Since it's only Marcus walking with us, I don't tell him the physical touch is unnecessary. I just walk alongside them, listening to their low conversation about Adrian.

Apparently, he was a surprise to them as well—inviting himself in at the eleventh hour and interjecting unfounded concerns into Mr. Calloway's mind.

The bungalow is a spacious two-bedroom, two-bathroom beachfront home. The flower arrangement and welcome basket aren't just thoughtful but beautiful. The open floor-to-ceiling windows bring the cool ocean breeze inside.

"You'll be okay for a while on your own?" Damien asks, setting my bag down on the bed in the guest room after I refused his offer of the primary bedroom.

"I'm fine. Good luck at your meeting."

I dismiss him and Marcus, who head off to the first of several closing conversations with Mr. Calloway.

Debating whether I should unpack his bag along with my own, I decide against it and instead try to call Lucian again.

After leaving another voicemail, I give Eve a ring.

"Hey, girl. How's the contract going?" she answers quickly. The thumping bass of music in the background tells me she's working out—something we do together often when we're both around.

"It's a shitshow."

"No! What's going on?"

The music turns down, and I imagine her sitting down, her brow creased in concern.

Eve is a fellow Ledger Companion. We started on the same day, both a little terrified, and were best friends in an instant.

"Adrian fucking Kingston is what's going on."

Her gasp is expected. Eve is the only person who knows everything about me—even what happened between Adrian and me.

"What did Lucian say?"

"To hold tight. Now he's ghosting me." I tip my head back, closing my eyes, and release a strained breath.

"No, things are blowing up at The Ledger." Her tone turns dark. "Someone hurt one of the girls."

Blood drains from my face, and I sit on the edge of my bed.

We all know the risks of a job like this. But Lucian goes to great lengths to protect his employees.

One of his girls being harmed by a client means retribution.

And Lucian will handle it personally.

That means I'm on my own with Adrian.

My problem is a big deal, but harm coming to a Ledger Companion is bigger.

So, I'll have to figure this out by myself.

Eve must sense my frustration because her voice softens. "Hey, Lucian will handle it. You know he will."

"I know," I sigh. "But this weekend just got a whole lot more complicated."

"Because of Adrian?"

"Yes, but..." I hesitate, and she picks up on it immediately.

There's a beat of silence before she hums, teasing but perceptive. "Or is it because of Damien Wolfe?"

I roll my eyes, but my heart betrays me with a little stutter.

"It's a high-stakes contract, Eve. That's all."

"Uh-huh." There's amusement in her voice. "It's Damien Wolfe, Elena. *The* Damien Wolfe."

I rub my temple. "I'm aware."

"And?"

"And nothing."

Eve makes an exaggerated scoffing sound. "You're lying to me. I know that tone."

"I'm not—"

"Oh my God," she gasps. "Don't tell me you have a crush on your contract."

I laugh at that—actually laugh—because the idea of having a crush on Damien Wolfe is absurd. He's a client. This is business. There are rules.

But then my laughter dies in my throat.

Because there are also exceptions.

And we've already made one.

Eve hears the silence stretch and knows. "Wait... no way."

I sigh, pinching the bridge of my nose. "It was before the contract started. I didn't know he was *him*."

"Shut up," she breathes, utterly scandalized. "You slept with Damien Wolfe before the contract even started?"

I groan. "Eve—"

"Oh my God, this is so much better than anything I was expecting. I thought maybe you were crushing, but no, you *fucked* him. Elena, that's—"

"Dangerous," I cut in. "It's dangerous, Eve."

She sobers, quiet for a second. "Yeah," she admits. "It is."

We both know what this means. The job works because of boundaries. Clear-cut lines.

This is a professional arrangement—it *has* to be—and yet, I've already blurred it.

"And now?" she prompts. "Is it just business?"

I exhale. "It has to be."

"Does it?"

I don't answer.

Because we both already know.

I just don't want to admit it.

"And now?" she prompts. "Is it just business?"

I exhale. "It has to be."

"Does it?"

I don't answer.

Because we both already know.

I just don't want to admit it.

Chapter 13
Damien

The room is supposed to be casual.

That much is clear from the leather armchairs arranged around the glass-top coffee table, the open bar stocked with top-shelf liquor, and the expansive view of the Calloway estate's pristine lawn through the floor-to-ceiling windows.

But it doesn't feel casual.

Not with the tension thick enough to strangle.

Mr. Calloway sits at the head of the informal gathering, nursing a glass of scotch as he leans back, completely at ease. He has the comfortable air of a man who owns everything in the room—including the men sitting in it.

To his right, Marcus occupies an armchair, equally relaxed, but I can tell he's assessing the room the same way I am.

And then there's Adrian Kingston.

The nephew.

The wildcard.

I don't let my expression betray anything as I study him. He's dressed the part—expensive loafers, tailored slacks, and a crisp button-down rolled up at the sleeves to feign effortlessness. But effortlessness isn't something you can buy, and his brand of casual reeks of trying too hard.

I've seen men like him before.

Men who want to be important but don't have the spine or the skill to get there.

He's a parasite. The kind that latches onto something greater because he knows he'll never build anything of his own.

The introductions are brief, and I offer a firm handshake, gripping just a little harder than necessary when he clasps mine. A test. A challenge.

Adrian meets my eyes with a smirk. He already knows who I am. He already doesn't like me.

Good.

The feeling is mutual.

"Damien Wolfe," he drawls as he leans back, spreading his arms across the chair like he owns the place. "I've heard a lot about you."

"Likewise," I reply smoothly, though we both know that's not true. I didn't bother learning his name until this morning, which is probably more thought than anyone else has given him.

Mr. Calloway, oblivious to the silent battle taking place, gestures toward the drinks on the table. "Pour yourself something, boys. This weekend is about relaxing and business."

Marcus reaches for the decanter, pouring himself a two-finger glass of whiskey before offering it to me. I wave him off.

"Not for me."

Adrian's eyes gleam like he's already found his first foothold. "Ah. Too disciplined for a drink? Or worried you'll lose your edge?"

The corners of my mouth twitch, but I keep my tone measured. "I don't need whiskey to sharpen my game."

Calloway chuckles, clearly amused, while Adrian tilts his head, still smirking like we're old friends.

The meeting begins, and for the first few minutes, it runs smoothly.

Calloway lays out his expectations, Marcus backs up our due diligence, and I present key points on why the merger is the best move for his company's expansion.

And then Adrian starts talking.

At first, it's subtle. A casual question here, a comment there, all under the guise of curiosity. But I see it for what it is—a slow, deliberate attempt to plant doubt.

"That's an optimistic projection," he muses, studying one of the reports we provided. "I'd love to see the analytics that back it up."

"You have them in front of you," I reply smoothly. "Page sixteen details the revenue forecast with a conservative projection alongside it."

He flips a few pages with exaggerated slowness. "Mmm. Even the conservative number seems ambitious."

"It's not. The industry trends are favorable, and with the increased market share this merger provides, the growth trajectory is well within reason."

Adrian hums like he's unconvinced. "Still... even with the right market conditions, the timing is aggressive."

"It has to be," I counter. "There's a small window to capitalize on these shifts before competitors move in. The sooner we finalize this deal, the better positioned Calloway Holdings will be."

He nods, considering, before turning to Mr. Calloway. "I assume you're comfortable with moving this fast? It's not rushed in your opinion?"

The bait is so obvious it's insulting, but it works.

Calloway leans back, stroking his chin. "I trust Damien's strategy, but it's a fair question. We are moving quickly. What's your response to that, Wolfe?"

Adrian hides his smirk behind his glass of bourbon.

Motherfucker.

I inhale through my nose, keeping my expression cool. "The timeline is aggressive because it needs to be. Calloway Holdings stands to make an additional fifteen percent ROI if we close before the next quarterly shift. If we hesitate, we lose leverage. If we lose leverage, we lose money. Period."

Calloway nods at that, but Adrian isn't done.

"I'm just saying, caution isn't a bad thing. There's a reason checks and balances exist," he continues. "After all, I imagine you'd hate to jump into a commitment prematurely and realize it wasn't what you signed up for."

I feel like there's a double meaning there, and my mind immediately runs to my contract with Elena.

My grip tightens around the armrest.

I remind myself that I don't know what his game is yet,

and there's no way he could know about my arrangement with her.

The pointed look from Marcus is a reminder that I can't rip his fucking throat out in the middle of a business meeting.

So I lean forward, resting my elbows on my knees. "The difference, Kingston, is that I don't hesitate when I see a good deal."

Adrian's smirk twitches. He wasn't expecting me to flip it on him so fast.

"Now," I continue, redirecting the conversation back to Calloway, "if we're ready to proceed, I'd like to go over the next steps for closing."

Calloway leans back, stroking his chin.

I wait.

Finally, he nods. "Agreed. Let's move forward."

But something lingers in his expression.

Not hesitation.

Something worse.

Doubt.

It's gone as fast as it appeared, but I saw it. And so did Adrian. Because the smug fucker has the audacity to smirk into his glass like he just won the first round.

But Adrian will soon realize I won't be as easy to undermine as he thinks.

Because I love a game of chess.

And he just sat down at the board with a fucking master.

Hours have passed.

The meeting dragged through lunch and into the late afternoon, and while the setting may have remained polished and refined, the undercurrents of tension only deepened.

Lunch had been served on the terrace—an immaculate spread of fresh seafood, chilled salads, and perfectly aged wines. An indulgence meant to suggest an atmosphere of ease. But the constant rounds of back-and-forth with Adrian made it anything but.

He never let up.

Every time I thought we'd moved past his concerns, he found a new one to introduce. A minor clause in the contracts. A logistical challenge that wasn't a challenge at all. A hypothetical risk so far-fetched it was laughable, yet each time, he managed to plant just enough hesitation in Calloway's mind to keep the conversation going.

By the time the meeting is officially adjourned, I'm two seconds from walking Adrian out to the ocean and seeing if he can swim his way back to New York.

I don't let my frustration show as Marcus and I take our leave, excusing ourselves with the polite, practiced ease of men who have been in these rooms for years.

We walk back toward the bungalows, the sun dipping lower in the sky, the scent of salt and citrus riding the warm summer breeze. The estate is quiet in the distance, but my mind is anything but.

Something about this doesn't sit right.

I can feel it.

I keep my gaze forward as I speak. "I want you to dig into Kingston."

Marcus snorts. "I'm offended you think I haven't been already. We both knew his interjection this late in the game spelled trouble."

"How deep?" he asks casually, slipping his hands into his pockets.

"As deep as it takes," I reply, my voice flat. "I don't give a damn if you have to go back to the day he was born. I want to know everything—his history, his investments, his failures. Find out who he owes money to and who he was fucking in college."

Marcus hums, considering. "You think he's trying to sabotage the merger?"

"I know he is," I say darkly, jaw tightening. "I just don't know how yet."

Because this isn't just some arrogant prick trying to flex his influence.

This is strategic. Calculated.

A man like Adrian Kingston doesn't insert himself into a billion-dollar deal at the last second without a reason.

He's not here to observe.

He's not here to help his dear old Uncle Calloway.

He's working an angle.

I just don't know what the hell it is yet.

Marcus exhales sharply. "I'll get our best guys on it."

"Good," I say, my voice cold, clipped.

For the first time in a long time, I have a feeling I'm playing defense instead of offense.

And I don't fucking like it.

I stretch my neck to each side, my eyes flicking back toward the main house.

Calloway isn't a fool. He's built an empire on knowing when to trust and when to question.

So why the hell is he entertaining this?

Does he actually trust Adrian?

Or is he using him?

Watching. Waiting. Testing me.

Or is Adrian bringing in another buyer who thinks they have more to offer than me?

If that's the case, then I need to be careful. Because if Calloway thinks Adrian has a point, I have more than just a deal to lose.

I don't break stride as I push open the door to the bungalow, stepping inside and scanning the open space automatically.

Elena isn't in the living room.

But I hear soft movement from the guest room.

I take my time.

Rolling my sleeves up as I walk toward the guest room, I tell myself it's just business. That I'm only going to check in.

I lean against the doorframe and find Elena sitting cross-legged on the bed, scrolling through her phone. Her hair is damp from a shower, the loose fabric of her silk camisole slipping slightly over one shoulder.

She looks up, eyes catching mine, and for a second—just a second—there's something easy in the air.

Something that doesn't belong here.

Something that feels a little too much like a routine we've done a thousand times. Me coming home from a long day of work. Elena, ready to hear about it while she tells me about her day.

Something I need to push to the back of my mind and bury.

"How'd it go?" she asks, tucking her phone away.

"Fine," I say automatically.

Her brow lifts, unconvinced. "Liar."

The corner of my mouth quirks before I catch myself.

I exhale, stepping into the room, sliding my hands into my pockets. "It was a waste of time. Adrian's an arrogant little shit with just enough access to be dangerous."

She hums, shifting slightly on the bed. "What's his angle?"

"That's what I'm trying to figure out."

I don't know why I say it out loud.

I don't usually think aloud, and I sure as hell don't unpack meetings with anyone who isn't on my payroll.

But Elena just watches me, waiting.

Unrushed.

Unbothered by the sharp edges of my mood.

And I realize—I fucking *like* that.

I rub a hand down my jaw, exhaling slowly. "He's not just here to observe. He wants control. Whether it's over Calloway or the deal itself, I don't know yet. But he's playing a long game, and I don't intend to let him win."

Elena tilts her head slightly, thoughtful. "Men like him don't play unless they think they already have an advantage."

I glance at her, curious despite myself. "And what do you think that is?"

She shifts again, tucking a leg under herself. "Leverage."

My silence must encourage her, because she continues.

"If I were guessing, I'd say he's new to the boardroom, but he's not new to the art of manipulation. He's testing boundaries, finding weaknesses. If he sees an opening, he'll exploit it. But he wouldn't be here—wouldn't be *this* confident—unless he already believes he has something on you."

I watch her carefully.

I like the way her mind works.

How easily she reads people.

But there's something else—something unspoken—hanging between us.

If I were Adrian Kingston, I'd realize the biggest advantage in this game is sitting right here in front of me.

And that means I need to keep an eye on Elena—especially where he's concerned. I won't give him the chance to get any ideas that involve Elena, let alone an opportunity to act on them.

I push off the doorframe, rolling my shoulders again. "I'll figure it out."

Elena studies me for a beat longer before exhaling.

"You should eat something."

I blink. "What?"

She nods toward the kitchen. "There was a charcuterie board in the fridge when I got back. You've been in that meeting for hours. Food won't kill you."

I huff a quiet breath, more amused than I should be. "Are you giving me orders now?"

Elena tilts her head, considering. "Technically, you're

the boss of this arrangement. But I get paid to take care of you, don't I?"

A short, surprised laugh escapes me.

She watches me for a second, then smirks.

"Go eat, Wolfe."

I shake my head, lingering just a little longer than I should. "You're awfully persistent."

"And yet," she calls as I turn back toward the kitchen, "here you are, listening to me anyway."

She's not wrong.

And that bothers me more than I'm willing to admit.

The morning is beautiful, but I can't feel it.

The sky is the kind of crisp blue that only exists in the Hamptons.

A warm breeze carries the distant sound of waves breaking on the shore. Sunlight streams through the open veranda doors, spilling golden light over the Calloways' long breakfast table.

It should be a perfect morning.

But my stomach is in knots.

Because I know Adrian is going to approach me at some point this weekend.

He always has a way—like a weasel.

A game he's played for a long time—twisting moments, warping the truth, doing everything he can to always appear in control. He hasn't changed.

I see it in the smug set of his mouth, the lazy, easy way he lounges at the far end of the table, as if he has all the time in the world.

He's waiting.

Waiting for the perfect moment to corner me.

I won't let him.

I focus on my plate, cutting into my eggs Benedict, listening to the quiet hum of conversation around me. The Calloways are in high spirits, chatting about the day ahead. Margo is already planning her victory in the afternoon's shuffleboard tournament. Marcus and Mr. Calloway are discussing a new development property in the city.

"Is your breakfast good?"

Damien's deep voice wraps around me, warm and effortless, as if we're the only two in the room.

It's such a normal question. A fiancé checking on his partner. He's playing the part perfectly.

He's finished with his plate, leaning on his elbow close to me.

So close that when I look over to answer, my breath catches in my throat.

Something about being here—surrounded by the ocean, maybe—pulls out the various shades of blue in his eyes.

He's so striking, I nearly forget the question.

His mouth quirks at my hesitation, amusement flickering there, but before I can answer, Adrian cuts in.

"So, Damien," he starts casually, leaning back in his chair as he stirs his coffee. "I assume you haven't had time to work through the concerns I raised yesterday. Will you be staying ashore today to get some work done?"

The table stills, tension creeping in at the edges of my awareness.

We're going out on the Calloways' yacht today, and the

thought of being stuck there with Adrian—without Damien —makes my cheeks flush.

I swallow my bite of food carefully, watching as Damien lifts his coffee cup, taking a slow sip before placing it back down with deliberate ease. He doesn't rush. Doesn't react.

He simply turns his gaze to Adrian, unreadable as ever. "Which concerns specifically?"

Adrian smiles, slow and self-satisfied. "Oh, you know— risk distribution, asset allocation, the minor oversights in your proposed terms. I imagine you were up all night revising your strategy."

It's bait.

An attempt to get under Damien's skin. To make him slip, even if just slightly, in front of Calloway.

But Damien doesn't take the bait.

He grabs the coffee pot, refilling my cup with a wink, then his own, and finally—*finally*—lets a smirk tug at the corner of his mouth.

"Nah, it took no time at all. Marcus and I went over everything in about ten minutes," he says smoothly. "We found your observations... interesting."

I bite back a grin at the calculated amusement in his voice, like he's indulging a child's attempt at chess.

"Interesting how?" Adrian pushes, his fingers tightening around his coffee cup.

Damien shrugs, utterly composed. "Turns out, you're using numbers that are decades old. Some pre-9/11 and— well—we all know how much New York shifted in that aftermath. It became a whole new world."

"That's for sure," Calloway agrees absentmindedly as he cuts into his eggs.

The simple statement—his uncle's approval—lands with the weight of a hammer, and I watch as Adrian's jaw tightens just slightly before he covers it with another smile.

Damien doesn't look away. Doesn't move.

Except to put his hand on my knee, sitting back like he's the one who *owns* the conversation now.

"In fact, we sent the updated projections and new reports validating our earlier statements last night just after dinner."

Damien takes another casual sip of coffee.

"You haven't looked them over yet?"

He's good.

Better than good.

The entire conversation is a masterclass in control, and I find myself quietly impressed—by his intelligence, by his ruthless ability to dismantle Adrian's every attempt at sabotage without breaking a sweat.

He isn't just a powerful businessman.

He's a strategist. A tactician. A man who always plays to win.

And Adrian—whether he realizes it or not—is already losing.

I lean my elbow on the arm of my chair, my hand wrapping around Damien's as he rubs my knee. Both of us looking to Adrian for his next quip.

A couple. United and supportive.

Exactly what Margo wants to see. And based on the way she looks at where Damien and I are touching, then gives her own husband an appreciative smile, I'd say we're on the right track.

The pissing match between them lasts the rest of breakfast, tension simmering beneath the surface of every exchange. Adrian smirks, Damien remains infuriatingly composed, and I sip my coffee, pretending not to notice the verbal chess match taking place between them.

Margo, enthusiastically unaware, finally claps her hands together. "Alright, enough business. It's time for a proper day on the water. Go change, boys. We're heading to the yacht."

I exhale, relieved as everyone starts to rise from the table.

It's beautiful out today, a perfect sky stretching over the horizon. The yacht, anchored just offshore, gleams in the morning light, its sleek white frame cutting a beautiful contrast against the blue.

I don't swim—I never learned—but I love being on the water.

Excusing myself from the table, I head inside to freshen up.

A moment alone. To gather my thoughts. To push Adrian's presence out of my mind.

I run cold water over my wrists, watching the drip of condensation from the porcelain sink, inhaling deeply.

Just get through the weekend.

I dry my hands, smoothing the plush towel over my palms before tossing it aside.

But the second I pull open the door, my stomach drops.

Adrian is leaning casually against the opposite wall, waiting.

Before I can react—before I can so much as inhale to tell him to *fuck off*—he rushes me.

A hand clamps over my mouth.

His other hand shoves the door open wider, pushing me backward as he steps inside, closing it swiftly behind him.

My back collides with the wood, heart hammering as I push against his chest, my fingers digging in, struggling.

"Shhh," he whispers, his breath hot against my cheek. "Shhh, now. You don't want your fiancé to hear you in here with another man, do you?"

I freeze.

Not because I'm scared—though fury burns through my veins like acid—but because right on cue, I hear Damien's voice from just outside the door.

"Elena is just freshening up before we head out."

His deep timbre rolls through the hallway, smooth and composed.

He has no idea what's happening on the other side of this door.

If he finds me locked in the bathroom with Adrian after this morning's charade, he'll get the wrong idea. That there's something between Adrian and me. Or worse—that I'm working with him.

I inhale sharply through my nose, locking my eyes on Adrian's.

There's satisfaction there. Victory.

But he has no idea who he's fucking with.

Slowly, he removes his hand from my mouth, but he doesn't step back.

Breathe. Stay in control.

I level him with a glare, my voice low but lethal. "What do you want?"

I shove against his chest, hard enough to make him take a step back, though his fingers remain curled around the door handle, still blocking my exit. Trapping me inside with him.

I refuse to shrink beneath his stare. Instead, I move with purpose, creating distance, my back straight, my chin lifted. If he thinks for a second he still holds any power over me, he's dead wrong.

Adrian watches me with the same smug amusement I remember too well. The look of a man who always thinks he's winning—even when he's seconds from losing everything.

Not this time.

"What do I want?" He repeats the question slowly, rolling it over his tongue like he enjoys the way it sounds coming from my lips. "You already know, Elena."

I cross my arms. "You're wasting your time."

"Am I?" He clicks his tongue, his gaze sweeping over me, cataloging every shift in my expression, looking for a crack in my armor. "I don't think so. I think you're going to hear me out because deep down, you know this is exactly what you need."

I scoff. "What I need is for you to step the fuck aside and let me leave."

His fingers tighten around the doorknob, but he doesn't

open it. Instead, he leans in slightly, lowering his voice like we're conspiring rather than standing on opposite ends of a war I never agreed to fight.

"You didn't tell him about us, did you?" His voice dips, condescending and coaxing all at once. "Does your fiancé know how many times I've fucked you?"

A hot coil of fury tightens in my stomach, but I don't let my face betray me.

Adrian smirks. "That's what I thought."

I hold his gaze, refusing to let him see the anger simmering beneath my skin. "I see you're still just as desperate to be relevant."

His smirk falters for the briefest second.

Good.

"And I see you're still as unreasonable as ever," he sneers.

"Better than being weak," I fire back.

His voice dips, taunting. "I just want you to keep him occupied. Distracted. Keep those pretty eyes on your *fake* fiancé while this deal falls apart, and I'll make you a very rich woman."

"You can throw your money around all you want, Adrian. But I don't need you. I never did."

He exhales sharply, his amusement dimming as something darker flickers in his eyes.

There. *The real Adrian.* The one who hates not getting his way. The one who lashes out when his control slips. The one who doesn't know what to do with himself when he *isn't winning.*

For a moment, we just stare at each other, the tension between us thick enough to suffocate.

Then, he smiles again. Slow. Calculated.

"Fine," he says, finally lifting his hand from the door and stepping back. "Play hard to get. But think about it, sweetheart. I'd hate for your fiancé to start hearing some nasty rumors about your past."

Asshole.

I survived my past. Something he never had to do.

I grip the doorknob, my entire body vibrating with the need to get out of this space, but I don't turn it just yet.

Instead, I meet his stare, calm and unwavering. "You should be careful, Adrian."

He tilts his head slightly. "Of what?"

My smile is sharp, razor-edged. "Of assuming I'm the same woman you left bleeding on a bathroom floor."

For the first time, his smirk falters completely.

"Don't forget what happened to your associates the last time you brought me into one of your deals."

I don't give him a chance to recover.

I turn the handle, stepping through the door into the bright hallway beyond, leaving him behind in the dim, suffocating shadows.

Chapter 15

The veranda is shaded from the morning sun, but the warmth of the day is already creeping in. A light ocean breeze ruffles the linen of my shirt as I lean against the railing, watching the waves roll in, slow and steady.

Margo chatters beside me, her easy warmth filling the space between us, but my attention shifts the second the door opens and Elena steps outside.

She looks different.

Still poised, still perfect, but something lingers beneath the surface—a flush high on her cheeks, the tension in her shoulders just a fraction too tight before she smooths it away like it was never there.

I push off the railing, straightening as she walks toward me, her smile bright, her hazel eyes catching the light like polished amber. If I hadn't just seen the ghost of something in her expression, I wouldn't suspect a thing.

"Are you excited for today?" I ask.

She steps closer, slipping her hands into mine, her fingers warm against my skin. "Yes," she says, breathless with enthusiasm, rising onto her tiptoes to press a soft peck to my cheek.

The gesture is unexpected.

Elena has been careful. Deliberate. She never gives more than what's necessary for the role.

And yet, here she is—giving more.

Margo watches us with a knowing smile, but before she can comment, a sharp blast from a boat horn sounds from below.

She turns, waving a hand toward the yacht anchored just off the shore. "Oh, for heaven's sake, I hear you! Give us a minute!" she hollers to the captain before spinning back around with a grin. "Impatient man, I swear. You two finish up and meet us at the dock."

As soon as she's gone, I pull Elena in, my hands firm at her waist, guiding her close until her chest brushes against mine. Her breath catches as I dip my head, my lips ghosting just below her ear, making it look as if I'm kissing her neck.

"You said no kissing," I murmur, my voice deliberately low, rich with amusement. "Are you breaking the rules, Miss Moreau?"

She exhales sharply, her fingers tightening ever so slightly on my forearm before she schools herself back into composure.

"I would never break the rules, Mr. Wolfe."

She steps back just enough to look at me, her expression smooth, unreadable. But something flickers there—something unspoken.

I let my gaze sweep over her, taking in the golden glow of her skin under the morning sun, the way her lips part just enough to make me wonder what it would feel like to press my mouth against hers, to taste her again.

Fucking dangerous thoughts.

"Physical affection is expected when we have an audience," she reminds me smoothly, tilting her head.

I narrow my eyes, but before I can respond, her expression shifts—her entire face lighting up with something close to genuine joy.

I glance over my shoulder just in time to see why.

James walks up the path, holding Marcus's hand and talking animatedly, likely about his L.A. photo shoot.

"Hey, you made it after all," I say with a nod, letting go of Elena.

James grins, sliding his sunglasses up onto his head. "Wrapped up the shoot early. Figured I'd crash your weekend in paradise." His smirk deepens as he turns toward Elena. "Besides, wouldn't want to miss a beach trip with my new friend."

She laughs, easy and warm, and for some reason, the sound settles something inside me.

"Come on, you lovebirds!" Mrs. Calloway hollers from the dock as others climb onto the smaller boat that will taxi us to the yacht.

Elena rolls her eyes at Mrs. Calloway's enthusiasm but lets out a small laugh as I take her bag from her shoulder. She slides her hand into mine without hesitation, letting me lead her down the dock.

"Time for some fun in the sun," I say.

The ride to the yacht is quick, and within minutes, we're stepping onto the deck of the impressive vessel. The Calloways spared no expense—pristine white leather seating, teakwood flooring, and a fully stocked bar under a shaded canopy.

It doesn't take long for Margo to challenge her husband to a competitive game of shuffleboard while others dive into the shimmering blue water, laughter echoing across the deck.

Elena and I settle onto a curved outdoor couch at the back of the yacht, and Marcus and James claim the spots beside us.

God, if Elena doesn't look fucking amazing.

She's wearing a red bikini, her toenails painted to match. Ledger red.

And I think of that fantasy when I jacked off with her dirty panties. The thoughts of that red dress. Red lipstick perfect for smearing.

Right now, I'm trying—and failing—to stop thinking about taking her to the back of the yacht. Slipping my hand into her bathing suit bottoms and feeling her smooth pussy, wet and wanting for me.

Making her gasp. Making her come.

The threat of someone catching us only makes it more exciting.

Fuck.

My thoughts shift the second I catch that walking prick, Adrian, with his eyes on Elena a little too long for my liking. Any fraction of time that shithead's eyes are on my fiancée is too long.

My—fake—fiancée.

I remind myself.

He moves his beady eyes to me. A smirk plays on his lips that makes me want to break his nose and throw him overboard.

He makes an obnoxious show of jumping off the diving platform with a flip into the ocean below. Margo applauds him like he's a child, which makes Marcus and me share an eye roll.

But it's a reminder of the familial connection they share.

The day of leisure moves on. Adrian moves out of my mind.

The air is warm, the sun casting a golden glow over the scene, and about one hour and several drinks later, I feel something close to . . . relaxed.

Which, of course, means my two idiot friends won't let me enjoy it.

"So," James drawls, lounging back and stretching his arms out over the back of the seat, "Elena, what has our brooding friend here told you about himself?"

She smiles so warmly I can't tell if this is really her or the Ledger Companion sitting with me. "Only what I need for our"—she stalls a moment, as if thinking of the right phrasing—"for our time together." She emphasizes the words, knowing my friends know the truth of our contract.

"Well, since Elena is obviously not getting the juicy details from you, I think it's only fair we tell her about your rebellious phase—on your behalf, of course."

I take a slow sip of my drink, shooting him a look over the rim. "There was no phase."

Marcus grins. "Oh, I beg to differ."

"Gasp!" Elena makes a show of her shock, turning her attention to me, interest sparking in her hazel eyes. "Rebellious? You?"

James chuckles. "See, this is why we need to tell her. No one ever believes Damien was once young and stupid."

"I was never stupid," I say dryly.

Elena stretches her legs, and it seems natural to put them in my lap. My hands knead her calves, the high arch in her soft feet.

Her cheeks blaze red, but otherwise, she follows my lead. Her eyes lock with mine for only a second.

"Okay, fine," Marcus follows, his eyes full of amusement at seeing my affections toward Elena. "But he was definitely reckless."

James leans forward, eyes twinkling with mischief. "Oh, Elena, this is a good one. Greece. Cliff diving. Our fearless Damien, proving he has more balls than brains."

Elena's brows lift, her gaze flicking to me with skepticism. "Cliff diving? You?"

Just before James can launch into my humiliation, a shadow falls over our small group.

Adrian.

Because of course it's Adrian.

"Elena," Adrian's voice is all practiced charm, oily and forced. "Need a refill?"

I don't even give her the chance to answer.

"She's fine."

Flat. Uninterested. Final.

Adrian chuckles, shaking his head. "Is the lady not able to speak for herself? Or just not allowed to?"

I'm already fucking turning, already ready to make it clear how close he is to getting thrown overboard, but Elena beats me to it.

"Clearly," she says smoothly, lifting her very full glass with a pointed flick of her wrist, "I don't need a refill."

She leans in, trailing her fingers along my jaw, her nails just barely scraping my skin as she turns my gaze back to her.

"But if I did, I'm sure my handsome fiancé would gladly take care of me."

She says it all while looking directly into my eyes, a look of admiration in her expression as her finger keeps tracing my jaw.

I smirk, taking her hand and placing a kiss on her knuckles. We thread our fingers together, our joined hands resting comfortably on her lap.

"You were saying, James?" she expertly dismisses the asswipe still blocking our sunlight.

After an awkward moment's hesitation, Adrian leaves. But the tension in my shoulders lingers a few moments longer.

Marcus nods solemnly, like he's about to deliver a tragic tale. "Santorini. Perfect summer. Perfect weather. And a cliff that made most people hesitate before jumping."

James huffs a laugh. "Enter Damien Wolfe—who apparently thinks hesitation is for mere mortals."

Elena's brow lifts as she turns to me. "I can't picture you jumping off a cliff without an extensive risk assessment."

"Right?" Marcus grins. "That's what makes it so good."

James smirks. "So, there we were, standing on the edge, looking down at crystal-clear water, maybe sixty, seventy feet below. People kept backing out."

Marcus shakes his head. "One guy spent ten minutes psyching himself up, then climbed back down the way he came."

I roll my eyes. "If you two are going to exaggerate, at least make it believable."

"Elena," James continues, ignoring me, "Damien didn't even look before he jumped. Just tossed his sunglasses at Marcus, ripped off his shirt, and—boom—gone."

She turns back to me, eyes wide. "You didn't even check the water?"

I take a slow sip of my drink, giving her a lazy shrug. "I had a pretty good idea of what was down there."

James laughs. "The hell you did! You were already midair when I saw the jagged rocks at the base."

Marcus grins. "You should've seen his face when he resurfaced."

"Triumphant?" I smirk.

"Try shocked," James fires back. "And probably a little grateful to be alive."

James nudges her. "And he'll never admit it, but he was definitely rattled when he climbed back up."

"I wasn't rattled," I say flatly.

Marcus snorts. "You were absolutely rattled."

Elena studies me like I'm an unsolvable puzzle. "So, what was it? A dare?"

James and Marcus exchange a look before James smirks. "Oh, absolutely a dare."

I glare at them both. "Don't."

Elena leans in, eyes alight. "Oh no, now you have to tell me."

James grins. "A French model named Claire made a comment about how real men don't hesitate."

Marcus sighs dramatically. "And our Damien, being the picture of restraint, just had to prove he was the most real man there."

Elena's laughter spills out, bright and warm, as she turns back to me. "So you jumped off a cliff to impress a woman?"

I drain the last of my drink, setting the glass down with an easy smirk, my free hand instantly going back to her smooth legs still resting comfortably in my lap.

"Seemed like the most efficient way to shut her up."

James and Marcus exchange another look before bursting into laughter, falling into their own conversation.

I shake my head, but I'm still smirking.

Elena leans back, still studying me with something unreadable in her eyes. "So," she says slowly, a hint of amusement in her voice, "do you still leap without looking?"

The way she says it makes my chest tighten, but I keep my expression relaxed. "I think you know the answer to that question."

She smiles, and I don't miss the way she bites her lip, like she's thinking about something.

Something that has nothing to do with cliffs and everything to do with a particular night spent in my hotel.

"I'm not sure I do, actually." She leans forward, setting her own drink down, and the lightness of the day captures me.

I smirk, shaking my head. "That sounds like a challenge."

Elena barely has time to react before I scoop her up into my arms, lifting her effortlessly against my chest.

"Damien!" she yelps, but her laugh betrays her. She's enjoying this.

With long strides, I move toward the diving platform, stepping past the railing with nothing but the vast ocean below us.

She stiffens instantly.

"Damien—" Her arms clamp around my neck, her breath hitching against my skin.

The panic in her voice is instant. "I can't swim."

The words, soft but sharp, cut through the moment in a second.

Every trace of playfulness vanishes as I feel the real fear in her voice. The way she's clutching me like she's bracing for impact.

My response is immediate. I turn around with my back to the water, setting her down and closing my arms around her, the railing behind her.

"Elena." My voice is quiet, careful. "I'm sorry. I didn't know."

She exhales shakily, her body still rigid. Her arms remain looped around my neck, and we're too close now—close enough that I can see the rapid rise and fall of her chest, the way her pulse flutters at her throat.

"Hey, look at me." I insist, my gaze trying to call hers to me. "I've got you, Elena."

She takes a deep breath.

"That's it. It's just you and me."

She gives me her hazel stare, her eyes bright but filled with fear, and it guts me for putting it there.

"Fuck, I'm sorry." I pant, wrapping my arms tighter around her waist and placing a kiss on the top of her head.

It happens without thought, but she doesn't protest. She doesn't step away from me.

In fact, her arms hold my neck tighter, and I run my hand up her back.

"I'm so sorry, baby," I whisper against her ear.

Shit. I didn't mean to say that.

But I'm not sorry I did.

The air shifts. Her breaths come out labored, but for an entirely different reason now.

The weight of something unspoken presses between us as she pulls back, looking at me, her fingers playing with the hair at the nape of my neck.

I run both hands down her back, gripping her hips. My thumbs almost toy with the thin waistband of her bikini bottoms.

Her breath hitches, my voice dipping lower, rougher.

"Do your rules still apply over the open ocean?" I murmur, unable to keep myself from looking at her full lips, pink, wet, slightly parted and begging for my kiss. "Or are there maritime exceptions?"

Her nipples pebble through the thin fabric of her

bathing suit as her eyes flicker between mine. For a second —just a second—I think she might say yes.

But a moment of clarity makes her straighten, tilting her chin just slightly. "The rules are the rules."

I grin, a slow, knowing smirk, when she quickly looks at my mouth, then back at my eyes.

She wants to kiss me as much as I want to kiss her.

But fine. If this is how she wants to play, we'll play by her rules.

"Okay then."

Stepping back, I let my hands fall from her waist, ignoring the way my palms itch to pull her back.

"Well, I suppose we should go show the Calloways who's boss on the shuffleboard."

Elena smiles, shaking her head as she adjusts the straps of her bikini.

And as we walk back toward the others, I can't help but think—

I'd jump a thousand cliffs for her.

Even if she never lets me.

Chapter 16

The estate's private spa is a haven of luxury, the kind of place most people dream about but never get to experience.

Everything is meticulously curated—the crisp white robes, the gentle trickle of a marble fountain in the background, and the lingering scent of eucalyptus and lavender.

Margo Calloway has spared no expense.

Not with yesterday's yacht event or our girls-only private spa day.

I stretch out on the massage table, my muscles melting under the skilled hands of the masseuse.

Across from me, Margo mirrors my position, her eyes closed in contentment as warm oil is kneaded into her skin.

It's heavenly.

And yet, I know this isn't just about indulgence.

The conversation started harmlessly enough—light, easy chatter about the St. James Orphanage.

I shared a few carefully chosen details—nothing too

revealing. Margo listened, nodding thoughtfully before shifting the conversation to the wedding.

A seamless transition. A natural one.

But I know where this is going.

At the end of this weekend, Mrs. Calloway's opinion will decide everything.

She may not sit on the board. She may not have an official title.

But Mr. Calloway listens to his wife.

And after this weekend, if she says Damien Wolfe is the right man to take over, her husband will sign the papers without a second thought.

So, I let her lead.

I answer her questions with ease, painting a picture of a woman hopelessly devoted to the man she's about to marry. But Margo Calloway is sharp.

I feel the shift before she even speaks—the way her words slow as the massage therapists press deep into the muscles along our spines.

"You know, my husband can talk numbers all day long. He can analyze market projections, dive into balance sheets, and play the long game with the best of them. But at the end of the day . . ." She pauses, turning her head slightly toward me. "He always says the same thing: *The man matters more than the numbers.*"

I keep my expression neutral, my tone even. "What do you mean?"

Margo's lips curve slightly. "You can have the most impressive business plan in the world, but if the man leading it isn't the right one—someone with integrity, vision, and a steady hand—it won't matter. The foundation will eventually crack." She studies me for a long moment. "I suppose that's why you're here, isn't it?"

My fingers tighten slightly against the plush towel beneath me.

"Damien has worked hard for this deal," I say carefully.

She nods, acknowledging that much. "And he's an impressive man. Brilliant. Ruthless when necessary . . . but controlled. My husband respects him. That's a rare thing."

Something about the way she says it makes me pause.

"And you?" I ask, watching her reaction. "Do you respect him?"

A knowing smile tugs at the corners of her lips. "I've been watching him. Watching the way he moves in these circles. He's different from the others."

Her tone shifts, her words slower now, deliberate. The therapists take it as a cue to prepare their supplies for facials, giving us this moment of focus.

"But I have to know . . . is he the kind of man who values legacy? Or just conquest?"

I don't answer right away, thoughtfully navigating through my mind, hoping to pick the right words.

The details of Damien's childhood and early years are a mystery to me.

I have no idea what drove him to the ambition he seeks as an adult, but I know he made every penny of his fortune on his own—one of the few men in the modern world who can make that claim.

It's something I respect about him immensely.

I know exactly what it means to crawl and fight for every

crumb, too—something I bet the Calloways know nothing about.

"Mr. Calloway had his fortune handed to him."

Margo has the good sense to hide her shock, but I can tell by the flash in her eyes that she wasn't expecting me to say that.

But she is quiet, allowing me to continue.

"He took that fortune and multiplied it, turning it into something greater. But that starting point—the Calloway name, the weight it carried—was given to him as a birthright."

I meet her gaze, steady and sure.

"Damien has had no such luxury. Every hill he has climbed, every mountain he's conquered, he's done it on his own."

She can see where I'm going with this, and I catch the subtle change in her calculated expressions.

"You see conquests, but I see something else." I exhale slowly, choosing my words carefully. "I see the first foundation of a legacy being laid—brick by brick, deal by deal—right before our very eyes. I wonder if the early Calloways didn't appear similar to those observing from the sidelines."

For a moment, Margo is silent. Then, finally, she lets out a soft, thoughtful hum.

"You are quite the persuasive woman, Elena."

She turns her head in the other direction just as our massage therapists return at the perfect moment.

"I like that about you." she says, her voice traveling across the room.

And just like that, the weight of the evening settles over me.

Because now I understand.

Tonight isn't just about business.

It's about proving—through every interaction, every glance, every whispered conversation—that Damien Wolfe isn't just here to win a game.

He's here to stay. And so am I.

The soft hum of conversation filters through the night air as I step onto the path leading toward the pavilion. Overhead, strands of delicate golden lights glow beneath the canopy of the outdoor tent, casting a warm, intimate ambiance over the evening's formal dinner.

Margo walks beside me, gushing over the perfect weather for our final gathering of the weekend.

Mr. Calloway is on the walkway, headed toward us. His eyes gleam as he watches his wife, and she beams back at him, her coral gown a perfect complement to his tailored white suit and matching bow tie.

A carefully curated image of unity—one I should have anticipated.

I run my hands down the beaded front of my gown, suddenly second-guessing my choice for the evening.

The soft seafoam-colored fabric is delicate, ethereal—Margo nearly died when I stepped out of the dressing room, saying it was perfect for tonight. I love the way it drapes over my frame, the way the light shimmers off the subtle beading, how the open back feels like the right mix of elegant and daring.

But I should have considered what Damien was wearing. We should have coordinated before leaving New York.

I internally scold myself. I'm a better Companion than this. These are the details I get paid to make perfect.

"Ladies." Mr. Calloway offers his arm to both of us—a gentlemanly escort the rest of the way to the tent. The sound of conversation, laughter, and the gentle clinking of crystal glasses drifts through the air.

My eyes dart from person to person nervously, until I find Damien—and the rest of the world falls away.

Standing near the elegantly set dining tables, dressed in a light-gray suit that fits his broad frame to perfection, he looks effortlessly powerful, undeniably in control. The crisp white of his shirt is open at the collar—a deliberate contrast to the more rigidly buttoned-up men surrounding him. His mother-of-pearl cuff links catch the flickering glow of candlelight, and he is, in one word, stunning.

But it isn't the suit, or the way we accidentally match, or even the setting that has my breath catching in my throat.

It's the way he is looking at me.

Damien Wolfe is a man who does not react easily.

A man who does not give anything away unless he intends to.

And yet, as his eyes sweep over me, there is no mistaking what I see in them.

His expression is unreadable, his stance deceptively relaxed, but his gaze is slow, deliberate—like he's taking his time, committing every detail to memory.

The way my floor-length gown shimmers under the lights, the seafoam color making my skin glow, my hazel eyes turn more green than gold. The way the low-draped back exposes the smooth curve of my spine, drawing attention to bare skin begging to be touched.

Something shifts in his posture, barely perceptible.

One hand slips into his pocket. The other swirls his crystal glass of amber liquor.

Heat licks up my spine, my cheeks warming despite the evening breeze.

He takes a step toward me, then another, placing his glass down on a nearby table.

I force myself to breathe, to focus, to close the distance between us.

We come together like two magnets, pulled by an invisible tether.

He wraps one arm low around my waist, his hold commanding, possessive.

The other slips beneath my hair, firm between my shoulder blades as he turns me, dipping me back ever so slightly—just enough that I am at his mercy.

My hands go to him on instinct. One around his waist, the other clutching his bicep.

His muscles ripple as he holds me.

Running his nose up the column of my neck, his lips barely touch the surface of my skin—the whispered memory of how they felt only a week ago.

He takes in the scent of my perfume in an almost reverent way.

"Damien." I gasp his name, and it doesn't come out as

the warning I intend. It's a breathy plea that sounds danger-ously like a cry for more—for those lips to place kisses along my neck, behind my ear. To mold to mine as a public claim of who I belong to.

A rumble in his throat sends a wave of chills down my body.

"Be careful saying my name like that, *Trouble*, when you look as beautiful as you do."

He sets me upright again, a triumphant gleam in his stare that looks almost boyish—carefree.

"Thank you." The smile that comes to my face is a real one. "You look quite handsome yourself."

My hand runs up his chest to the piece of his lapel that is tucked under, out of place.

I correct it, my mind going back to the evening at Ember & Ash.

"There. Perfect." The last word is a whisper, and he takes in a sharp breath, stepping closer to me.

"Elena," he starts, catching my wrist as it retreats—just like he did when he asked me to stay with him. The moment stretches, pulling tight between us, and I'm afraid if one of us doesn't break it soon, my rules will become nonexistent.

His eyes move to my mouth, and I know he's thinking the same thing.

Wondering what will happen if he pushes through the invisible barrier of my rules to taste me again.

Our savior comes in the form of Margo. Her voice cuts in smoothly, distracting us both.

"I do love a couple who knows how to dress in sync," she muses, sipping her champagne.

Damien doesn't release my wrist right away, his thumb brushing once against the delicate skin before he finally lets go. But he doesn't step back. Instead, he turns slightly toward Margo, his expression shifting into something effortlessly composed—though the heat behind his gaze doesn't fully disappear.

His hand drifts down to my lower back, resting there in a way that feels both protective and possessive.

"When something"—he pauses, his eyes flicking back to mine—"or *someone* is meant to stand beside you, things tend to align naturally."

Margo, ever perceptive, lifts a knowing brow, pleased by the sentiment.

But I know the words aren't for her.

They're for me.

And the slow, deliberate way Damien's fingers trace the curve of my spine before finally falling away tells me—he knows I know it too.

Chapter 17

Elena

The guests have begun to mingle, the hum of conversation blending seamlessly with the soft notes of the live string quartet playing in the background.

With Damien momentarily pulled into a discussion with Mr. Calloway, I find myself drifting, my eyes scanning the candlelit terrace—until they land on James and Marcus.

The two of them stand a few feet away, glasses in hand, watching me with the kind of amused smirks that make my stomach tighten.

I narrow my eyes at them in silent warning, but their expressions only deepen in mischief as they approach.

Marcus reins in his smirk, joining Damien and Mr. Calloway. James leans in, his voice low and teasing. "That little display back there? The way Damien couldn't take his eyes off you? Yeah, we saw it. And we're not buying your act for a second."

I give his arm a playful smack. "It's all part of the gig," I whisper back, my eyes darting to make sure no one heard.

James lifts his brows in mock disbelief, while Marcus simply takes a sip of his drink, the glint in his eyes making me roll mine.

"Sure it is, sweetheart."

My cheeks warm, and I turn away, cursing them both under my breath as we're called to dinner. "Behave yourself," I scold, but it's all in good fun.

"I should be telling you that, apparently." He leaves with the last word, joining his husband as we take our seats.

The arrangement is a careful orchestration of power and influence. Mr. and Mrs. Calloway are seated to Damien's right, while I am on his left. The rest of the long table is a mix of Calloway and Wolfe associates, key figures in the merger, and a few esteemed guests meant to add to the prestige of the evening.

Unfortunately, Adrian is directly across from me.

Even more unfortunately, the floral centerpieces are low and unobtrusive, ensuring a perfectly clear view of the man I'd rather pretend didn't exist.

I feel his eyes on me, so I don't even bother looking up.

He's sure to have a smug smirk in place the entire evening—wanting, waiting for me to react to his proximity.

I don't. I won't.

Instead, I place my napkin on my lap, keeping my posture poised as the servers begin presenting the first course.

I don't even realize I'm reaching for Damien's hand. My arm snakes beneath his, my fingers mingling between his.

Still talking with Mr. Calloway, he raises my hand, kissing my knuckles as if it's the most natural thing in the world—like we do this every day.

It's a small, subtle touch.

Part of the charade because Margo is right there, watching our every move.

Damien puts my hand back in his lap, his fingers still threaded between mine, and he gives me a gentle squeeze.

A reminder.

We're in this together tonight. It's the final game, and he's in my corner as much as I am in his.

The servers move seamlessly around us, placing down the first course with practiced precision. The presentation is impeccable—a silver charger set before me, the pristine white plate showcasing a decadent display of escargot in their shells, each nestled in a bed of herbed garlic butter.

The scent alone is mouthwatering—rich, warm, laced with the intoxicating aroma of butter and white wine, mingled with the faintest hint of freshly chopped parsley.

The escargot are perfectly prepared, their shells gleaming under the candlelight, each one a tiny treasure chest of indulgence. The delicate spiral grooves hold pools of golden butter, shimmering under the glow of the overhead chandeliers. A sprinkle of sea salt and finely minced shallots adds to the anticipation curling low in my stomach.

A small hum of approval escapes me before I can stop it, and I hear Damien's low chuckle beside me. I glance up, only to find his amused gaze fixed on me.

"You're a fan," he muses, watching as I take the special

two-pronged fork in one hand and the snail tongs in the other, securing my first bite with practiced ease.

I smile. "One of my favorites."

The conversation around us resumes as I focus on my plate, maneuvering the tongs around the smooth curve of the shell to keep it steady while I spear the tender meat.

But just as I lift it to my plate, the shell slips—snapping free of my grip and launching across the table.

Time slows.

I watch in horror as it spins through the air, bouncing once against the rim of a wine glass before Mr. Calloway, with reflexes impressive for a man of his age, reaches out and catches it midair.

The conversation around me stops.

Heat crawls up my neck, spreading fast across my cheeks as every eye in our immediate vicinity lands on me.

Then, without thinking, I flash a smile. "Slippery little suckers."

Silence stretches for the briefest moment before Damien lets out a low, rumbling chuckle beside me.

Margo joins in, her laughter light and genuine.

Mr. Calloway grins, placing the rogue shell back onto my plate with a wink. "Happens to me all the time," he assures, his voice warm and indulgent.

The table relaxes, the moment passing as others chuckle and return to their meals. I let out a breath, willing my pulse to steady, and glance sideways at Damien.

He sets me at ease with a quick wink, his grin pulling out the dimple on his left cheek. I look at it quickly before meeting his blue eyes once again.

His smile only gets bigger for just a beat before he turns back to his plate and the conversation. "So, what were you saying, Richard?"

The courses continue, each one as exquisite as the last. Every plate is a masterpiece—tender filet with a red wine reduction, delicate seafood bisque with a hint of saffron, a fresh citrus sorbet to cleanse the palate before the next indulgence.

I pace myself, knowing meals of this caliber are meant to be savored, not rushed.

The conversation at the table remains mostly business, the merger still the center of attention, though a few personal remarks are thrown in between bites. Mr. Calloway reminisces about his early years in the company, Margo chimes in with her own perspective, and Damien holds his own, his words confident and assured. I listen, nodding where appropriate, inserting small, strategic remarks to keep Margo engaged.

The servers move seamlessly around us, clearing the last remnants of dinner. I take a sip of my wine, thinking the evening is winding down, thankful for the lack of dramatics.

Then Adrian speaks.

I clearly celebrated too early.

"It's an ambitious plan," he says smoothly, swirling his drink lazily in his hand. "But I have concerns about the developments in those lower-income areas. We've all seen projects like this before—big promises, even bigger failures. Sink money into them, and before long, you're looking at a ghost town of half-finished buildings and a PR nightmare."

He leans back, the picture of nonchalance, but his words

are pointed. A calculated jab meant to shake Calloway's confidence in Damien.

I set my wine down and meet Adrian's stare head-on.

Damien takes a breath to respond, but I beat him to it.

"Actually, I'd have to disagree," I say smoothly, my voice carrying across the table with certainty. "There was a real estate development in a struggling district just over ten years ago—similar scale, similar concerns. And yet, here we are a decade later, and that same project is now widely credited with revitalizing the entire area. Job creation, infrastructure improvements, increased property values— by all accounts, it was a resounding success. The Lennox Square Redevelopment, if I'm not mistaken."

Adrian scoffs, shaking his head. "I wouldn't put too much stock in what your fiancé tells you, Elena. He's going to make sure you hear exactly what he wants you to believe."

Damien physically tenses beside me, but I place my hand on his thigh, a silent signal. I keep my expression poised, unaffected. Then, with a knowing smile, I lift my glass.

"On the contrary," I counter, tilting my head slightly. "That wasn't one of Damien's investments."

I let the words settle, enjoying the slight flicker of confusion in Adrian's gaze before I deliver the final blow.

"That was an initiative led by Margo." I look to her with a proud smile.

Adrian's jaw tightens as Margo lets out a soft laugh, utterly delighted.

"Oh, Elena, you've done your research," she muses,

lifting her own glass. "That project was one of the ones I was most proud of."

"You set a precedent that makes it easy for others to follow. I have confidence the impressive Wolfe Industries CEO has accounted for this in his plans."

I turn my warm smile to Damien, my hand moving from his leg to his cheek. I tuck a short tuft of hair behind his ear and brush my thumb along his jaw.

His returning expression is one of awe, mixed with something that looks too much like adoration.

I push away the warmth settling over me, bringing my structured rules back to the forefront of my mind.

It's all part of the gig.

Calloway, watching the exchange with obvious amusement, chuckles and shakes his head. "Damien, you really have found yourself a sharp one, haven't you? A woman who can keep up with you."

He looks at Margo, his expression softening as he lifts his own glass.

"Reminds me of us."

Margo smiles at her husband, touching his arm affectionately.

Adrian stays silent, barely masking his irritation.

"Well, I think this calls for a toast." Calloway raises his glass higher.

"To Damien and Elena—two forces to be reckoned with. This is not just a match for love, but a match of prowess and power. A partnership that will shape our city in ways we've yet to see."

He grins, nodding toward Damien and I feel him tense.

At something Calloway said? Or perhaps the toast in general, I'm not sure.

"New York better get ready."

The rest of the table follows suit, glasses clinking together as they echo the toast.

I feel Damien's fingers thread through mine again beneath the table, a small squeeze of approval.

He holds my stare and that tension eases away.

We clink our glasses together, our eyes never leaving each other as we take a sip.

And as I meet Adrian's gaze across the table, the sour downturn of his mouth telling me exactly how much he hated losing this round, I can't help the small, satisfied smile that curls at the corner of my lips.

"In fact," Mr. Calloway stands and nods to the musicians who have been playing softly in the background of our meal. "I demand the first dance with the blushing bride-to-be."

Calloway rounds his chair and holds his hand to help me up.

"Need to show these young ones how it's done." He teases, his words a playful jab at Damien as he pats his shoulder twice, escorting me to the dancefloor.

The music swells, the soft hum of a jazz standard filling the air as Mr. Calloway leads me effortlessly across the dance floor. His grip is firm but gentle, the kind of steady confidence that comes from years of practice.

I expected this to be awkward, but it isn't.

He's easy to talk to, his conversation lighthearted as he spins me with ease.

"You're a natural," he compliments, his voice warm with amusement.

I smile. "You're a very good lead."

"Decades of keeping up with Margo will do that to a man." He grins.

"Speaking of which, I mean it when I say, you and Damien make quite the pair."

I don't let my smile falter.

"I'd like to think so."

"True love can be rare for men like us," he continues, guiding me into another smooth turn.

"A woman with beauty and brains? That's a once-in-a-lifetime treasure. I knew Margo was the one the moment I saw her handle herself in a room full of men who underestimated her. She proved them all wrong."

He eyes me with approval.

"And I suspect you're no stranger to doing the same."

The compliment is genuine, and I tuck it away like a small victory.

"That's very kind of you to say, Mr. Calloway."

He laughs.

"Oh, none of that. We're past such formalities. Call me Richard."

I don't miss the way Damien's gaze lingers on me from across the room.

He's standing with Marcus, but his attention is solely on me.

The weight of his stare is something I can feel even with my back turned.

The song winds to an end, and before I can return to my seat, another hand extends toward me.

"May I?"

James' eyes twinkle with mischief, and I can't help but smile as I let him take my hand.

"Of course."

Richard claps him on the shoulder before heading toward Damien and Marcus, likely to return to business.

James pulls me in with an easy grace, his touch light as we fall into step.

"Well, you know how to liven up a dinner party," he teases, his voice pitched low.

I roll my eyes playfully. "If by *liven up* you mean nearly taking Calloway's eye out with a snail projectile, then yes— I'm a real showstopper."

He throws his head back in genuine laughter.

Dancing with James is effortless.

He makes me laugh, relax even.

And I know that if circumstances were different—if I were allowed friendships outside of this contract—he and I would be fast friends.

But then, just as the song shifts into something slower, a shadow looms over us.

"Mind if I cut in?"

The tar-like sound of Adrian's voice oozes down my back uncomfortably.

The lightheartedness I felt just moments ago vanishes, replaced by a sharp tension curling in my stomach.

My body goes rigid, but I don't want to make a scene.

James hesitates, his eyes flicking to mine as if asking if I'm okay to be left with him.

I nod once. "It's fine."

Reluctantly, James steps back, giving me one last glance before turning toward Marcus and Damien.

Adrian's hand finds my waist as he pulls me closer than necessary.

I resist the urge to shove him away, keeping my expression carefully neutral.

"I have to admit," he murmurs, his breath warm against my ear, "I didn't expect you to play this role so well. It's almost believable."

I inhale through my nose, forcing myself to stay composed.

"Let go of me."

"Now, now." His fingers tighten slightly on my waist. "No need for theatrics. We're just two old friends catching up, aren't we?"

I grit my teeth.

"You and I were never friends."

He chuckles.

"That's true. We were so much more than that."

His fingers trail slightly lower, and I jerk away from him.

He only smirks.

"Tell me, Elena . . . have you given my offer some thought?"

I meet his stare, unblinking.

"I don't need to."

"Why not?" His tone is smug.

"What's he offering you, Elena? A pretend ring and an NDA? A condo, maybe?"

He leans in, his voice a low whisper against my ear, and I grit my teeth so hard it hurts.

"I'll give you something real. One hundred million dollars, Elena. Something life changing."

The number is outrageous.

Just like his desperation.

And his misguided belief that anything he could ever say would make me consider his offer for even a second.

I lift my chin, meeting his gaze with unwavering defiance.

"I'd rather set myself on fire, you stupid piece of shit."

Chapter 18
Damien

Calloway is talking.

That much I am aware of. The words he says, whether he is directing them at me—no fucking idea.

Marcus responds when I don't, his expression clearly questioning me, but I don't register a single word.

Because my focus is locked elsewhere.

On her.

On him.

Adrian's hand rests too low on Elena's back, his grip firm, possessive in a way that sets my teeth on edge. His lips move close to her ear, whispering something meant only for her, and the way his fingers linger against the delicate fabric of her dress makes my grip tighten around my glass.

I know his type.

The ones who take because they think they can. The ones who wear their arrogance like a second skin, convinced the world owes them something.

And right now, I can see it—the way he's toying with her, testing her boundaries, pushing just enough to see how far he can go before she pushes back.

The sharp burn in my chest is immediate, creeping up my throat, my jaw locking tight as I watch the interaction unfold.

I don't do jealousy.

It's pointless. Useless. A distraction at best.

But this?

This isn't jealousy. This is something else.

Something far more dangerous.

I should look away.

I should stay focused on the larger picture, on the merger, on the endgame we're so close to achieving.

But I don't.

Because I fucking can't.

Adrian shifts closer, his fingers pressing slightly into the curve of her waist.

She tenses, her body language giving away more than she realizes.

That's it.

I set my glass down with a little more force than needed, already moving before I've fully processed the thought.

Elena catches sight of me just as I reach them. Relief flashes in her eyes for the briefest second before she smooths her expression into something composed. Unreadable.

I don't break stride.

"Mind if I cut in?"

My voice is calm, deceptively smooth, but there's no mistaking the weight behind it.

Adrian, predictably smug, offers a lazy smirk.

"Actually, we were just—"

"I wasn't asking."

I step forward, sliding an arm around Elena's waist, pulling her against me in one fluid movement.

The shift is immediate—she's in my arms, and he's dismissed.

Adrian exhales sharply through his nose, clearly irritated but not foolish enough to press the issue. Instead, he salutes lazily with two fingers on his forehead, some mock acknowledgment before strolling away.

I swear to God, I've never wanted to wipe a look off someone's face more.

Exhaling slowly, I fight the tension coiling inside me, redirecting my focus to the woman now in my arms.

Her pulse is racing beneath my fingertips. Her pupils blown wide, a clear sign of high adrenaline.

"Are you okay?" I murmur, my voice lower now, meant only for her.

She hesitates, just barely, before forcing a small smile.

"It's fine."

It's not.

"Elena," I press gently, tightening my hold just slightly.

She exhales, her lashes lowering before she speaks.

"I just don't want to cause a scene," she admits, her voice quieter now. Then, after a beat, she adds, "But . . . Adrian makes me uncomfortable."

Those words are all it takes.

A slow, simmering protectiveness flares inside me, raging in an instant to a boil, and I look for him.

My mind immediately rewinds—to the yacht, to the way Adrian looked at her in that bikini, his eyes lingering too long, like he had any fucking right.

To his hands on her just now, holding her too tightly, too familiarly.

To the way she tried to lean away, her shoulders stiff, every muscle locked in discomfort.

The thought of it burns through me like gasoline on an open flame.

I clench my jaw, forcing my grip to remain steady, controlled, even as my blood simmers with something dangerously close to rage.

I want to go find him, smash his smug face into a brick wall.

Elena must sense it because her hands come up, palms pressing gently against the sides of my face.

"Hey, eyes on me, Wolfe."

It stops me cold.

My focus shifts, locking onto hers as my heart stutters in my chest.

"That's it. It's just you and me."

They're the same words I said to her when I scared the shit out of her on the yacht.

Her calm, sweet voice is a soothing balm, cooling the heat threatening to explode within me.

"He's not worth it," she whispers.

But you are.

She's calming me, her thumbs barely brushing against my skin in quiet reassurance, grounding me in a way nothing else could.

And in return, my hands move against the smooth, bare expanse of her back, stroking up and down, a silent promise that she is safe.

That no one will ever hurt her while she is in my arms.

Something about the moment shifts everything in my mind.

She isn't just my contract.

She isn't just part of the game we're playing.

She's Elena.

And I would burn the fucking world down before I let anyone make her feel unsafe.

I lean in, lowering my voice so only she can hear.

"No one will hurt you," I vow. "Not him. Not anyone. Not as long as I'm here."

Her fingers press slightly into my skin, and I feel the tension in her frame begin to ease.

The weight of the moment lingers between us, stretching too tight, pulling too close.

But I don't want to be the one crashing through her barriers.

I want her to meet me there, at that line her rules have drawn in the sand, and I want the both of us to cross them together.

So, I do the only thing I can before I do something I shouldn't—I shift it.

My lips curve slightly, my tone feigning casual consideration.

"But if you'd like . . . there are a few alternative solutions we could consider."

Her brows pull together slightly. "What?"

I exhale, as if weighing the options.

"Drowning. Spoiled little rich boys drown all the time."

She smiles, catching onto my teasing as it has its intended effect.

"A tragic croquet accident."

I look at her as if I just had a bright idea.

"I saw him go to the bathroom kind of quickly after the snails. We could feed him a bunch and make him shit himself to death."

Her eyes widen in shock as a genuine laugh escapes her, the sound breaking through the tension and sending a surge of satisfaction through me.

"Damien," she chides, shaking her head, but she's smiling now, and I feel the tension in my own shoulders ease in response.

I smirk, leaning in just enough to murmur, "What? I'm a problem solver."

Her laughter is soft, breathless, still lingering as she shakes her head.

I should leave it at that. Should let this moment slip by before I do something I shouldn't.

But I don't.

Because I can't.

Instead, I study her. The way her lips are still parted slightly, the way her eyes are warm but guarded, like she's not sure whether to let her walls down or rebuild them higher than before.

I want to tell her she doesn't have to.

Not with me.

But I'd be the biggest fucking hypocrite that ever lived.

Instead, I settle for something lighter. Something that won't shatter whatever fragile thing has been built between us tonight.

"You're beautiful when you laugh, Trouble."

The nickname slips out effortlessly, my voice quieter now, rougher.

Elena's smile falters slightly, and something flickers in her hazel eyes—something I can't quite grasp before she hides it away.

Her lashes lower, and she exhales softly, her fingers still resting lightly against my chest.

"Careful, Wolfie," she murmurs. Her gaze lifts to meet mine, something almost wistful in her expression. "You almost sound like you mean that."

I don't blink. Don't breathe.

Because fuck.

I do.

I mean every damn word.

But before I can say anything, before I can do anything, a crack of thunder rolls across the sky, the distant storm drawing closer.

Elena glances up, distracted, her lips parting slightly as she watches the sky flicker with lightning over the ocean.

I take the out she's given me, exhaling slowly as I step back, creating space between us.

"We should head out before it downpours," I murmur, running a hand through my hair.

She nods, like she's been snapped back into reality, and I recognize the way she swallows thickly, how she subtly puts distance between us.

Like she needs to.

Like she's afraid of what might happen if she doesn't.

Still, she lets me take her hand as we move away from the dance floor, making our way down the wooden deck and onto the moonlit beach that leads back to our bungalow.

I slip off my shoes, holding them in one hand, and Elena follows suit, lifting the hem of her gown as she steps barefoot onto the cool sand.

For a while, we walk in comfortable silence, the sounds of the distant party fading behind us, replaced by the steady rhythm of the waves.

After a beat, Elena stops, glancing at me before holding out her shoes.

I lift a brow, and she smirks.

"You're already carrying yours," she points out. "Might as well add mine to the collection."

I huff out a low laugh, but I take them, adding them to mine.

She watches me for a moment, something unreadable in her expression before she finally asks, "Tell me why?"

I glance at her, brow lifting slightly. "Why what?"

She hesitates, then gestures vaguely with her free hand, the motion encompassing more than just the merger—the empire, the relentless drive, the insatiable hunger for more.

"Why do you chase all of this so much?" she asks, her voice curious, not judgmental.

Something about the way she asks—like she genuinely wants to understand me—makes my chest tighten.

"What made little Damien Wolfe want to grow up and own half the world's biggest cities?" she presses, tilting her head slightly.

I let out a slow breath, my eyes fixed ahead on the ocean as I consider her question.

She's not the first person to ask.

But she is the first person I actually want to answer.

"You talk about it like it was always inevitable," I muse, my tone dry but not unkind.

She shrugs, a small smile playing on her lips.

"Well, you don't exactly do anything halfway, Mr. Wolfe. From where I'm standing, it seems like every move you've ever made has been leading up to this. Like you always knew exactly where you were going."

I hum, shifting the shoes in my hand before tucking my free hand into my pocket.

"I didn't."

She waits, patient, giving me the space to continue if I want to.

I exhale, my gaze tracing the horizon before I finally say it.

"My father was a mid-level corporate man who lost everything on a bad investment."

Her brows furrow slightly, but she doesn't interrupt.

"He made a bet on something too risky. Didn't hedge it properly. And when it crashed, so did we."

I shake my head slightly. "Lost the house. The savings. Everything."

Elena stays quiet, listening.

"My mother . . ." I swallow, my voice steady, but the memory burns like an old wound.

"She never recovered from it," I continue. "She fell into a deep depression. Eventually, she took her own life."

Elena sucks in a quiet breath, but I don't look at her.

This part has always felt so detached from me.

"I had no idea, Damien," she whispers.

"You won't find any records of it. No stories. No head-lines. Just . . . gone."

I keep my voice flat, because if I don't, something inside me might crack open completely.

"When I was able to, I paid a lot of money to make it that way."

I finally glance at her, my lips twitching into something humorless.

She doesn't say anything, but I can feel the weight of her sorrow as she looks at me.

I turn back to the ocean, the water black and endless under the stormy sky.

"After that, it was just me and him. My father. But he didn't even try to put us back together. He just . . . drank himself into a coffin a few years later."

"Damien."

Her voice is barely carried by the wind, soft and aching with something I don't want to name.

I shake my head. "I raised myself. After he lost everything, he was content to sit in the wreckage, pretending the world owed him something. I wasn't."

My jaw locks, that old familiar burn settling deep in my gut.

"I was never going to be like that. Never again was I going to go to bed hungry for the third day in a row."

Her grip tightens on my arm.

I glance down at where her fingers wrap around me, the contrast of her delicate touch against the tension still coiled in my body.

I hadn't even realized she was holding onto me.

"I clawed my way out of there," I continue, my voice quieter now.

"Finance. Mergers. Acquisitions. Turning failing companies into powerhouses. I built everything I have from the ground up."

Silence stretches between us, but it's not empty.

It's full.

When I look at her, I expect pity, maybe sympathy—but all I see is warmth.

Something deep. Something real.

Like she sees beyond the ruthless, untouchable man I've spent years crafting—the one people fear, the one who doesn't break, doesn't bend.

Like she sees the boy I once was.

And fuck if I don't want to throw these shoes down, take her in my arms, and kiss her until there's nothing left between us but this thing we both refuse to name.

As if the universe itself is conspiring against me, the sky opens up.

A torrential downpour hammers down in an instant, soaking us to the bone within seconds.

Elena gasps, laughing as she shrinks into herself, hands lifting in a useless attempt to shield herself from the rain.

Water streams down her shoulders, her dark hair already flattened against her skin.

"Let's run for it!" I call out, offering my hand.

She doesn't hesitate.

Her fingers slip into mine, gripping tightly. She pulls her dress up with the other, and together, we take off across the beach, our feet kicking up sand as we sprint toward the bungalow.

Her laughter follows us, mixing with the steady rhythm of the rain, and for once, I'm not thinking about business, deals, or the next move I have to make.

I'm just here.

Running through the rain, laughing with a woman who is completely unraveling me.

By the time we reach the deck, we're both drenched, water dripping from our clothes, our hair, our skin.

Elena lifts the hem of her gown as we take the stairs, but the slick wood betrays her.

She slips with a curse, and my hands fly out to catch her.

Our shoes are forgotten, clattering on the ground around us.

My arms wrap around her waist, anchoring her against me before she can fall.

Her hands clutch at my chest, her breath shallow and uneven.

Now, we're too close.

But not nearly as close as I want us.

The sound of the rain fades into the background, drowned out by the pounding of my pulse.

Her dress clings to her like a second skin, the soft fabric molding to the curve of her waist, the swell of her breasts.

Water drips from her lips, down the line of her throat, trailing over her collarbone.

And her eyes—hazel and burning with passion—tilt up to mine, like she's daring me to push further.

Daring me to take what we both want.

I lean in.

I don't care about her rules.

I don't care about this fucking contract.

I just want her.

But just as my lips nearly brush against hers, she steps back.

"Damien."

Her voice is full of breath, and I know it's not all from our run.

"My rules."

A muscle in my jaw tightens.

I exhale slowly, my fingers still gripping her waist, unwilling to let go just yet.

My thumb drags over her full bottom lip, watching as arousal washes over her at my touch.

My voice is gravelly, low.

"I've thought about breaking your fucking rules a dozen times tonight."

Her breath catches, and for a second, I think she'll let me.

That she'll let me pull her in, kiss her the way I've wanted to since the moment I laid eyes on her at The Ledger.

Hell, since I woke up alone in my hotel suite.

But she doesn't.

She forces herself to step away, clearing the space between us, and I see the effort it takes.

Elena keeps her beautiful eyes on me, and I wish I fucking knew what she was thinking.

I'm goddamn desperate for it.

Then—finally—"Good night, Damien."

She turns, walking smoothly toward the door of the bungalow.

But just before she disappears inside, she hesitates.

Looking back at me over her shoulder, her expression softer now.

One hand rests on the doorframe, like she needs it to keep her from running back to me.

"Thank you . . . for telling me."

She's talking about my past. My parents.

Everything I told her tonight.

She leaves me standing there in the rain, my hands aching to pull her back.

I run a hand through my soaked hair, exhaling sharply as the storm continues to rage around me.

My chest is tight, my pulse unsteady, and for the first time in a long time, I feel completely out of control.

This woman.

She's inside me now. Beneath my skin, in my fucking head, making me want things I swore I didn't need.

I should go inside.

I should shake this off, pour myself a drink, get my mind back where it belongs—on the merger, on Calloway, on anything but the way Elena Moreau just looked at me.

But I don't move.

I just stand there, fists clenched, watching the door she disappeared behind, knowing that sleep will be a long, long way off tonight.

Chapter 19

Damien

The vibration in my pocket pulls me out of the rain and into the bungalow.

I reach for my phone, swiping away the droplets still clinging to the screen. A message from Calloway.

> Calloway (Group Text—Marcus & Me):
> Conference call—five minutes.

That was three minutes ago.

I exhale sharply, shaking off the lingering tension from the storm, from her, from everything. My clothes are soaked through, clinging uncomfortably to my skin, and the last thing I need is to sit through this call looking like I just crawled out of the Atlantic.

I head to my bathroom, peeling off the wet fabric and tossing it onto the counter. The muscles in my back protest as I scrub a towel over my skin, trying to wipe away the chill that has settled deep inside me. But it isn't the cold that's gotten under my skin. It's her.

It's the way she looked at me when I told her about my past.

The way her hands settled on my face when she was trying to calm me down.

The way she almost let me kiss her.

I rub a hand over my face, forcing my mind to shift. Focus, Wolfe.

Sliding on a dry shirt and comfortable lounge pants, I run my fingers through my damp hair just as the conference call rings.

From the living room, I answer, and the flatscreen flickers to life.

And just like that, my mood sours because sitting next to Calloway, smug as ever, is Adrian Kingston.

Of course, he's here.

Marcus's face appears in another box, his usual easy expression slightly more alert. He notices Adrian too. The flicker of irritation in his gaze is subtle, but I catch it.

Calloway leans forward, folding his hands on the table in front of him. "All right, gentlemen, let's get this squared away before the night is over."

I settle onto the couch, gripping the remote a little tighter than necessary. I already know exactly what this is about.

And I already know I'm not going to like it.

The second Calloway clears his throat, I know exactly where this is going.

I lean back against the couch, arms stretched along the top, my posture deceptively relaxed. I've played this game long enough to recognize when a man is gearing up for yet another round of Adrian's bullshit.

Sure enough, Calloway sighs, rubbing a hand over his jaw before speaking.

"Adrian has raised another concern," he starts, his voice measured. "Something about the long-term scalability of the Wolfe Industries development strategy as it pertains to—"

I cut him off, my patience already running thin. "Why don't we let Adrian explain it himself?"

Adrian shifts slightly in his chair, adjusting his cuffs like the extra second will help him find an answer worth saying. His smirk is still there, but I see the crack in it.

"Of course," he says, clearing his throat. "I just think we need to take a closer look at the, uh... the projected growth model, particularly in the—"

"Which model?" I ask smoothly.

His lips part slightly, like he wasn't expecting to be put on the spot so quickly. "The... uh, the one outlining—"

I cock my head. "You mean the one already vetted by Calloway's board? The one that's been analyzed, projected, and confirmed three times over?"

His mouth clamps shut.

I press forward, my voice silk over steel. "Or do you mean the alternate model you proposed yesterday? The one that—remind me—was missing half its financial projections and fundamentally misunderstood market demand?"

Marcus lets out a barely contained chuckle.

Adrian's jaw tightens. "That's not what I—"

"Cut the bullshit," I say, my patience snapping. "Every so-called 'concern' you've raised has been nothing but an attempt to derail this deal. And quite frankly, I'm done entertaining your amateur-hour tactics."

Adrian bristles. Calloway sits back, watching me carefully.

I level my stare at him through the screen. "Your nephew has tried to lob bombs at our plans that, frankly, have no merit. So make a choice, Calloway: Are we doing this, or are we going to keep playing twenty questions while your competitors circle you like sharks?"

Silence.

Then—Calloway lets out a low chuckle, shaking his head as he beams.

"You've got a spine, Wolfe," he says with something like pride. "Damn good trait in a partner."

I lift my glass to the screen in mock salute. "Then let's get this merger done. And you'll have the biggest shark in the tank on your side."

His laughter is warm, genuine. "Hell yes, we will."

Before Adrian can muster another weak attempt at interference, Margo enters the frame, settling gracefully onto the arm of her husband's chair, her arm slipping around his shoulders.

"Smartest decision you've ever made, darling," she tells Calloway, her eyes flicking to mine with something close to satisfaction. "This isn't just about numbers. Wolfe Industries isn't just building an empire—it's building a legacy."

She looks directly at me as she says it.

And for a reason I don't quite understand, it hits.

Harder than I expected.

Legacy.

Not just holdings. Not just assets but something that goes on longer.

A family.

For the first time, I realize that's what Calloway sees when he looks at me. Not just a business partner—but a man with a future. With a wife.

With Elena.

I swallow, my grip tightening around the remote in my hand.

Except she isn't mine.

Not really.

And each moment I remind myself of that truth, it sours more and more in my mind.

The screen goes dark, the room sinking into silence.

This is it. The victory I wanted. The one I've worked for nearly a year to finally hear.

And yet, as I sit there, staring at my own reflection in the now-black television screen, it feels... empty.

The triumph I should be reveling in is missing something. Someone.

My phone buzzes in my pocket, Marcus's name flashing across the screen.

MARCUS: "You finally put that little shit in his place. About damn time. Congrats, buddy."

I let out a slow exhale, half-grinning as I type out a simple "Well fought. Congratulations to you too."

The words feel hollow.

I should be celebrating. Should be pouring myself a drink, savoring the win, but instead, I find myself thinking of Elena.

Because she's as much a part of this as I am.

Every dinner, every event, every carefully placed interaction—she was there. She played the role flawlessly, not just standing beside me but elevating me in ways I never anticipated.

And all I can think about is how I want to tell her.

I want to swoop her into my arms, feel the warmth of her body against mine as I tell her, We did it.

I want to hear her laugh when I spin her around.

I want to feel her lips on mine as she kisses me in celebration, like this is our victory, not just mine.

My grip tightens around my phone, Marcus's message still glowing on the screen.

Margo's words come back to me.

Legacy.

And I don't know exactly how, but I can't stop thinking Elena had something to do with affirming that legacy to Margo.

I run a hand through my hair, pushing up from the couch with sudden resolve.

She deserves to hear this news.

Not in the morning when we're packed into the helicopter, heading back to New York, the real world creeping back in, but now.

I cross the bungalow, my steps quiet against the wooden floor. When I reach her door, I hesitate just a second, listening.

The rain batters down hard outside, making it difficult to tell if she's still awake.

Then, I knock—gently.

And wait.

The knock goes unanswered, and as I raise my knuckles to try again, I hear a faint, broken sound inside her room.

A sharp edge of protectiveness flares in my chest, and my mind races to the piece of shit that's been a thorn in my side all weekend. If Adrian made her more upset than she let on. If he said something to her, threatened her.

I hear it again, and it breaks my resolve.

I can't stand out here, walk away from her knowing she's in distress. Not when I can do something about it.

She's here because of me. Thrown into a weekend with a man who made her uncomfortable for me. Keeping her unease a secret to put my needs, the merger, our contract first.

I turn the knob slowly, pushing the door open with care.

"Elena?" My voice is low, just in case she is sleeping. Maybe crying out in her dreams.

Her bed is still made, a breeze coming in through the open door that leads to the terrace. The salty night air, damp from the raging storm, rushes around the room.

I take a step toward it, thinking she may be outside, but another sound comes from behind, and I turn around.

The door of her bathroom is ajar just enough that I can see her, and the sight freezes me.

Steam billows around the shower, fogging up the glass enclosure. But I can see enough.

Another gasp escapes her. It's so quiet, yet it blares around me.

The blood is rushing through my body, going straight to my cock. My pulse hammering, my mind screaming at me to leave.

I shouldn't be here, watching her, but fuck if I can't look away.

Her body is moving, writhing and beautiful.

One hand is on her breast, and I can imagine her pinching the peaks of her nipples.

My mouth goes dry, wanting to suck that breast, nip at her while she cries out.

But it's her other hand making me jealous, driving me to near madness.

She's holding a shower wand. The spray of the nozzle is centered on her pussy, and fuck if she doesn't look like a goddess.

The way she moves is hypnotic. Sensual, unguarded, fucking devastating.

Her body arches into the spray of water, head tipped back against the tile, droplets racing down her flushed skin. Her dark hair clings in damp waves over her shoulders, and fuck, I should turn away, should give her the privacy she deserves—but I can't.

Not when she looks like this.

Her free hand leaves her breast, trailing over her stomach, sliding lower, her thighs parting just enough to give me a glimpse of where she's touching herself. Slow, teasing strokes, drawing out the pleasure, building it. I can see the way her muscles tighten, her breath catching as she moves the showerhead in tight little circles, sending the jet of water straight to her clit.

I swear, my fucking knees nearly buckle.

My fists tighten at my sides, my pulse hammering, my cock already painfully hard. Every sound she makes hits me like a wrecking ball—low, breathy gasps, the softest moan slipping past her lips as she tilts her hips, chasing the release she's on the verge of falling into.

And then, my name.

Not a whisper. Not a passing thought. A plea. A fucking surrender.

The sound slams into my chest, steals the breath from my lungs. Need surges through me like a violent storm. The final thread of control holds on tight as the sight of her threatens to eviscerate it.

I want to be the one pulling those sounds from her. Want to replace that fucking showerhead with my fingers, my tongue, my cock. Want to slide inside her, stretch her open, make her beg like that for real.

For me.

The thought alone nearly undoes me, and I take a staggering step back, dragging in a ragged breath.

But I don't go to her.

Because as much as I want her—as much as I want to bury myself so deep inside her that she forgets she ever had rules to begin with—she has to be the one to break them.

Not me.

Not yet.

The feeling is there. That thought of just falling over the edge of the cliff and surrendering to the crashing waves below. I could just take one step, and she would see me.

She would either send me away... or not.

That version of the fantasy where she invites me in, hands me the nozzle, and gives herself over to me is nearly impossible to ignore.

And just when I think I might actually do it, her phone buzzes on the bedside table.

The sound is a gunshot in the silence, breaking the haze I've been drowning in. I retreat fast, backing away from her door, my breath still ragged in my chest.

The screen glares up at me, the words sinking in like a dull knife.

UNKNOWN NUMBER: *Think about my offer. I'll be in touch soon.*

Next week.

Next week, she won't be mine anymore.

Except, she never was.

I inhale slowly, my grip tightening around my phone. *She's an escort. This was always going to end.*

But for the first time, the thought *sits differently.*

It sits *wrong.*

A bitter taste rises in my throat, and suddenly, I'm not standing in this bungalow. I'm back in Manhattan, five years ago, watching a woman I once thought I loved *fuck another man in our bed.*

I remember the sharp edge of betrayal cutting through me, the way I told myself *never again.*

Never again would I let a woman inside my walls. Never again would I put myself in a position to be the fool.

And yet, here I am.

Standing outside Elena's door, wanting something I have no right to want.

Because at the end of the day, I signed the contract knowing exactly what this was. I paid for her presence, for her time, for her careful companionship in a world where everything is a calculated move.

But the truth?

I don't just want her in my bed.

I don't just want her for a fucking contract.

I want her.

Not because she makes me look good in front of Calloway.

Not because she plays her role flawlessly.

Not because our names on a paper will make us a power couple feared by everyone.

But because *she's the only person who's ever made me feel anything real in years.*

Because when I look at her, I don't see a woman who can be bought—I see the only woman I've ever fucking *wanted.*

I exhale sharply, my pulse hammering.

I've spent the last five years locking the door on anything resembling real intimacy. But she's already inside. *She's already inside, and she's burning the place down.*

And the worst part?

I want to let her.

I want to give her the gasoline and matches and watch her set fire to it all.

Let her ignite every tarnished memory and destroy every brick in the walls I've built.

I've secured my empire. Now, it's time to secure the one thing I never saw coming.

Her.

Chapter 20

Elena

The stupid smile won't leave my face, and it's all Damien Wolfe's fault.

DAMIEN: You did great this weekend.

DAMIEN: I mean it.

A simple text. Nothing elaborate. Nothing flirtatious. But as I stare down at my phone, the warmth it spreads through me is anything but simple.

I lean back in the town car, tapping my reply as the driver navigates through the late-morning Manhattan traffic.

ELENA: You weren't too bad yourself.

It's light. Nonchalant. But still, I watch the screen, waiting, because the three little dots appear instantly.

DAMIEN: 😐

A laugh escapes before I can help it.

The car rolls forward, heading toward the real estate office where I'll be meeting my realtor, Nina. I've looked at the property sheet for the bakery a hundred times, memorized every detail, run through every scenario of how I'll make it mine.

But today, it feels different. Like it's finally happening.

This time next week, I'll be signing my offer.

This time next month, the keys will be in my hands.

The idea makes my heart race, anticipation curling around me like a warm embrace.

ELENA: Okay… you were swell.

I imagine Damien rolling his eyes.

DAMIEN: 😐😐

ELENA: Fine. You were incredible. I've never seen anything like it. Stupendous… comes to mind. Magnificent, perhaps.

My grin widens.

DAMIEN: This is more like it.

DAMIEN: We should focus a few minutes on my magnificence.

ELENA: Ooh… would love to. Super busy, though.

DAMIEN: Doing?

Oh, why do you want to know, Mr. Wolfe?

ELENA: Things. 

I watch the screen. The dots appear, disappear. Appear again. Then disappear once more.

Is he in a meeting, texting me under the table, hiding his phone and his smirk? Or is he alone in his office, leaning back in his chair, smiling as he types?

DAMIEN: Will those 'things' be over by five p.m.?

My brows pull together, and I swipe up, checking the schedule for our contract. There's nothing planned until tomorrow.

His next message pops up at the top of my screen.

DAMIEN: It's not on the schedule.

DAMIEN: I know you were just looking.

ELENA: Was not.

The dots flicker again. Then stop. Then start again.

I press my lips together, biting back a laugh.

DAMIEN: So... tonight?

All that for this?

ELENA: Depends.

ELENA: May I ask what we'll be doing?

DAMIEN: We'll be making a detailed presentation on all the qualities of my magnificence. It could take us all night.

I chuckle, shaking my head.

ELENA: That sounds riveting.

ELENA: What outfit would one wear for such an occasion?

I stare at the message, my stomach flipping as I hit send.

The back-and-forth is too easy. Too effortless.

And I shouldn't like it.

Shouldn't like the way my pulse kicks up every time my phone buzzes with his name. Shouldn't like the way my fingers hover over the screen, thinking too long about what to say next.

But I do.

I like it too much.

DAMIEN: Let me take care of that.

My breath catches.

My mind betrays me instantly, flashing back to last night's rainstorm. The almost kiss. The tension so thick between us it could have swallowed me whole.

And then, later—alone in the shower, the fantasy unfurling behind my closed eyes.

The way I imagined him finding me, watching me, stepping inside, pushing my hand away to take over.

His hands, his mouth, his beautiful fucking cock—

I wouldn't have been able to tell him no again.

If he had come to me one more time, I would have shattered my own rules.

And I can't afford to do that.

Because we only have a few more days left.

One last outing—Mr. Calloway's birthday dinner. Then the merger is complete, the deal signed.

Then, Damien and I will go our separate ways.

The thought burns more than I want to admit.

So I do the only thing I can.

I end the conversation.

> ELENA: Then it's a date.

A pause.

> DAMIEN: I hope you have a good day, Elena.

It's my name at the end of the sentence that pulls the knot in my stomach tighter. That makes it feel more intimate than it should.

I shouldn't reply.

I do anyway.

> ELENA: You too, Wolfie.

The dots appear immediately.

DAMIEN: I don't think so.

ELENA: Too late.

DAMIEN: No.

ELENA: That's your name now.

DAMIEN: Never.

ELENA: For all time. 😏

ELENA: See you at five, Wolfe.

DAMIEN: See you… Trouble.

I let him have the last word.

Because I need to focus.

I'm meeting Nina at the real estate office, and after that, we'll head over to the bakery to take another look.

I can't stop smiling as I step out of the car, fully expecting the driver to pull away, but he stays put.

"Mr. Wolfe's instructions," he says before I can ask. "I'm at your service all day, Miss Moreau. Wherever you need to go."

A warmth unfurls inside me, but I push it down.

I don't have time to think about Damien Wolfe today.

I need to see to my future.

Walking into the building, energy is buzzing inside me as I step through the lobby. Nina is near the elevator, waiting, and my smile stretches wider.

"Nina!" I call out, waving.

She turns, but instead of smiling back, confusion flickers across her face.

"Elena..." she hesitates. "Did you see my text?"

A chill slithers down my spine.

I pull out my phone.

Two unread messages.

> NINA: I'm not sure what happened, but someone purchased the bakery last week.

> NINA: I'm so sorry, Elena. I know you had your heart set on this place, but we'll find something else.

The words on the screen blur as I read them over again.

Someone purchased the bakery last week.

No. That's not possible.

This was supposed to be mine.

I had a plan. I was so close.

I worked for this. Saved for this. Dreamed of this.

A numbness creeps up my spine, spreading through my limbs as my pulse pounds in my ears. My fingers tighten around my phone, my grip turning white.

This can't be happening.

"Elena?" Nina's voice is soft, cautious. "I'm so sorry."

I blink, forcing myself to meet her gaze. Her brows are drawn together in concern, but I can't focus on that.

Because my mind is racing.

Who bought it? Why now? Was there another buyer all along?

I swallow hard, the lump in my throat thick and heavy.

My stomach churns, twisting into knots so tight they feel like they might strangle me from the inside out.

Nina's voice filters in through the haze of my spiraling thoughts. "We'll keep looking, okay? There are plenty of properties. I know this one was special, but—"

But it won't be the same.

She doesn't say it, but we both know it.

Nothing will be the same.

This wasn't just any building—it was the building. The one where I had worked, where I had been saved when I had nothing else.

The place that made me believe in more for myself.

The bakery where I had planned to build my future, to finally create something that belonged to me.

Another property won't replace that.

Nina gives me another gentle look, squeezing my shoulder. "I really am sorry, Elena."

I nod, but I don't respond. Because if I do, I might break.

She checks her watch. "I have another appointment, but I'll call you as soon as I have any updates, okay?"

I barely register her words before she turns to leave, heels clicking against the polished tile floor as she disappears into the elevator.

The lobby is quiet now, too empty, too hollow.

Like something was just ripped out of me, leaving nothing but an aching, gaping hole behind.

I step outside, needing air, but it does nothing to clear the fog pressing against my ribs.

The driver looks at me expectantly, waiting for my next instructions, but I shake my head.

"I just want to walk for a moment," I murmur, voice barely above a whisper.

He nods and stays put as I take a few steps down the sidewalk.

The sounds of the city swirl around me—cars honking, people chatting, the distant hum of a street performer's saxophone—but it all feels muted.

My head is too full. My chest too tight.

I was so close.

I had a plan. The money was coming. I was ready.

It was supposed to be mine.

But it's not.

Someone else owns it now.

The weight of that realization sinks deep, wrapping around my ribs and pulling tighter, like a cruel, invisible vice.

I saw it. I imagined every detail—the display case that would showcase my cheesecakes, the espresso machine steaming behind the counter, the laughter of customers filling the air.

I pictured my name on the awning. My hands locking the doors at the end of the night, turning off the lights, knowing I had built something for myself.

I was ready to put down roots.

To have something stable, lasting.

To prove—to myself, to the world—that I was more than what I had been.

That I wasn't just another girl passing through, making temporary plans in someone else's life.

I feel stupid now, for letting myself believe it could all

fall into place so easily.

That for once, something I wanted wouldn't be just out of reach.

I let out a slow breath, pressing my fingers against my temples.

Crying won't change anything.

Raging won't get the building back.

I could call Nina, demand answers. Who bought it? Why now? But even if I knew, what would it change?

The contract with Damien is almost over. The money is coming. But it won't come fast enough.

It's done.

Over.

I lost.

The thought cuts deep, but there's nothing I can do.

So, I won't stand here on the sidewalk, looking like a lost little girl who just had her favorite toy snatched away.

No.

Instead, I'll do the only thing that has ever comforted me.

An hour later, I'm in Damien's kitchen.

Music playing.

Mixer on.

My best friend is on the phone, talking me down, and I'm blending a smooth and creamy cheesecake batter.

The scent of dark chocolate and espresso fills the kitchen, warm and rich, wrapping around me like a cocoon. The music plays softly in the background—something smooth, low-tempo jazz, the kind of music that would fill the air of an intimate café. The kind of place I wanted to build.

The kind of place that was supposed to be mine.

I push the thought down, focusing on the rhythm of my movements. Mix, pour, smooth, bake.

Baking has always been my escape, my therapy. There's comfort in the precision, in the control. The way the right balance of ingredients, time, and temperature can transform something raw into something exquisite.

That's what I do. I create.

And tonight, I need to create something extraordinary.

I think of the dessert Damien ordered that first night at Ember & Ash—the indulgent, over-the-top chocolate espresso mousse cake.

Of course, he would pick the most decadent thing on the menu.

A smirk tugs at my lips as I pour the glossy, dark chocolate filling into the crust, the aroma of coffee threading through the air.

A Dark Chocolate Espresso Cheesecake with a Salted Caramel Drizzle.

It's not just dessert. It's an experience.

Every element has a purpose—the bittersweet intensity of the chocolate, the bold, velvety espresso, the buttery, crisp crust, and the final touch... the caramel, slow-cooked with the perfect balance of sugar and sea salt, drizzled over the top in elegant swirls.

I know how to make people crave something they never even knew they needed.

And for the first time all day, I feel like I have control over something.

"It's fine," I say, feigning optimism. "It's just a building, right? I'll find something else."

"You don't have to pretend with me," Eve counters, her voice laced with knowing. "You wanted that place."

I inhale sharply, my grip tightening on the spoon as I swirl another pass of caramel.

"Yeah," I admit, my voice dropping, letting the truth slip through the cracks. "I did."

There's a pause on the other end, the quiet understanding only a best friend can give.

Then, softer, "I'm sorry, babe. That fucking sucks."

I swallow past the lump in my throat. "Yeah. It does."

But what else is there to say?

She doesn't offer false optimism or try to sugarcoat it. She knows me too well for that.

Instead, she lets out a slow exhale. "So... you baking it out?"

A small smile touches my lips. "What else?"

"Cheesecake?"

"You know it."

Eve hums approvingly. "That's my girl. What kind?"

I glance down at the glossy surface, the delicate swirls of caramel gleaming in the warm kitchen light. "Dark chocolate espresso with salted caramel."

Eve whistles low. "Damn. You're pulling out the big guns."

I scrape the last bit of batter into the pan, smoothing it

to perfection before placing it in the oven. "Figured I'd make something indulgent enough to distract me from the soul-crushing disappointment of my life."

Eve snorts. "That sounds dramatic."

"It's cheesecake, Eve. It demands drama."

"Fair."

A beat of silence stretches between us, not uncomfortable, just... there.

Then, she sighs. "I wish I could say something that would make you feel better."

I lean against the counter, looking at the cheesecake sitting in the oven.

"You already did."

lean against the counter, the oven's warmth pressing against my legs.

"You already did."

We sit in that quiet moment together, connected across the miles, until she finally says, "All right, well, I gotta go be a person or whatever. But keep me posted, okay?"

"I will."

"Take care of you."

Our mantra.

"Take care of you."

We say our goodbyes, and I hang up, staring at the cheesecake through the oven window.

Golden edges. Perfect rise. It'll need time to cool, but it's already shaping up exactly how I imagined.

Maybe not everything is lost.

Maybe some things just take a little longer to rise.

With a deep breath, I push off the counter and head toward my bedroom.

The cheesecake will take time to set, which means I have time to take a shower.

And if I'm being honest... I'm more than a little curious about what Damien Wolfe has planned for tonight.

Chapter 21
Damien

The quiet hum of the jewelry store surrounds me, the air thick with the scent of polished wood and luxury.

Light refracts off rows of diamonds and rubies, catching the gleam of precious metals encased in pristine glass. It's all wealth and excess—the kind of place where status is bought, and sentiment is wrapped in velvet.

I've bought gifts before. Jewelry, cars, clothes—they were obligations. Expected.

But this?

This isn't about a price tag or a duty.

It's about seeing her wear something beautiful. Knowing that every time she takes the piece out of the little velvet box, she'll feel them, think of me. And I like the idea of that.

Something that keeps me on her mind because she's fucking living rent-free in mine.

The jeweler—a seasoned professional with a practiced,

knowing smile—moves with silent efficiency, carefully selecting a few pieces to present on the black velvet display before me.

First, a bracelet—thin, elegant, with a line of emeralds catching the light like fractured stars in her hazel eyes. It's beautiful, but not quite right.

Marcus's voice crackles through my Bluetooth earpiece.

"I'm digging into the nephew," he says. "Guy's got skeletons. I just need to find where they're buried."

"Good." I keep my voice low as the jeweler begins wrapping the earrings, his movements efficient from years of practice. "Your guy is on him?"

"About that…"

I stop rolling my cuff, tension lacing through my shoulders.

"What does that mean?"

Marcus exhales. "He lost him."

Next, a ruby necklace—a delicate chain with a single pendant, subtle yet striking. I almost consider it. Almost.

I grit my teeth. "Marcus."

"I know," he mutters. "But he's calling in a favor to get a track on his cell phone. Won't be exact, but close enough."

Not good enough.

"Has he been spotted anywhere useful?"

"Couple of times." A pause. "He's been meeting with Norwood & Ellis."

The name sends a slow, simmering heat through my chest.

"Tell me you're joking."

"Wish I was."

Norwood & Ellis was a predatory investment firm I dismantled years ago—parasitic bastards who preyed on struggling businesses. I didn't just run them into the ground; I lit the match and watched them burn.

"He's trying to gather allies," I mutter.

"Yeah, but even if he did, he doesn't have the firepower to compete with us."

Maybe not. But that doesn't mean he isn't planning something.

The jeweler studies my expression, then seems to get an idea. His fingers move to another case, unlocking it with a quiet click before pulling out something else.

A pair of diamond threader earrings. The white gold chains are sleek, elegant, the diamonds catching the light at just the right angle.

Perfect.

I nod once, and the jeweler inclines his head in understanding, setting them aside without a word.

"Hold on, Wolfe. I'm getting another call—it's James." Marcus puts me on hold, and I set my phone on the glass counter, stretching my neck and releasing a heavy breath.

The jeweler clears his throat subtly, stepping forward to offer the carefully wrapped package.

"I take it your proposal went well, Mr. Wolfe?"

I hesitate a second too long.

Then, my lips curve into a slow, practiced smirk. "It did," I say smoothly, exhaling through my nose. "With a ring so beautiful, how could she say no?"

The jeweler beams. "A beautiful addition to your beautiful bride, Mr. Wolfe."

I don't correct him.

Because the thought of Elena wearing these—knowing I picked them for her—

Yeah. I like that too much.

I nod to the jeweler, accepting the bag before heading toward the exit. The town car is waiting at the curb, the driver already stepping out to open the door.

I slide into the backseat, loosening my tie just enough to breathe.

A few moments pass before Marcus's voice returns. "Back. Where were we?"

"Adrian's making a play, but we don't know what it is yet," I remind him.

"Right," Marcus hums. "I'll keep pushing, but let's be honest—he's just another trust fund dickhead trying to play in a league too big for him."

"True."

A pause. Then—his tone shifts.

"Anyway... let's talk about something more interesting."

I don't like where this is going. "Marcus."

"Elena."

I pinch the bridge of my nose.

"You gonna pretend you're not interested?" he continues, amused.

"I don't pretend anything," I say dryly.

Marcus chuckles. "Uh-huh. That why you've got the sappiest goddamn smirk on your face right now?"

I glance at my reflection in the tinted window. Sure enough—there's a fucking smile. I school my expression, jaw tightening. "You can't even see me right now."

"Don't need to, Wolfe." Marcus is loving this.

"There's nothing there, so stop reading into things." I try to act nonchalant, toying with a thread on the seam of my slacks.

"So," Marcus presses, "you wouldn't mind if I set her up with James's brother?"

I freeze.

Marcus's voice drips with feigned innocence. "He's single, you know. And she'd be a great sister-in-law."

A muscle in my jaw ticks.

The mere thought of Elena with someone else—with someone's fucking hands on her, making her laugh, making her bite her lip the way she does when she's trying not to smile—

No.

Absolutely not.

"Marcus," I say evenly.

"What?" he drawls, all smug amusement. "If she's just part of the contract, then what's the problem?"

I exhale slowly, dragging a hand through my hair. "You're annoying."

"And you're dodging the question."

I glance at the navy-blue bag sitting beside me.

Elena has no idea it's coming. No idea I picked them just for her.

"Look, I need you to keep an eye on things tonight," I deflect.

"Why? You got plans?"

"Yeah." I'm thinking about Elena's reaction seeing the earrings. Her putting them on. Me putting my lips on the curve of her neck while she's wearing them.

Fuck.

Marcus keeps pushing because—he's a nosy asshole. "You taking Elena out?"

"I didn't say that."

"But you didn't say no."

I rub my temple.

Marcus hums knowingly. "You're going on a date."

I don't answer.

"...Damien?"

"Goodbye, Marcus."

"Have a goo—"

He's still laughing when I hang up.

I check my watch.

The other package I sent should be arriving soon.

I wish I could be there to see her open it. To see the surprise on her face, the way her lips might part slightly, the way her fingers would graze over the silky fabric.

But that can wait.

Because the real pleasure will be later tonight—when I get to see her in it.

Chapter 22
Elena

The shower is scalding, the steam thick in the air as I methodically move through each step of my routine—washing, exfoliating, massaging lotion into my skin. This ritual calms me, resets me.

In light of everything going on, it still does the trick.

There is still a pang in my heart when I think about the bakery.

Soon, it won't hurt so much. I know I'll find something else.

I'll still make my dream come true. It will just look a little different than what I've been dreaming about.

I step out of the shower, toweling off before wrapping another around my damp hair. Picking up my seaweed mask, I remember the other day when I was getting ready for our first night out with the Calloways.

It seems like a year ago, but it's just been a week.

Damien came back to the penthouse, and I didn't know. He nearly scared me half to death.

Before I get back to my skincare, I peek my head out of my room and call out, just to be sure.

"Hello?"

I wait. Silence is the only thing answering me.

And something unexpected.

A large, pristine white box sits on the kitchen counter, wrapped with a sleek black satin bow. On top of it, an envelope with my name written across it in bold handwriting.

It must be from Damien.

I reach for it slowly, running my fingers over the thick cardstock before slipping it open.

"Five o'clock."

Signed simply: Damien.

The corners of my lips lift despite everything weighing me down.

Lifting the lid, my breath catches at the sight of what's inside.

A gown.

Not just any gown—a masterpiece.

The fabric shimmers under the soft light, deep red with an almost liquid sheen, pooling like molten silk as I unfold it. The cut is breathtaking—sophisticated but daring, with delicate straps and a plunging neckline, a slit that promises just enough temptation without being obvious.

I trail my fingertips over the fabric, savoring the feel of it, my stomach twisting in an unfamiliar kind of excitement.

I don't try to suppress the small smile curving my lips. No one is here to see it, so I allow myself to feel the moment, to enjoy the beautiful gown.

Returning the lid, another envelope catches my eye.

My name is also written on this one.

Perhaps it's more instructions for this mystery night Damien is slowly letting me in on.

As soon as I pull out the contents, I know who this is from.

A cold shiver races down my spine as my fingers tighten around the stack of glossy photographs.

My pulse slows, my mind struggling to process what I'm seeing.

A night I've worked so hard to forget.

The strip club.

Dim neon lighting. The grainy quality of a surveillance camera.

A shot of the VIP lounge.

And me.

A younger version of myself—barely nineteen, still so naïve, still believing I had control over my world.

The next photo makes me tremble.

I'm straddling the lap of a man whose face I can't forget, no matter how many years have passed.

The man who took everything from me.

Who left scars no one could see.

There are a dozen pictures here.

Me, dancing. His hands on my hips. The exact moment before everything changed.

The moment before the door locked.

The moment before I lost all control.

The moment I stopped belonging to myself.

A wave of nausea rolls through me, my breath shuddering as I force myself to look at the last image and the note scrawled across the bottom in sharp, slanted handwriting.

"Thursday. Ten o'clock."

No name.

No signature.

But I can hear Adrian's voice saying it, dripping with smug satisfaction.

My fingers tremble, the photographs crinkling in my grip.

He's not just threatening me.

He's reminding me.

Reminding me of what he did—what he allowed to happen.

The bargain he made, including me in the price without telling me.

He wants me to relive it.

To feel small. Helpless.

Like I did that night.

My pulse thunders in my ears, and I clutch the envelope tighter, my breath suddenly too shallow, my skin crawling.

How did this get here? How did he get this here?

A chill rakes down my spine. I rub my arms, a sick feeling settling in my gut as I glance around the room, half-expecting to find him lurking in the shadows.

The Hamptons felt like a shield, a bubble of safety where Adrian's reach couldn't touch me. But this? This is different. This is an invasion. A threat. A message, clear as day.

I grab my phone with shaking fingers and dial Lucian's number.

Fuck.

No answer. Again.

"Lucian," I rush, my voice uneven. "I don't know where you are, but I need you to call me back. This—this is getting worse." I exhale sharply, gripping the phone tighter. "Call me, please."

I hang up, pressing my palm to my forehead, willing myself to stay calm, to breathe.

I'm still on my own for this.

I can do this. I'm trying to convince myself more than anything. But I can't solve every problem today. I still have time before Thursday.

I can figure this out. Lucian will call me back by then, and we'll figure something out together.

Damien just secured the merger, but there is no ink on the contracts yet. Things could still turn to shit, and if Adrian gets what he wants, that's exactly what will happen.

The clock on the wall reads three forty-five.

I don't have time for this right now.

I fold the note and tuck it back inside the envelope, carrying it to my dresser and shoving it into the bottom drawer.

Later. I'll deal with it later.

For now, I need to focus.

I check on the cheesecake, running my fingers lightly over the smooth surface before adding the final drizzle of salted caramel. The dark chocolate espresso filling is rich, the crust perfectly crisp, the scent curling around me like a warm embrace.

It's perfect.

Satisfied, I slide it into the fridge, my chest rising with a deep breath.

The weight of the envelope still lingers in the back of my mind, a splinter pressing into my thoughts, but I push it aside.

Not now.

Instead, I reach for the large white box, fingers skimming over the black satin bow. My smile returns, softer this time, but still real.

I pick up the gown and head toward my room, anticipation curling low in my stomach.

As I step into my room, I let the fabric spill through my fingers, the silky weight of it grounding me, reminding me of something beyond the shadows creeping at the edges of my mind.

Tonight, I don't have to think about Adrian. About threats scrawled across old photographs or ghosts clawing their way back into my present.

Tonight, I can focus on Damien.

On whatever he has planned.

Helping him enjoy the victory of winning his merger.

I smooth my hands over the gown one last time, exhaling slowly.

For the next few hours, I'll let myself have this.

Tomorrow, I'll fight my battles.

Tonight, I'll let myself forget.

Chapter 23

Damien

I step into the penthouse, the city lights flickering beyond the floor-to-ceiling windows, but it's not the skyline that stops me in my tracks.

It's Elena.

The New York skyline silhouetting her, bathed in the soft glow of the chandelier, and for the first time in a long fucking time, I forget what I was about to say.

The gown fits her to perfection, the deep-red fabric draping over her curves in a way that should be illegal.

The slit teases the line of her leg, the delicate straps exposing the smooth expanse of her shoulders, and when she turns at the sound of my footsteps, her hazel eyes catch the light, gleaming with something unreadable.

Christ.

I've seen beautiful women. Been with beautiful women. Women who worked hard to be perfect, poised, polished. But this? This is something else entirely.

She isn't just beautiful.

She's breathtaking.

I walk toward her, loosening my tie just enough to find my breath again.

"You're staring," she murmurs, the ghost of a smile playing at her lips. Her eyes run down my body, taking in my black tux.

I stop just short of her, my fingers itching to reach for her, to trace the delicate straps on her shoulders, to follow the curve of her spine where the fabric dips scandalously low.

"You're impossible not to stare at," I reply, my voice rougher than I intended.

Her lips part slightly, and I take advantage of the moment, reaching into my jacket pocket and pulling out the small navy-blue box.

"Before we go," I say, flipping it open, "one last thing."

Her gaze drops to the box, and for the first time tonight, I catch the flicker of surprise in her expression.

Nestled in the velvet are the pair of diamond earrings, set in white gold—elegant, timeless, refined.

The moment stretches between us, tension thick in the air.

"Damien..." she exhales, her voice softer than before. "You didn't have to—"

"I know." I cut her off, my tone steady. "But I wanted to."

She hesitates, her fingers twitching as if she's unsure whether to accept or refuse.

"Elena." I lower my voice just slightly, letting it drop into something quieter, more coaxing. "Let me."

She presses her lips together, and I know she's about to agree before she even says it.

Finally, she reaches out, her fingers brushing the edge of the velvet.

And just as she's about to lift them, I snap the box shut with a quick flick of my wrist.

She jumps slightly, her head snapping up, her eyes narrowing in exasperation.

"Seriously?" she huffs, crossing her arms.

I smirk. "Couldn't resist."

She tries to look unimpressed, but the corner of her mouth twitches, betraying the amusement lurking just beneath.

I open the box again, this time holding it steady as she picks up the earrings, her fingers tracing over the delicate settings.

She lifts them to her ears, securing each one, and the second she turns back to me, I swear the breath leaves my lungs.

They're perfect.

Simple but striking, luminous against the soft glow of her skin, catching the light as she tilts her head slightly.

I take her in, from the gown to the way the diamonds gleam at her ears, and something deep inside me tightens.

She doesn't need expensive jewelry to be beautiful.

But fuck, does she wear it well.

"How do they look?" she asks, and I realize I haven't said a damn word.

I clear my throat, steadying myself. "Stunning."

She watches me for a moment, something unreadable in her expression, before smoothing her hands over her dress.

"Well," she says, tilting her head. "It seems we're not curating a list of your admirable traits after all. And there is no merger event today." Her eyes narrow in speculation. "So, are you going to tell me where we're going?"

A slow smirk pulls at my lips. "You'll see."

She narrows her eyes further. "You're not going to tell me?"

I offer my arm, my other hand placing the navy-blue box onto the counter. "It's a surprise."

She doesn't argue this time.

With a small shake of her head, she slips her fingers around my arm, letting me lead her toward the elevator.

As the doors slide shut behind us, I steal another glance at her, watching the way the diamonds catch the light, the way she carries herself with effortless grace.

The night hasn't even started yet, and I already know—

No matter how this ends, I'll never forget the way she looks right now.

The limo pulls up to an exclusive restaurant, discreet and understated, tucked away on one of the quieter streets of Manhattan. The kind of place with no sign out front, where reservations don't exist because only a select few even know it's here.

I step out first and help Elena from the limo, her gaze

drifting up the length of the sleek, modern façade before she turns to me, one brow arched.

"Of course," she muses, amusement flickering in her eyes. "Let me guess—Wolfe Industries is stitched into the linens somewhere?"

I smirk, offering my arm as I guide her inside. "I like to have options."

The maître d' greets us without a word, simply nodding before leading us toward an intimate, candlelit table near the back. The space is warm, ambient, the sound of soft jazz floating through the air.

The moment we're seated, the tension of the day seems to bleed away.

We take our time.

There's no rush, no formality. No pressure to perform for anyone else.

Conversation flows between us as effortlessly as breathing.

And for the first time in a long time, I feel—light.

Happy.

Like I've finally realized just how empty my life was before her.

Work, mergers, money—powerful, yes. But hollow.

I don't know when I started measuring my success in bank accounts and acquisitions instead of in moments like these. The kind where laughter sneaks up on me. Where the taste of a drink lingers a little longer because I don't feel the need to rush to the next thing.

Where a woman sits across from me, holding my gaze,

my attention, and I want to stay in this moment just a little while longer.

She takes a sip of wine, and I watch the way her lips press against the glass before setting it down, licking the faint taste of red from the corner of her mouth.

"So," I say, cutting through the lull in conversation, "your turn to tell me."

She blinks, tilting her head. "Tell you what?"

I lean back in my chair, swirling the amber liquid in my glass. "I told you about little Damien. Tell me about little Elena."

For the first time tonight, she stiffens.

It's subtle, almost imperceptible, but I catch it.

The slight way she tenses, the flicker of something unreadable in her eyes.

I know that look.

It's the look of someone deciding whether to let a secret slip or to bury it deeper.

I'm about to brush it off, tell her to forget it, when she exhales softly and lifts her gaze to meet mine.

"Well," she starts, voice even but quiet, "there's not much to tell."

She pauses.

"Mostly because I don't remember much of anything."

Something in my chest tightens.

She hesitates, and I know—whatever she's about to say, it's significant.

"When I was seven years old," she continues, voice softer now, "I was found on the steps of St. James Orphanage with a note that said my name was Elena."

For the second time tonight—I'm speechless.

I stare at her, my grip tightening around my glass, the warmth of the whiskey suddenly meaningless.

She says it so simply. Like it's just a fact. Something ordinary.

But there's nothing ordinary about being abandoned.

Nothing ordinary about being seven years old with no past. No family. No home.

Elena keeps her expression smooth, controlled, but I see it now—the way she holds herself together like she's used to keeping this story locked away, like she's practiced saying it in a way that makes it sound like it doesn't matter.

But it does.

It matters.

The way she said seven years old rattles something inside me.

I was twelve when my own world fell apart. Fourteen when I had to start raising myself because no one else would.

But—fuck. Seven.

Too damn young to be left with nothing.

I set my glass down carefully, pressing my elbows onto the table, studying her. "That's all you know?"

Her lips twitch like she's considering a smile, but it never fully forms. Instead, she just lifts one shoulder in a shrug.

"That's all anyone knows."

There's a note of finality in her tone, but I don't miss the way her fingers toy with the stem of her wine glass, restless, like the weight of what she just said is pressing down on her more than she wants to admit.

"The nuns tried to place me in foster homes, but you can imagine, I had separation issues. None of them lasted long."

She's opening up the darker parts of herself. Likely the parts that should stay hidden when she's on the job.

Elena is paid to be what her contract wants. Never herself.

It stirs something in me, thinking I may be the only one she's given this side of herself to. That it makes me different from the others.

"The older children get, the less likely adoption is for them."

My heart keeps breaking, thinking about the small girl, the teenager who called an orphanage home. Alone. With no one but strangers to look after her.

"When I turned eighteen, I aged out, and that was that."

I watch her closely as she rolls the stem of her wine glass between her fingers, her gaze drifting somewhere distant. Somewhere I can't follow.

"When I was little," she says, voice even but quiet, "I thought I'd been abandoned. That whoever left me on those steps didn't love me enough to keep me."

She exhales softly, shaking her head. "But as I got older, I started thinking... maybe that wasn't it. Maybe leaving me there was the only thing they could do to save me. Maybe wherever I came from, whoever left me... there was nothing left. And that was their way of giving me a shot. The only shot they had to give."

She meets my eyes then, something deep and searching

in her expression, as if she's measuring whether I understand.

And fuck, do I understand.

Most people wouldn't see it that way. Most people wouldn't have the strength to look at their past and find something more in it—something beyond the pain. But she does. And it's just another thing that makes her different. That makes her special.

"So if someone did that to save me," she continues, tilting her head slightly, "they had to care about me. And I wasn't going to waste it."

A small, sad smile plays on her lips, her voice softer now. "Maybe someone out there is wondering what happened. If I made it. If I survived."

I take a slow sip of my whiskey, studying her. When I set my glass down, my voice is quiet, firm. "I'd say you've done more than survive."

She watches me carefully.

"You've thrived."

Her brows lift just a fraction, lips parting like she wasn't expecting that.

For a moment, we just sit there, the city humming softly around us, the world narrowing to this conversation, to this moment.

Then, I raise my glass, tilting it toward her.

"To thriving."

Her lips curve—not the full, teasing smiles I've pulled from her before, but something real. Something that makes my chest tighten in a way I don't want to examine too closely.

She lifts her own glass, clinking it softly against mine before taking a slow sip.

I see the sadness still lingering in her eyes, the weight of a past that has shaped her but never broken her. And I know it's time to move on.

I set my glass down and push back from the table, rising to my feet before extending a hand toward her.

She eyes me warily. "What now?"

I smirk. "You'll see."

She places her hand in mine, her touch fleeting, barely there before I lead her through the restaurant, out into the night.

The city is quieter now, the distant hum of traffic muted by the stillness between us. I open the car door, watching as she slips inside, the soft rustle of silk against leather filling the space.

I slide in beside her, the limo gliding smoothly into motion, the glow of the skyline flickering against the tinted windows.

Neither of us speaks.

Her hand drifts down to the seat between us, resting lightly against the leather. I don't move mine, but I don't pull it away either.

Our pinkies are so close they could touch.

Almost.

I feel the warmth of her skin, just within reach. It would take nothing to close the distance, to slide my hand over hers, to offer her something—reassurance, comfort, a tether to the present instead of the past she just let me see.

I want to. Fuck, do I want to.

But I don't.

Instead, I sit in the quiet, letting it stretch, letting it settle.

Letting her know she doesn't have to fill the silence with anything at all.

And maybe that's the real difference between us.

I spent my whole life clawing for control, for power, for something to hold onto.

She learned how to exist in the spaces between.

So I let her have this one.

Let her sit in the stillness.

Let her breathe.

And for the first time in a long fucking time, I do the same.

My breath catches the moment I lift my gaze to the grand entrance before me. The Met. New York's infamous opera house, its towering columns and gilded lights standing proudly against the night sky.

I've seen it before, of course—walked past it, admired it from afar, even lingered outside once or twice, watching as elegant patrons filed inside.

But I've never stepped through its doors. Never had the luxury of sitting beneath its chandeliers, listening to voices so powerful they could shake the walls.

And now, not only am I here, but I have it all to myself.

Or rather, we do.

I glance at Damien, who stands beside me, calm and composed, as if buying out the Met for an evening is as easy as making dinner reservations.

He barely blinks as the doorman opens the grand entrance for us, as if this isn't a big deal. As if this isn't—

"Damien," I murmur, still taking in the sight before me. "You did not rent out the Met for the night."

His lips twitch, but he keeps his expression neutral. "I may have."

I turn fully toward him now, eyes narrowing. "You may have?"

He tilts his head slightly, that signature smirk tugging at the corner of his mouth. "I already had this arranged. It was supposed to be for... something else."

I arch a brow, waiting.

He hesitates, then clears his throat, adding, "I just forgot to cancel it."

I let out a breathy laugh, shaking my head. "Right. Like you could ever forget you rented out one of the world's most famous opera houses."

He shrugs, his hand resting at the small of my back as he guides me inside. "What can I say? My calendar is very full."

I roll my eyes, but I can't stop the warmth spreading through me, the way my pulse flutters as we step into the lavish, gold-lined lobby. A stunning red carpet stretches up the grand staircase, leading to opulent balconies overlooking the main floor.

The theater is empty, silent, yet full of a hushed magic. Like it's waiting for us.

For me.

I swallow, my fingers tightening around the folds of my gown. I've never felt this way before—dressed in something breathtaking, wearing diamonds I have no business owning, on the arm of one of the city's most powerful men, walking into a place I've only dreamed of.

It's not real.

I know that.

It's a fantasy, a life I only get to indulge in for a few more days. But standing here, under the soft glow of chandeliers, surrounded by velvet and gold, with Damien's touch warm against my back—

It feels real.

And that's what makes it dangerous.

The opulence of the Met is almost overwhelming—the rich reds and golds, the towering chandeliers, the intricate carvings adorning every surface.

It commands a kind of reverence, the kind of place that feels like it belongs in fairy tales rather than real life. It's breathtaking, magnificent, everything I imagined it would be and more.

But none of it holds my attention the way he does.

Damien Wolfe, who rented out one of the most famous opera houses in the world just for tonight. Just for us.

For me.

I smooth a hand over the fabric of my dress, trying to ground myself, trying not to let the weight of the moment press too deeply into my chest.

The dazzling beauty of this place, the gown I'm wearing, the diamonds in my ears—it's all temporary. A fleeting glimpse into a world that isn't mine.

I can't afford to get swept up in it.

Still, I feel his eyes on me before I even turn my head, the weight of his gaze warm, unwavering.

"Why did you really do this?" My voice is quiet, barely

above a whisper, but in the hush of the grand, empty theater, it carries between us.

He doesn't look away. "To celebrate."

I arch a brow, unconvinced. "To celebrate your merger?"

He exhales, tilting his head slightly as he studies me. "Not just mine."

I shake my head, a small scoff escaping. "I was just along for the ride."

"That's bullshit," he murmurs, and the certainty in his voice makes my breath catch.

Before I can counter, he leans in, bringing with him the dark, clean scent of him, something rich and expensive, something that makes my pulse stutter before I can stop it.

"Margo wouldn't have given it to just me," he continues, his voice softer now, almost contemplative. "You know that."

And I do.

The realization settles into me, undeniable, humming in the space between us.

Damien Wolfe is a man who doesn't need anyone. He commands rooms, bends people to his will, shapes entire industries with a single decision. But that wasn't enough for Margo Calloway.

She needed to believe in more than his ambition.

She needed to believe in us.

He watches me closely, waiting for me to challenge him, to tell him he's wrong.

But I don't.

Because he isn't.

Still, I force an easy smirk, needing to pull this conversation back to safer ground, needing to shake off the way he's looking at me, like he sees something in me I don't know how to give. "So what you're saying is... I'm your secret weapon?"

The corner of his mouth curves, but there's something different about his smile this time, something softer, something that makes my stomach flip in a way I'm not prepared for. "That's what I'm saying."

I should let it go. Let the conversation drift away, laugh it off, shift to something lighter.

But I don't.

Because he's still watching me like that.

Like I matter.

Like I mean something to him.

His hand moves before I can think, his thumb grazing over the silky fabric just above my knee. It's the barest touch, barely anything at all, but it steals my breath, the warmth of it sinking beneath my skin, setting fire to something I can't name.

He lingers, his fingers brushing together after, like he's memorizing the feel of me against them.

Like he knows he shouldn't have touched me but couldn't stop himself.

My heart pounds, but I manage to keep my voice light. "Well, if I forget to tell you later..." I pause, letting myself take him in—the sharp edges of his jaw, the way the dim light softens him in a way I'm not used to seeing. "I had a really great time tonight."

The air between us tightens, the weight of something unsaid pressing down on my chest, making it harder to breathe.

His expression shifts, the usual sharpness replaced by something softer, something I don't think I've ever seen on him before.

He looks happy.

Genuinely happy.

And for a moment, I forget that any of this is temporary.

That the contract ends soon.

That none of this is real.

I can't look away and neither can he.

The space between us could vanish so easily. His minty breath would mingle with mine.

Damien drops his gaze to my mouth, and I know he's thinking about it too. The tension stretches, so tight it might snap, and I know—if he leans in, I won't stop him.

But I'm not going to be the one that makes it happen. I'll not be the paid escort who seduces her Contract. Who could be blamed for taking things too far, coercing the agreement for some kind of gain.

He demanded the contract have no physical aspect to it. The sexual bargaining that is common in a profession such as mine. A Ledger Companion.

He didn't want it. Didn't want it to complicate the arrangement.

But now—the way he is looking at me—

The lights dim.

The hush of the opera house fills the space between us,

shattering the fragile moment before it can break me completely.

A waiter appears, setting down two delicate flutes of champagne, the bubbles rising in tiny streams.

We take the flutes. Our glasses sharing a soft clink before we both take a sip. Damien nearly drains his. A look of exasperation in his eyes nearly makes me chuckle but I tamper it down.

Thankful the darker theatre is helping to hide the rosy burn creeping up my cheeks.

The first notes rise, thick with emotion, wrapping around me in waves. It's powerful in a way I hadn't expected, the rawness of the voices, the way they carry through the vast space, filling every empty corner.

I sit frozen, my lips parting slightly as the performance unfolds before me.

I've never been to the opera before.

Never had something like this done for me.

Never felt so completely *swept away*.

The performance is breathtaking and somewhere between the second and third act, I realize my hand is resting against something warm and solid.

Damien.

The second I notice, I begin to pull away, but before I can, his hand moves over mine.

Catching it. Holding it.

Not letting go.

I still, my pulse hammering in my ears, but he doesn't move. Doesn't speak.

His attention stays forward, eyes locked on the stage, his thumb tracing slow, absentminded circles against my skin.

Like he doesn't even realize he's doing it.

Like touching me is the most natural thing in the world.

And I let him.

I shouldn't. But I let him.

Chapter 25
Damien

I didn't check my phone once tonight.

Marcus is handling anything that comes up, and he was more than happy to do it—glad, even, that I was taking a night for myself. And for once, I let it happen. No meetings, no endless schedules, no work creeping into the corners of my mind.

It was just her.

It was a night unlike any I've had before.

One I don't want to admit meant something to me.

Back at the penthouse, Elena made sure there was no more temptation, no more lingering moments to pull us closer than we already are. The moment we stepped inside, she told me goodnight and disappeared into her room.

I should go to bed too. I should let this night settle, let it remain what it was—a moment in time, temporary and fleeting, just like our contract.

But I can't sleep.

I've been staring at the ceiling for too long, my mind

replaying the way she looked in that dress, the way her lips parted in awe when the first notes of the opera filled the air, the way she smiled softly and said she had a great time.

She meant it.

That does something to me.

With a sigh, I push out of bed and pad toward my study, the glow of the city spilling through the towering windows, slicing through the darkness. The space is quiet, heavy with the kind of silence that should bring peace but doesn't.

My feet carry me toward the grand piano without a second thought.

It's been a long time since I played.

My fingers hover over the keys for a moment before pressing down, coaxing a single note into the stillness. Then another. And another.

The melody comes on its own, slow and deliberate, stretching through the room like a whispered secret.

My mother had made me play as a child.

"Fortune favors the bold, Damien. Play boldly."

She said it like a mantra, like the notes of each piece were more than music—they were control. Mastery. Another way to shape me into something untouchable.

When my father crashed the family, the piano disappeared with everything else.

And for a while, I let it stay gone.

There was no room for music when I was clawing my way out of the wreckage. No space for anything that didn't drive me forward, keep me moving, keep me fighting for something more than the nothing I had been left with.

But when I finally had money—real money—this was one of the first things I bought.

I didn't question why.

Didn't examine what it meant that I wanted it back.

Now, as my fingers move over the keys, something shifts in my chest. The tension I've been carrying, the storm of thoughts that won't let me sleep—it all starts to dissolve, carried away by the music, by the rhythm, by the memory of her eyes on mine, shining under the soft glow of the opera house.

And for the first time in years, I remember what this feels like.

Not an obligation.

Not a strategy.

Just something that belongs to me.

A soft creak pulls me from my trance, the melody faltering as I turn my head.

Elena stands in the doorway, watching me.

She's wrapped in a short silk robe, the tie loose at her waist, her damp tresses falling over her shoulders. The city lights catch the curve of her bare collarbone, the delicate diamond earrings I gave her still glinting in her ears.

In her hand is a small dessert plate, a slice of dark choco-late cheesecake resting in the center. A fork in the other.

She stays in the doorway, not daring to move an inch inside the study.

"I didn't know you played."

I lean back slightly, resting my forearms on my thighs, letting the softness of her voice settle around me.

"It's been a long time."

Elena tilts her head. "Did you love it?"

I consider that, my gaze flickering down to the keys.

"I don't know," I admit after a moment. "I think I might have."

She watches me for a long moment, and I swear there's something unspoken in the way she looks at me.

Something neither of us should be feeling.

She shifts on her feet, her hands coming together, the fork clanging against the plate with a soft ding.

I look at the plate, then her.

"I—made this for you." The hesitation makes my chest tighten, like she's doubting if she should have done it.

I can't look away from her. Words are lost to me. My chest rises hard with each labored breath, and I know this is the moment. The moment we cross a line—one way or another.

"Come here," I say before I can stop myself.

She wavers just for a second, and I stop existing.

If she tells me no, returns to her room, that has to be it. I have to let her walk away.

Not just tonight. But at the end of this contract.

But if she doesn't. If she takes a step toward me—

Then she does.

She walks toward me slowly, carefully, as if afraid that one wrong step will shatter the fragile restraint between us.

But she never looks away. And neither do I.

Whatever this is, wherever it's going—I'm already too far gone to stop it.

The soft glow of the city casts light over her, illuminating the smooth planes of her skin, the dark waves of her still-damp hair spilling over her shoulders. The tie of her robe loosens with each step, slipping free, the silk parting effortlessly.

The nightgown underneath is black, delicate, a second skin that barely covers her. Lace teases across her chest, the thin straps leaving her shoulders bare, her nipples taut against the fabric. A slit runs up her thigh, exposing the smooth, toned length of her leg as she closes the distance between us.

She stops beside the bench, breathing unevenly, a flush warming her cheeks.

She wants this.

She just doesn't want to be the one to break the rules because I also had stipulations in my contract request. No intimacy.

Okay, little Trouble.

We'll break these rules together.

Slowly, I widen my legs, making space for her between them. My hand trails up her bare thigh, feeling the slight tremor beneath my touch, the tension in her stance. Then, with a firm but gentle pull, I guide her to stand directly in front of me.

She sets the plate, the fork on the piano, and it's like a bell, marking the shift in the moments between us.

Her scent surrounds me—faint traces of vanilla, her lotion, the floral hint of her shampoo. I press my forehead to her stomach, breathing her in, savoring the warmth of her body so close to mine.

She doesn't move.

Doesn't touch me.

But she doesn't pull away either.

My lips brush against the smooth plane of her stomach, just above her navel, then move closer to her hip.

A barely-there sigh escapes her lips, so quiet I almost miss it.

I pull back slightly, reaching for the plate beside me, taking the fork and spearing a bite of the dark chocolate cheesecake. The moment the rich, velvety texture hits my tongue, I groan low in my throat, closing my eyes for a brief second.

It's fucking perfect.

Decadent. Sinful. The kind of dessert that lingers, that demands to be savored.

When I open my eyes again, she's watching me, her lips parted, her breathing uneven.

A shiver runs through her, and I know it's not from the cold.

I set the fork down and drag my finger slowly along the side of the cheesecake, gathering a thick smear of chocolate and caramel on the tip.

I stand. My other hand moves higher on her thigh, taking the hem of her nightgown with it, the soft silk rising under my touch.

She doesn't stop me.

"Tell me, Elena," I murmur, my voice rough, thick with need. I hold my finger just shy of her lips, tracing the sticky sweetness across them. "Is eating dessert against the rules?"

Her breath hitches.

I press my finger gently to her lips, the warmth of her mouth sending a sharp jolt straight through me.

She hesitates, and I see the war in her eyes. But I wait. The next beat of my heart is tied to what she does next.

I see the second her resolve breaks. Her shoulders drop, and she exhales the tension she's been retaining all week.

The moment her tongue flicks out, tasting the chocolate, I nearly break.

She closes her lips around my finger with a moan, sucking gently, licking until every trace of dessert is gone.

I exhale sharply, my jaw clenching, my cock throbbing with need.

She knows exactly what the fuck this is doing to me. But I can't break all the way.

My little troublemaker needs to throw out these rules with me.

When she finally releases my finger, her gaze lifts to meet mine, something unreadable swirling in those hazel depths.

A silent question.

A silent dare.

And I'm more than fucking willing to see how much longer she will keep holding back—lying to herself, to me about how much she wants this. Wants us.

Her breath is uneven, her chest rising and falling in a rhythm that matches mine. She's waiting. Wanting. But she still won't break.

Not yet.

So I'll keep inching forward. Keep teasing. Keep testing exactly how long she can lie to herself before she gives in.

My fingers skim the edges of her robe, pushing the soft silk past her shoulders. She doesn't stop me. Doesn't even hesitate. The fabric slides down, pooling at her feet in a whisper of luxury, leaving her bare except for the thin slip of black lace and silk that barely covers her.

I lean in, my breath fanning over the delicate skin of her neck. She tilts her head, offering it to me without a second thought.

I don't kiss her. But I'm fucking dying to.

My lips hover, just shy of contact, dragging slowly down the elegant curve of her throat to her shoulder.

She exhales sharply, her body swaying toward mine, her hands bracing against my abdomen.

I don't give in.

Instead, my fingers find one of the thin straps of her nightgown, toying with it, letting it slip off her shoulder in a slow, torturous reveal.

Her skin is warm beneath my touch—soft, smooth.

I move to the other side, repeating the action, my lips grazing her neck, the top of her shoulder, a featherlight touch that makes her shiver.

I slip the second strap down, watching as the silk nightgown slides over the curve of her breasts, catching only in the crook of her elbows, leaving her half-exposed, bared to me.

I inhale sharply.

"Fuck."

The word is more breath than sound, more reverence than control.

Her breasts are full, round, perfect. The soft light catches on her skin, illuminating the peaks of her nipples, already taut, begging for attention. I watch as a wave of goosebumps rolls down her body—a clear sign of the emotions raging within her.

The ones she is so carefully trying to hide.

I reach for the plate, gathering another smear of dark chocolate cheesecake onto my finger.

Her breath hitches as I bring it to her skin, circling her nipple with the rich, decadent dessert, spreading it in slow, teasing strokes.

She lets out a soft, broken sound, her body arching ever so slightly toward me.

"Answer me, baby."

My lips hover just beneath her ear, my voice a whisper of control and hunger, a thread away from snapping.

"Is eating dessert against your rules?"

Her breath is shaky, her fingers twitching where she grips my shirt.

Then, finally—finally—she exhales a long, trembling sigh and shakes her head.

"No."

One word.

One simple word, and it's like she's granted me the keys to heaven.

"It's not against the rules." She's fucking panting for me.

I don't waste a second.

My tongue drags a slow, torturous circle around the hard peak of her breast, the lingering taste of dark chocolate and espresso blending with the warm, addictive sweetness of her skin.

She moans loudly, arching into my touch, her hands

clutching at my shoulders, seeking something to ground her.

I run my thumbs beneath the soft weight of her breasts, remembering how they felt in my hands that night in the hotel. How they filled my palms, how she trembled beneath me.

Another slow swipe of cheesecake across her other breast. Another moan as she shudders under the sensation.

I need more.

Both hands find her thighs, squeezing, caressing, before sliding around to grasp her hips.

In one swift movement, I lift her, setting her onto the cool surface of the piano.

Her thighs press the keys.

The shift sends a discordant ripple of notes into the air, a soft, haunting melody beneath the sharp hitch of her breath.

A gasp leaves her lips, her fingers tightening in my hair, her legs instinctively parting just enough for me to step between them.

My mouth finds her skin again, tongue flicking over her nipple before sucking it between my lips, savoring the way she writhes against me.

The sounds she makes—the soft, breathy moans, the way my name leaves her lips in a quiet plea—send fire through my veins.

I rise, pressing my forehead against hers, breathing her in, letting the heat between us coil tighter, heavier.

She's watching me, her hazel eyes glazed, her lips parted. That beautiful flush has spread down her chest, her body betraying the restraint she's still desperately trying to hold onto.

She's still fighting it.

Still keeping herself from surrendering completely.

I reach between her legs, sliding my fingers along the silk of her panties, groaning at the heat, at the unmistakable wetness soaking through the fabric.

"Fuck, baby." My voice is rough, full of raw, aching need. "You're so fucking wet."

She shivers, barely parting her legs for me. Just a fraction.

Not enough.

Never enough.

I pull the nightgown over her head in one smooth motion. The black silk joins her robe on the floor, leaving her bare before me.

Jesus Christ.

She is the most beautiful thing I've ever seen.

My hands grip her thighs tighter.

"Lay down."

It's not a request. It's a command.

My hands frame her torso, my lips ghosting over her skin as she slowly reclines, her back meeting the cool surface of the piano.

She gasps at the sensation, her skin pebbling, her body arching slightly, instinctively, as if already reaching for me.

I trail my palms over her, fingers tracing the delicate dip of her waist, the soft curve of her hips.

Up, over her ribs, teasing at the underside of her breasts

before moving down again, savoring every inch of warm, flushed skin.

When I reach the thin straps of her panties, I hook my fingers beneath them, dragging them down her legs, slow, deliberate.

She lifts each foot, helping me.

Fuck, she's perfect.

I press my hands to the insides of her thighs, coaxing them open, baring her to me completely.

She's stunning like this—laid out on my piano, bathed in the glow of the city skyline, breath shallow, pupils blown wide with need.

And I'm about to ruin her.

I dip my finger into the cheesecake once more, scooping just enough to spread across her skin, dragging it downward, watching her shudder.

Her hazel eyes lock onto mine, filled with something raw, something desperate.

"Damien."

A plea. A prayer.

She's losing herself, and fuck if I'm not right there with her.

"I've got you, baby."

I rub the cool, decadent mixture over her clit—slow, deliberate circles—spreading it across the delicate bundle of nerves. The contrast between cold and heat makes her body jolt, a strangled moan escaping her lips.

My thumb joins in, pressing just the right amount of pressure, coaxing more slickness from her, mixing her arousal with the lingering chocolate and caramel.

I want her messy. Want her undone for me.

"Fuck," I breathe, my hands sliding down to grip the backs of her thighs.

Then I lower myself, sitting on the piano bench, shifting one of her legs over my shoulder.

She doesn't move or push me away.

She just watches, breathless, waiting.

I run my lips up the inside of her thigh, my stubble dragging against her sensitive skin, inhaling the intoxicating scent of her arousal.

The second my mouth gets close, I groan, my eyes rolling shut for half a second.

She's so fucking sweet.

Better than any dessert. Better than anything I've ever tasted.

I press my tongue flat against her, licking a slow, firm strip up her pussy, gathering every last trace of chocolate, caramel, and her own addictive flavor.

The sound that leaves her—half gasp, half whimper—drives me insane.

I repeat the motion, savoring the way she squirms, the way she clenches her fingers into the piano's glossy surface, her knuckles white.

Then I close my lips around her clit, sucking gently before flicking my tongue over the sensitive bud.

She cries out, her hips bucking, chasing the sensation, needing more.

"Jesus, baby, you taste so fucking good."

I tighten my grip on her thighs, holding her in place as I feast on her, taking my time, unraveling her piece by piece.

My tongue explores every inch of her, alternating between deep, slow licks and rapid, teasing flicks.

She's drenched, her arousal slick against my lips, and I want more of it.

I want all of it.

I slip one finger inside her, groaning at how tight and warm she is.

Her walls clamp down around me, her body begging for more, and I oblige, adding another finger, curling them upward as I continue working her clit with my tongue.

Her back arches off the piano, her thighs trembling around my head.

She's close.

I can feel it.

"Damien—"

My name on her lips is pure sin—breathless and broken.

"Keep going."

I double down, my pace relentless, my fingers pressing against that spot inside her that makes her body seize.

She gasps, her head thrown back, her body shaking as the orgasm crashes over her.

I don't stop.

I don't let up.

I lap up every aftershock, savoring every drop of her as she writhes beneath me.

Not until she's whimpering, too sensitive, too spent.

Only then do I slow, pressing one last lingering kiss against her, my hands smoothing over her trembling thighs, grounding her.

I look up at her—her chest heaving, her lips parted, her eyes heavy with pleasure.

And fuck, if she's not the most beautiful thing I've ever seen.

I take her hand, helping her sit up, my fingers wrapping around hers, grounding her as her body trembles with the aftershocks of her orgasm.

She watches me, her breaths still uneven, her lips slightly parted. Her hazel eyes—darkened with desire—meet mine, and something unspoken lingers between us.

Satisfaction. Seduction.

Something far more dangerous.

I bend at the waist, picking up her nightgown and robe, the silk cool between my fingers. I straighten, locking my gaze with hers.

"Arms up, Trouble," I murmur, my voice just above a whisper.

She hesitates—just for a second—before obeying.

The way she lifts her arms so effortlessly, trusting me to dress her after I've just unraveled her—it does something to me.

I slip the nightgown over her head, my fingers grazing her heated skin, lingering a second longer than necessary.

She shivers.

My hands find her hips, then her thighs, guiding her off the piano, steadying her, setting her carefully on her feet.

She's pressed against me, her body warm, soft.

My cock is still painfully hard, throbbing between us, demanding relief I won't take.

Not tonight.

Not until she shatters those rules on her own.

I don't look away, and neither does she.

I hold out her robe, and she takes it slowly, glancing down at it, then back up at me, something unreadable in her gaze.

I don't speak. Just watch her.

Waiting.

Testing.

"Good night, Elena."

A faint smile—barely there—tilts the corner of my mouth, gone just as quickly as it appears. My expression evens out, unreadable once more.

I only shift back an inch or so, giving her just enough space to move.

She hesitates again.

Then she steps away.

Slowly.

Deliberately.

Sliding her body past mine so closely that I feel the whisper of silk against my skin—the ghost of her warmth where I want it most.

Her eyes never leave mine as she walks toward the door.

She reaches it, stopping just before crossing the threshold.

Then—she looks back at me.

Her teeth catch her bottom lip, the movement hesitant, contemplative.

It's the last thing I see before she disappears into the

hallway, leaving me standing there—fists clenched at my sides, pulse hammering, mind completely fucking wrecked.

And I know—without a doubt—I'm gone.

Completely fallen into her.

Chapter 26

The next morning, I sit on the edge of my bed, staring at my phone, waiting. My fingers hover over the screen, my mind looping through last night—the way I let go, let myself feel.

I should regret it.

I should feel guilty for letting myself get swept up in Damien.

But fuck, I loved every second of it. Every word he whispered. Every touch. Every look.

My skin still tingles where his hands were, where his mouth was. Just thinking about the way he devoured me makes a shiver ripple down my spine.

I close my eyes and take a deep breath, shaking off the haze of last night's pleasure.

Because today is a new day.

And I need to be in control.

Damien wasn't looking for complications. I wasn't supposed to be, either. Between Adrian, the pictures, and the gutting loss of my bakery, there's already too much happening.

I exhale, rolling my shoulders before checking my messages.

Still nothing from Lucian.

Annoyance prickles under my skin, but just as I'm about to text him again, a response finally comes through.

LUCIAN: Sorry, got busy. Looking into it now.

That's it?

Not exactly reassuring.

I clench my jaw, my irritation mounting, but I don't have time to dwell.

Tonight is Mr. Calloway's birthday, and we're going to a Giants game. Margo rented out one of the luxury suites, and I need to be flawless.

I shove away every thought that doesn't serve me and slip into form-fitting, high-waisted blue jeans, a red crop top, and simple white wedges. On my way out, I grab the floral arrangement I ordered—something elegant but not too sentimental.

By the time I step into the towering glass lobby of Wolfe Industries and the elevator doors open on the seventieth floor, my head is clearer.

But the second I approach the receptionist's desk, something shifts.

The woman behind it—tall, stunning, and immaculately put together—barely glances up from her screen.

The cliché attractive assistant who wears too-short

skirts and too-high heels for her CEO boss—it makes me roll my eyes.

"He's not available." Her tone is clipped, dismissive, like I'm some random visitor who doesn't belong.

She still doesn't check. "And he won't be for quite some time."

Something in her tone isn't just dismissive. It's personal.

My grip tightens around the flowers, the delicate paper wrapping crinkling loudly in the vast space.

"You make it sound like you're referring to more than just today's calendar," I muse, my voice light, amused.

The receptionist—Vanessa, according to her nameplate—finally looks up, eyes scanning me in a slow, deliberate sweep.

"Leave the flowers. I'll see he gets them." She goes back to her keyboard, clacking away loudly as if that settles it.

"Thank you, but I'll deliver them personally."

I'm about to tell her my name when she stands, placing both hands on her desk and leveling me with a look that says she's had enough.

My eyebrows shoot upward, and I fight back the grin threatening to push the last of her thin patience over the edge.

"I'm sure you have high hopes that Damien will put you on his rotation, but unfortunately"—she sighs dramatically—"he claims to have a surprise fiancée. One that makes him forget his assistant of two years' birthday."

That last part was more for herself than for me. The scoff and roll of her eyes nearly make me laugh.

Oh.

Poor thing.

I school my features, letting my lips curve into something sharp and knowing. "Damien, huh? Not Mr. Wolfe? You seem quite friendly with your boss... on a first-name basis."

Vanessa doesn't waver, her smirk deepening.

"Mr. Wolfe and I have an understanding." She leans in slightly, lowering her voice like we're old friends sharing secrets. "I fully intend for him to remember that I'm the only stable woman in his life. And I suspect I won't be working here very long once he does."

My blood heats, but I don't react.

"But I'll be sure to personally deliver these flowers to him on your behalf, Ms....?"

She holds her arms out as if to take them from me.

With deliberate ease, I move the flowers to my other arm, holding them like a baby, careful not to squish them.

"That won't be necessary."

Then, without breaking eye contact, I pull out my phone.

I've never called Damien before. But I know he'll answer.

It barely rings twice before his voice comes through—smooth, low, instant.

"Elena?"

"Hi, honey." I keep mine just as even. "Your assistant seems to think you're too busy to see your fiancée. Oh, and she hopes to be fucking you soon. Anything you'd like to come and clear up, or shall I just wait in the lobby?"

The shift in the air is immediate.

Vanessa freezes.

Her eyes widen in panic. "I—I didn't..."

A door slams open.

Damien strides out, his presence crackling with barely restrained fury.

Every conversation in the lobby dies.

His gaze locks onto Vanessa, his expression lethal. "What the fuck did you just say to my fiancée?"

His voice is dangerously low, controlled—but I can feel the storm rolling beneath it.

Vanessa stammers, taking a step back. Her bravado evaporates in an instant.

I cross my arms, arching a brow. "Vanessa was just talking about the... arrangement you two have."

Damien reaches for my hand, pulling me behind him. His grip is firm. Protective.

"Mr. Wolfe." She's pleading now. "Damien."

He turns his head slightly, his voice dropping into something low and final.

"Vanessa," he says, her name a death sentence. "You mistook my patience for interest. That was your first mistake."

He takes a slow step closer, his expression unreadable, lethal in its restraint.

"Your second?" His voice softens, a mockery of kindness. "Speaking to my fiancée like you were ever competition."

Silence razor-sharp. All color drains from Vanessa's face.

A woman in a sharp navy suit—HR, I assume—steps forward with two security officers.

Damien takes the flowers from me, his hand still in mine

as he finally looks at me. The intensity in his expression nearly takes my breath away.

When he turns back to the older woman, his expression shifts—bored, already dismissing the situation.

"Ms. Bradley no longer works for Wolfe Industries."

Vanessa stares at Damien, eyes darting around, realizing—it's over.

She opens her mouth, like she wants to fight, like she wants to beg, but nothing comes out. She knows she's lost.

Damien doesn't spare her another glance as he pulls me into his office, slamming the door behind us.

The second it shuts, he places the flowers on his desk with slow, deliberate care. Every movement is controlled, precise—like he's forcing himself into restraint.

Then, arms crossed over his chest, he leans back against the desk, watching me with an infuriatingly smug expression.

I know that look.

The one that says he's enjoying himself way too much.

I fold my arms, mirroring his stance, tilting my chin slightly. "What?"

His smirk deepens. "You were jealous."

I scoff, my lips parting in an incredulous laugh. "Don't flatter yourself."

Damien tilts his head, his gaze flickering over my face like he's cataloging every detail, every subtle reaction I don't want him to see.

"You think I didn't notice the way you bristled when she called me Damien?"

His voice drops lower, smooth as silk, coaxing me into his game.

"Admit it, Trouble." He reaches out, the back of his fingers skimming over my forearm, barely a touch at all. "You didn't like her thinking she could have me."

The way he says it—low and deliberate—makes something flicker hot inside me.

I hold my ground, refusing to let him see how much I'm still irritated, how much I hated the sound of her voice wrapped around his name.

I should leave it. I should brush it off, let him think he's wrong, keep my dignity intact.

Instead, I step toward him.

His brows lift slightly, but he doesn't move back.

Another step.

He shifts just enough to press against the edge of the desk, giving me space—but not much.

Another step, and I'm close enough to feel the heat radiating off him, close enough that his scent—his cologne—is all I can breathe in.

"During this contract, Mr. Wolfe," I murmur, my voice steady, smooth. "You are as much mine as I am yours."

His jaw tightens, that flicker in his blue eyes turning molten, burning beneath his careful control.

His tongue darts out to wet his lips, like he's considering something dangerous. "That almost sounds like a promise."

I lift a hand, let my nails drag lightly down the crisp fabric of his dress shirt, down the center of his chest. "Think of it as an expectation."

His muscles tense under my touch, his control tightening like a coiled spring.

"So you want to own me now?" His smirk is lazy, but his breathing isn't.

I let my fingers toy with the first button of his shirt, slipping it free. "Just reminding you where you stand."

Another button undone. My nails rake gently over his skin, dragging down to his abdomen, his breath growing heavier. The muscles in his forearm shift as his grip on the desk turns lethal.

I lean in just enough that my lips nearly brush his ear. "Reminding you of the rules."

He exhales sharply, his knuckles nearly white as he keeps his restraint.

"Your rules," he corrects, his voice dark. "Aren't as firm as you pretend they are."

He's right, and we both know it.

My fingers move lower, undoing another button, feeling the flex of muscle beneath my touch.

I barely brush against his belt, letting my fingertips trail just along the hem of his slacks.

His breath hitches, his restraint pulled so tight it's a wonder he's still standing still.

I smirk. "That was a mis—"

Two knocks followed by the door opening rip the intensity of the moment away.

I yank my hand back, stepping away just as Marcus and James stroll in, wearing matching Giants jerseys with bold lettering across the back:

MR. & MR. LANGSTON.

My body tenses instantly, and my face burns.

Damien is all cocky grins and boasting chest as he shrugs out of his shirt entirely, pulling it from his arms with smooth, easy confidence—like this moment wasn't just teetering on the edge of something reckless.

Like my hand wasn't about to graze over his cock to see if he was hard for me.

Like I wasn't going to sink down to my knees and swallow every inch of Damien Wolfe's infamous control.

James raises a brow, grinning like he just walked into something extremely interesting.

"Are we interrupting?"

"No." I clear my throat.

"Yes," Damien counters at the same time, his smirk downright sinful.

I shoot him a glare, but he just leans casually against the desk with a shrug, utterly unbothered.

James gives me a knowing look. "Mmm."

Marcus, ever the gentleman, steps forward, handing me a gift box. "From Mrs. Calloway."

Thank God for Marcus.

I take the box, eager for a distraction, but I can still feel Damien's gaze on me, watching as I lift the lid.

Inside, folded neatly, are two jerseys. One in Damien's size and one in mine.

I pick mine up, turning it over, and my breath catches.

FUTURE MRS. WOLFE.

My stomach drops.

It's just a gift. A party favor. A costume for the night.

But somehow, seeing it written out—bold and clear—makes something in my chest squeeze.

My eyes lift—instinctively—to Damien.

He's staring at the jersey, then at me.

And fuck, his expression...

There's something behind it, something raw. Dark. Like the words on the jersey aren't a joke to him at all.

His lips part slightly, like he has something to say, but he doesn't speak. He just watches me, watches the way I'm holding the jersey, how I haven't put it down.

James is the one to break the silence. "Mrs. Calloway insisted. She thinks it'll be a nice touch. A little... couples-themed apparel for her birthday boy."

I barely register his words, still caught in the heat of Damien's gaze.

It's just a jersey.

It doesn't mean anything.

Now, if only I could believe that lie.

Then maybe I could also convince myself that I'll be ready to walk away from Damien Wolfe in three days.

End this contract and never look back.

For some reason—a reason I know but don't want to admit—the idea of that sickens me.

Chapter 27

Damien

The ride to the stadium is torturous.

I should be focused on the game, on Calloway's birthday, on anything other than the woman sitting next to me.

But all I can think about is how close she was to falling apart for me in my office.

If James and Marcus hadn't walked in when they did, how far would Elena have let herself go? How far would I have let her take me?

She was unbuttoning my shirt, dragging her nails down my stomach, her hand so close to wrapping around my cock. The moment her fingers barely grazed me, I knew—I was fucking done for.

And now we're in the back of my limo, rolling through the city, exactly how I imagined it the night I took her panties.

That night, I pictured it in excruciating detail—Elena,

pressed against the cool leather seats, her legs spread for me, her head thrown back as I devoured her.

I thought about her gasping my name, moaning for me, her body trembling under my hands as I licked, sucked, and fucked her into oblivion.

I thought about pulling her into my lap, yanking that silky dress up around her waist, and slamming my cock inside her as the city blurred past us.

I thought about all the ways I'd ruin her.

And how much I'd fucking love every second of it.

I came so hard that night, fisting her panties in my hand, her name on my lips.

And now she's right here.

Next to me.

So fucking close.

Her thigh brushes against mine every time the limo turns.

She's chatting with Marcus and James, laughing, completely unaware that I'm sitting here, gripping my own knee to keep from grabbing her and finishing what she started.

She smells like vanilla and something sweet, something decadent—and I swear to fucking God, if I look at her lips one more time, I'm going to lose my mind.

Marcus is talking. James is making a joke. Elena is smiling.

And I?

I'm sitting here, drowning in frustration, shifting slightly in my seat because my cock is aching against my slacks, throbbing with the memory of her mouth, her hands, the fucking control she had over me in my office just now.

It's ridiculous.

I'm ridiculous.

Because she is right here.

And I can't touch her.

And it's driving me insane.

Elena's voice is soft, barely above the hum of the city outside, but it rips me out of my spiraling thoughts.

"Are you okay?" Her fingers graze my knee, a light, gentle touch. "You're sweating."

I blink, forcing myself to breathe, to register where the fuck I am—who I'm with.

Her.

Marcus and James.

Not in my office with her on her knees. Not in my penthouse, with her moans echoing across my home. Not in my damn fantasies, where I'm sinking inside her, claiming her.

I clear my throat, forcing my body to relax, my grip loosening from where I hadn't even realized I was clenching my own knee.

"Yeah, I'm good," I manage, my voice steady, controlled.

Her brow furrows slightly, but she doesn't push.

She's still watching me, though. That calm, steady focus in her gaze—like she can feel the way my pulse is hammering beneath my skin.

I want to cover her hand with mine. Just... sit there, touching her, feeling that warmth, the way we had at the opera.

But Marcus and James are here, and I know she wouldn't

want to play into the performance of this contract any more than necessary. They know what this is.

And yet, she's relaxed around them.

She enjoys their company. Genuinely.

Especially James.

They hit it off that first night at The Scallop, when we had dinner with Calloway, their easy conversation filling the space between my own careful, measured words.

That feels like a lifetime ago now.

Like we've been in this contract for years, not just a little over a week.

Three more days.

That's all the time I have left with her.

Three more days until she walks away from The Black Ledger, until she takes her money and finally builds the future she's been working toward.

A future that, until recently, I hadn't pictured myself in.

Now?

I want to be there.

I want to be included in the future she's carving out for herself. I want to see her bakery open its doors, to watch her build something that belongs only to her.

But more than that—I want her to be mine.

Not just for three more days but for as long as she'll fucking have me.

Marcus mutters a curse under his breath, sharp and low, slicing through the easy rhythm of conversation.

I glance over, instantly on alert.

"This might be bad, Wolfe," he says, his tone weighted with something that makes my spine stiffen.

The atmosphere in the limo shifts instantly—the light-hearted ease evaporating, replaced with something thick, heavy.

Marcus turns his phone toward me, the glow of the screen casting shadows across his face.

I take it, eyes locking onto the subject line first—an official email from a city planning commission member.

My gut tightens.

Then I read the first line.

Environmental review on the East River project site.

My grip tightens.

I don't need to read the rest. I already know this is bad.

But I do anyway.

Mr. Wolfe,

Following our preliminary assessment of the proposed development site at the East River location, surveyors have identified critical environmental obstructions that may impede construction. Due to protected wetland status and recent soil integrity concerns, the feasibility of the development as outlined in your proposal is now under formal review. A full report is pending, but alternative site evaluations are strongly recommended at this time.

We will be in touch as soon as additional information is available.

A slow exhale pushes through my nose.

Protected wetland status?

Soil integrity concerns?

Bullshit.

We did the work. We were prepared. Every clearance, every permit, every environmental study—approved.

This was not an issue. This should not be an issue.

But now, suddenly, it is.

I think back to the Hamptons, to Adrian's smug little comments about our *ambitious* timeline. How he chastised us, hinting that we were *cutting corners.*

I shut him down that night—told him, in no uncertain terms, that he was a fucking idiot if he thought we hadn't done our due diligence.

Because we had.

And yet, here we are.

A major piece of our development plan—the key site our financial projections are hitched to—is now suddenly in question.

If this site is pulled...

If Calloway catches wind before we have a solution...

This merger could be dead in the water.

My fingers flex against the phone before I shove it back at Marcus.

"Get our land-use attorneys on this," I say, my voice calm, clipped, controlled. "I want a full breakdown of every environmental study, every clearance we obtained before this project was approved."

Marcus nods, already typing.

James exhales slowly. "What about who ordered the new survey. Who signed off on it."

He's right. If this was pushed now, there's a reason.

But I don't have time for speculation.

I need facts.

I glance at Elena, expecting concern, maybe unease—but instead, her expression is sharp. Focused.

Like she's already thinking five steps ahead.

Good.

Because this could change the game.

And I have three days to make sure I don't lose.

***

The energy of the stadium is electric, a steady hum of excitement woven through the roar of the crowd. The scent of buttered popcorn, grilled hot dogs, and freshly cut grass lingers in the air, mixing with the crisp evening breeze filtering through the open VIP suite.

The luxury box is tucked away from the main concourse, offering privacy, yet the pulsing atmosphere still surrounds us—a steady thrum of anticipation in the background.

Marcus and I linger near the entrance, our conversation still circling the land survey issue, voices low but edged with tension.

Elena and James walk ahead of us, enjoying a much more casual conversation.

She throws her head back, laughing at whatever James said, and it seems like Marcus and I come to the same realization.

This can wait until tomorrow.

A headache builds at my temples, tension winding tight across my shoulders, but I force myself to push it aside.

This isn't the time to let it consume me. Not tonight.

I release a frustrated sigh, hoping I can push this to the back of my mind for a few hours.

Elena appears at my side, her fingers grazing the bend of

my arm—a barely there touch—and warmth spreads through me.

She doesn't say anything.

Her presence alone is enough to tether me back to the moment.

We're at a public event, surrounded by people who believe she's my fiancée, which means we can appear to enjoy these small touches. These little embraces that any typical couple would do, and I get the sense that she's using that excuse to pull me out of my own head.

As we move through the suite, mingling with guests and making our way through the buffet, she continues to keep that thread of contact between us—her fingers slipping into mine, the gentle pressure of her hand resting lightly on my forearm, the warmth of her body close enough to brush against mine.

They're small gestures, casual enough to anyone looking, but with each fleeting touch, I can feel the tension draining from my muscles, the sharp edges of my thoughts softening.

By the time Calloway steps onto the field for the ceremonial first pitch, I'm no longer thinking about the merger or the land surveys or the dozen ways this could go sideways.

I'm thinking about her and the way the golden light inside the suite seems to follow her.

Within minutes, Calloway joins his party guests, his wife linking her arm through his with a radiant smile. He waves off the applause, ever the composed businessman, greeting and thanking everyone.

Margo, however, is practically glowing.

"I think it's time for presents," she announces, clapping her hands together, her excitement effortlessly commanding the attention of the room.

Calloway smirks, shaking his head as if already resigned to whatever extravagant display she has planned. "Darling, you know I don't need anything."

She waves him off, her expression playful yet utterly self-assured. "I know. That's why I had to get creative."

A small black box is handed to him, and a hush falls over the suite as he lifts the lid.

Inside, resting against the velvet lining, is a single key.

Calloway's brow furrows slightly, his sharp gaze flicking up to meet his wife's.

Margo merely smiles. "And what, Mrs. Calloway, does this key unlock?"

"The stadium," she purrs, her hands gesturing around her. "You are now the proud owner of the New York Giants."

For a beat, the room is silent before it breaks into chaos.

Laughter, applause, murmured disbelief. Someone swears under their breath, clearly grasping the sheer magnitude of what just happened.

We're off to the side, watching the spectacle, me sitting in a chair as Elena's fingers trace slow, absentminded circles along my back.

It's instinctive, that touch. Natural.

And I let myself lean into it.

She leans in as well, her voice laced with amusement. "She bought him a fucking baseball team. You billionaires— I swear."

The corner of my mouth lifts, my hand trailing in slow

strokes along the back of her thigh. "Well, what else do you get a man who has everything?"

"I suppose." She scoffs softly. "But now I have to know—what's the most absurd gift someone's ever given you?"

I arch a brow, considering.

Without warning, I pull her down into my lap. A small yelp escapes her lips, her hands flying to my shoulders as she steadies herself.

Her breath catches, but she doesn't get up.

I should let her go.

But I don't.

Because this—her in my arms, her weight pressed against me, her warmth seeping into my skin—feels too fucking good.

I let out a slow breath, my thumb brushing along the outside of her thigh, fingers flexing as I grip her just a little tighter.

She's watching me now, searching my face, waiting for my answer.

"Well…" I finally say, my voice quieter now. "Don't be sad for the poor little billionaire, but… I don't really receive gifts of a personal nature."

Her brows knit together slightly. "What do you mean?"

I hesitate, then tilt my head slightly, my gaze steady on hers. "They're always business-related. Impersonal. Practical."

She doesn't speak right away, but I see something shift in her expression.

Sympathy.

And fuck, I don't want that.

"What about your family?" Her voice is softer now, careful, as if she already knows the answer.

My fingers brush a lock of hair behind her ear, a deliberate touch to help soften my answer.

"There is no family."

Her lips part slightly, the realization sinking in.

Because suddenly, she understands.

When my parents died, I didn't just lose them. I lost everything.

I became an orphan, just like her.

When my mother was buried, my father should have just climbed into the grave with her. I was eighteen when he died, but he had been vacant for years. And then it was just me—for real.

A slow ache burns behind her gaze, but she doesn't say anything.

I offer a small, almost amused smile, rubbing my hand up and down her thigh, as if I can wipe that look from her face.

"But I had Marcus," I say, my gaze flicking toward where he and James are engaged in conversation. "And now James."

Her expression softens just a fraction, the hint of something warmer behind her eyes.

"And I prefer experiences over gifts anyway," I continue, my lips curling at the corner. "So... maybe swimming with the sharks off the coast of South Africa?"

Elena laughs, shaking her head. "Of course. Just a casual, heart-stopping near-death experience."

I smirk. "Adrenaline rush. Better than a gold-plated watch."

I say it like it's nothing. Like none of this is a big deal.

But she's still looking at me like it is.

And the way her fingers toy with the soft hair at the nape of my neck—like she's trying to give me something, even if it's just this moment.

I shouldn't let it get to me.

But it does.

And all I can think about now...

Is what I would give her.

If she would let me.

If we were different people.

If this weren't just a contract.

There isn't anything in this world I wouldn't give her.

Chapter 28

Damien

Nearly an hour passes, and somehow, we've successfully managed to avoid any talk of the merger.

The game continues in the background, the suite filled with easy conversation, laughter, and the occasional burst of cheers from the stands outside.

Across the room, Elena is tucked into a quiet conversation with Margo, their heads tilted toward each other as they giggle like they're sharing secrets.

It's a simple moment, an unassuming one, but as I watch them—Margo's warm, maternal presence, Elena's soft, unguarded expression—it strikes something deep in my chest.

For a second, they could almost be mother and daughter.

The thought cuts through me, unexpected and visceral, breaking something open inside me that I'm not ready to acknowledge.

I swallow hard, forcing my attention elsewhere, focusing on Marcus and Calloway as they talk through something lighthearted, something easy—until *he* joins us.

Adrian.

The cocky piece of shit sidles up like he belongs here, hands in his pockets, a smug grin tugging at the corner of his mouth.

I know that look.

And I know exactly what's coming next.

"So," he starts, his tone all casual charm, but I hear the sharpness beneath it, the calculated edge, "any recent developments on the merger sites? Any last-minute changes?"

The fucker is baiting me.

Marcus stiffens beside me. Calloway's expression remains neutral, but I see the way his attention sharpens, waiting.

I could lie. Say no and brush him off.

I could give a half-truth, something vague, something noncommittal, and pray to fucking God that Calloway doesn't read into it.

I take a slow breath, about to respond—

But before I can, Elena moves.

Her conversation with Margo halts abruptly, her gaze snapping toward us, and before Adrian can press any further, she shifts the entire fucking moment on its axis.

"Richard," she says smoothly, pulling a small box from her purse. "I have a small gift for you. It's nothing much."

I blink, caught off guard.

I hadn't even realized she'd thought to bring anything other than the flowers for Margo.

That smart, beautiful fucking woman.

She was over there waiting, talking to Margo but still in tune to what was going on around her. Biding her time and holding off to use the moment as a distraction to save my fucking ass from the shit show we just learned about on the way over here.

God, if it doesn't take everything in me to stay right here and keep myself from finally giving in to every agonizing temptation that's driven me nearly mad all fucking week.

She turns toward him, smiling, and there's something genuine in her eyes, something bright and excited, like she truly wants to give this to him—not because it's expected, not because it's part of the contract, but because it matters.

"Though," Elena continues, shooting Margo a knowing glance, "it seems like it was meant to be, considering your wife's gift."

Margo tilts her head in curiosity, and Calloway, clearly intrigued, takes the box and carefully opens it.

His mouth pops open in shock.

We all lean in slightly, trying to see what's inside.

"Oh, Margo. Look."

His voice is thick with emotion as he pulls out a simple silver keychain. One side holds a small picture—an old photograph, slightly faded, of a young couple in the prime of their youth.

The other side holds the exact same couple, only older.

A perfect then-and-now image of Richard and Margo Calloway.

"That's from our first date," Margo breathes, eyes wide with disbelief. "How on earth...?"

Elena smiles, warmth radiating from her expression. "The Global Future Fund still had the pictures you submitted when they did that piece on you," she explains. "And I noticed the recent photograph in *Fortune* magazine was the exact same pose. It seemed too good to pass up."

"Elena."

Calloway is beyond touched; his voice is thick with emotion as he swipes at his eyes before pulling her into a hug.

Margo lets out a quiet gasp, tears spilling freely as she, too, embraces Elena.

And just like that, Adrian is completely forgotten.

Hell, even the fucking merger is forgotten.

I can see it in Adrian's face—the way his jaw tenses, the way his fingers twitch at his sides, barely restraining his frustration. He fucking hates it.

Hates that Elena just effortlessly stole the spotlight, that she's the one Calloway and his wife are wrapped up in right now, that she's the one making this moment unforgettable.

It's poetic, really.

And when he tries to shift the attention back, his voice all forced charm as he attempts, yet again, to circle back to business—

Margo shuts him down without a second thought.

"No talk of work tonight." She dabs at her tears, smiling at Elena before squeezing her husband's hand. "That's an order."

Adrian clenches his jaw, swallowing whatever smart remark he had ready.

And I sit back, taking in the scene—Elena still tucked in

Margo's embrace, Calloway fitting his new key onto the keychain, Adrian fuming in silence.

Elena's laughter still lingers in the air, wrapping around me like a thread I don't want to cut.

Margo is still wiping at her eyes, showing off the new keychain with a fond smile, while Calloway beams, clearly moved by Elena's thoughtful gift.

I barely hear any of it.

Because the second they step away, I move to Elena.

Crossing the short space between us, I wrap an arm low around her back and pull her flush against me. Her body fits against mine effortlessly, like she belongs there.

I bury my face in her hair, inhaling the scent of her perfume—warm, soft, fucking intoxicating.

She chuckles, a quiet sound, but I don't miss the way her breath hitches slightly.

"Damien," she whispers, my name a soft admonishment, but there's no real bite to it.

I tighten my grip, my fingers pressing into the dip of her spine.

"You're fucking incredible."

My voice is low, rough, and even I can hear the longing in it.

I don't know if she catches it.

I don't know if she realizes how completely I'm losing myself in her.

But before I can dwell on it, before I can even think about what the hell I'm doing, a voice I fucking despise cuts through the moment.

"Touching little display."

The smirk on Adrian's face is one I want to rip clean off. He strolls up with that easy arrogance, his hands in his pockets, his eyes flicking between us before settling on Elena.

His gaze lingers too long.

And I feel the barely contained violence coil tight in my chest.

My fingers twitch at my sides before instinct takes over, my grip tightening around Elena's waist, pulling her closer —a silent warning.

He doesn't take it.

Adrian's smirk deepens, his eyes flicking between Elena and me like he's enjoying some private joke at my expense.

"I have to say, Elena, you've got quite a talent for keeping powerful men entertained."

The words hit like a match to gasoline.

My jaw tightens, my fists flex at my sides. I don't know what pisses me off more—the audacity of the statement or the way he's looking at her, like she's something to be passed around, like he has the right to talk about her at all.

It takes every ounce of control I have not to knock the smugness clean off his face. Instead, I step forward, positioning myself between them, my body blocking his view of her entirely. My voice is low, controlled, lethal.

"Watch the way you talk to my fiancée."

Adrian lifts his hands in mock surrender, but the smirk never falters.

"Relax, Wolfe," he drawls, voice dripping with condescension. "I meant it as a compliment."

Lying bastard.

My fingers twitch at my sides, every muscle in my body coiled tight, ready to snap.

Calloway's voice carries across the suite, drawing Adrian's attention. The older man waves him over, gesturing for him to join their small group at the far end of the room.

Adrian lingers.

He should just walk the fuck away. Take whatever shred of dignity he has left and leave.

But instead, he steps in, just close enough that no one else can hear.

His voice is low, laced with poison, looking around me, right at Elena.

"When he's finished with you... tell me how much."

He winks. Smiles.

And I lose it.

The growl rumbles from deep in my chest before I can stop it. My vision narrows, my body moving on instinct, fists clenching as I lunge for him.

I don't care about the setting, the crowd, the fact that Calloway is just feet away—none of it matters.

I'm going to break this bastard.

But before I can get my hands on him, Elena is there.

Her body presses against mine, her hands splaying against my chest, my face.

Her touch grounding me, pulling me back from the edge.

Elena's eyes lock onto mine, a silent plea written in their depths.

"Damien," she murmurs, voice quiet but firm. "Remember. He's not fucking worth it."

I'm breathing hard, my blood still boiling.

"But you are," I grit out, the words barely controlled. "You're fucking worth it, and he can't—"

"He can."

She rubs my jaw with her thumbs. Her hands slide down my neck, gripping my shoulders, making me feel her touch before they rest on my chest again.

"Damien. Don't play his game. He's goading you. If you snap, he wins."

I close my eyes, exhaling a slow, uneven breath. I don't want to back down.

Every instinct in me is screaming to finish what Adrian just started.

To wipe that smug fucking look off his face.

But Elena's right.

Adrian walks away victorious, chuckling under his breath.

I don't watch him go.

I don't give him the satisfaction of my attention.

Instead, I keep my focus on Elena.

On the way her hands still rest against my chest, the way she's holding me together without even realizing it.

She doesn't look back at Adrian or acknowledge him at all.

She just looks at me.

And somehow, that's enough to settle the storm inside me.

I blow out another breath, muscles still tight beneath her hands, and drop my forehead against hers.

My grip tightens at her waist, keeping her close, needing her there.

"Come on," she whispers, her voice softer now. "Let's go home, okay?"

I don't answer right away.

I can't.

I'm still too wound up, my mind already moving a mile a minute, plotting exactly how I'll make Adrian regret this.

She tilts her head, watching me carefully. "Hey, Wolfie."

The nickname pulls my eyes to hers.

A small smile tugs at her lips, but the worry is still there, flickering behind her gaze.

"Take me home?"

It takes me a second longer than it should, but eventually, I nod.

She exhales, relaxing against me.

But even as I turn, leading her toward the exit, one thing is certain.

Adrian won't fucking get away with this.

That smug asshole is going to pay.

Chapter 29

Elena

The city lights filter through my bedroom window, casting a soft glow that reflects off the full-length mirror in front of me.

I stare at myself, fingers toying with the buttons of my jersey—the one Margo gifted me, the words FUTURE MRS. WOLFE pressed bold across my back.

The lettering feels heavier than fabric, like it's pressing into my skin, branding me with something I shouldn't want.

But I do.

I exhale slowly, my breath shaky as I undo the buttons one by one. The soft material parts, revealing smooth skin, the delicate lace of my bra.

My pulse kicks up as I reach behind me, unhooking the clasp, slipping the straps from my shoulders, and letting it fall to the floor, where it joins my discarded shoes and jeans.

Now, I stand there in nothing but the jersey and my black lace panties, the cool air teasing across my bare skin.

My fingers skim the fabric, adjusting it, feeling the absurdity of wearing something so oversized yet feeling so exposed.

I should talk myself out of this.

I should turn around, get under the covers, and pretend that this is just another night.

But I don't want to.

I'm tired of lying to myself. Tired of pretending I don't know exactly what I want.

Damien.

The thought sends a heat curling low in my stomach, and before I can overthink it, I step out of my bedroom, barefoot, moving on instinct.

The penthouse is dark, the city skyline the only thing illuminating the space. A quiet stillness lingers in the air, and for a moment, I wonder if he's already gone to bed.

He was quiet after we left the ballgame—brooding, his mind still caught on Adrian's words.

I know he wasn't upset with me, but still, I didn't like seeing him that way—tense, locked in his own head.

A soft gust of wind stirs the living room, and I realize the large sliding doors are open.

The sheer curtains billow gently with the night breeze, their ghostlike movement pulling my gaze to the verandah.

Damien is sitting outside, his posture relaxed but his grip tight around a dark-amber beer bottle, fingers flexing around the glass.

He's leaning back in his chair, long legs stretched out in front of him, head tilted slightly as he stares out over the city.

In an almost lazy motion, he lifts the bottle to his lips, taking a slow drink, his throat working as he swallows.

The movement is unhurried, but there's something about it—something raw, something starved.

I step forward, pushing the curtain aside, letting the fabric brush against my skin as I walk onto the terrace. I don't say anything. I simply lean against the frame of the door, waiting, letting the moment stretch.

The wind lifts my hair, a soft whisper of movement, and he notices.

His head turns toward me, and everything inside me tightens at the way his breath hitches.

His eyes darken as they rake down my body, slow and deliberate, taking in the way the jersey hangs open, the way the fabric shifts as I move, teasing glimpses of bare skin beneath.

I see the way his grip on the bottle tightens, the flicker of tension in his jaw as he drags his tongue along his bottom lip.

Heat coils low in my stomach, my confidence solidifying, my resolve firm.

I walk toward him, slow and measured, each step deliberate.

The jersey shifts with my movements, the cool air brushing over my exposed skin, tightening my nipples beneath the soft fabric.

His gaze tracks every inch of me, his breathing deepening, his pupils dilating as I draw closer.

I stop just in front of him, the space between us humming with anticipation.

The wind carries the faint scent of his cologne, and suddenly, I don't want to wait. I don't want to think.

I just want him.

I know he wants me too.

He wants me to break my own rules.

He won't push me—won't be the one to cross that final line—but he wants me to.

I see it in the way his body tenses, like he's holding himself back from reaching for me. He's waiting, silently daring me to be the one who finally snaps.

So, I do.

With deliberate slowness, I lift one knee onto the lounge chair, then the other, sinking onto his lap, straddling him.

His breath hitches, his hands instantly finding my thighs, his grip firm and warm as he drags them up, cupping my ass in both palms.

A low, guttural sound rumbles in his throat, like he's been starving for this—waiting for me to do what he's craved from the very beginning.

I reach for the beer bottle in his hand, prying it from his grip as his fingers flex against my skin, his hold tightening as though he needs to feel me, to reassure himself that I'm really here.

Tilting the bottle to my lips, I take a slow sip, my throat working as the cold liquid slides down—a stark contrast to the heat simmering between us.

Damien watches me like a man on the verge of losing control, his lips slightly parted, his breathing uneven. He looks drunk—not on alcohol, but on me.

On my proximity.

On the fact that I've finally given in.

I don't set the bottle down just yet. I want to savor this, to let it stretch.

His hands move, slow but deliberate, trailing up my spine, guiding me closer as he presses his lips, then his nose, to the column of my throat.

He drags his mouth up the length of my skin, his breath hot, teasing, sending shivers cascading down my spine.

I take another sip, my hand slipping to the back of his neck to steady myself, and the moment the bottle leaves my lips, I set it down on the side table, both my hands now free.

Free to touch him.

Free to feel him.

I grip his shoulders, my nails digging into the firm muscle as I shift, arching against him, grinding against the thick length pressing beneath me.

The friction is intoxicating.

The heat unbearable.

I'm soaked, aching, clenching around nothing as my body begs for more—for him.

His hands tighten on my ass, fingers digging into my flesh as he pulls me harder against him, guiding my movements, making sure I feel him.

The pressure, the way his body meets mine in each slow, grinding thrust—it's too much and not enough all at once.

A moan spills from my lips, unbidden, helpless against the way he's unraveling me with something so simple.

His breath is ragged, his lips brushing against my jaw as he curses under his breath.

"Fuck, Elena."

His voice is breathy, raw, desperate.

"Put me out of my fucking misery."

His forehead drops against mine, his hands still locked on my hips, guiding, controlling, pulling me down against every rock of his hips.

His patience—his infamous control—is dissolving right before my eyes, unraveling thread by thread.

We're so close.

So close that our breaths mingle, our lips barely a whisper apart.

I open my mouth, teasing him, hovering on the edge of that final barrier, daring him to take it.

He tilts his head, chases the space, his mouth a fraction away.

"Elena," he rasps, thrusting up against me as I grind down, the sensation making both of us shudder. His voice is a plea, a promise, a demand all at once.

"Please, baby."

He wants me to say it.

He needs me to say it.

And fuck, I need it too.

My lips brush his.

The smallest touch.

I exhale, my voice nothing more than a whisper.

"Kiss me."

And before I can finish the word, his mouth claims mine.

Damien breaks.

There is no hesitation, no restraint—just raw hunger.

His mouth crashes against mine, his tongue sweeping

in, claiming, devouring. There's nothing soft about the way he kisses me. No tentative exploration, no slow unraveling.

This is possession. This is obsession. This is Damien Wolfe finally taking what's his.

A desperate sound rips from my throat, swallowed by the relentless press of his lips, the way his fingers tangle into my hair, tilting my head back so he can kiss me deeper, harder.

I moan into his mouth, rolling my hips against his already hard cock, feeling the rigid length pressing up against me through the thin barrier of my panties.

The sensation sends a pulse of heat straight between my thighs, and I do it again—harder, grinding against him, desperate for friction.

His growl vibrates against my lips, sharp and possessive, before he suddenly stands, gripping me tight against his chest. My arms wrap around his shoulders on instinct, my legs clenching at his waist as he carries me effortlessly toward the verandah.

The city stretches behind me, lights twinkling, a thousand stars burning beneath us, but all I can see is him.

Damien sets me down onto the wide ledge, the cool metal biting into the backs of my thighs, and his hands don't stop moving—gripping my waist, sliding down my thighs, pulling me closer.

My legs lock around him as he steps between them, his large hands splaying across my ribs, thumbs brushing the undersides of my breasts, teasing, coaxing.

"Elena." His voice is a warning. A plea. A demand.

His lips trail along the column of my throat, his breath hot, his control hanging by a thread.

He wants permission.

He wants me to break the final barrier between us.

I shift, arching against him, my fingers trailing up his chest, nails dragging lightly across his bare skin.

"Damien." My breath is uneven, shaky. "Take it off."

He doesn't ask if I'm sure.

He doesn't hesitate.

His fingers find the collar of my jersey, peeling the fabric down inch by inch.

The cool night air kisses my bare skin, sending a shiver racing down my spine as the jersey slips lower, exposing my breasts to the open night.

He groans, a deep, reverent sound.

"Jesus, fuck."

His hands drag up my sides, his thumbs grazing over my nipples, making them tighten further.

His mouth follows. Hot and starved.

His lips close around one peak, sucking it into his mouth, his tongue swirling, licking, teasing.

I gasp, fingers threading into his hair, my body shaking as he devours me.

His teeth graze the sensitive bud before he sucks harder, his other hand squeezing the soft weight of my other breast, kneading, teasing, rolling the peak between his fingers.

A moan rips from my throat, and I roll my hips against him, grinding against the thick, hard length straining against his pants.

His breath shudders against my skin, and his hands

move—gripping my hips, guiding me against him, rolling his own hips in time with mine.

The barrier of my panties and his pants is unbearable. Too much and not enough all at once.

I need more.

I need him.

And from the way he's breathing, from the way his hands are shaking—Damien Wolfe is barely holding on.

He fists my hair, tilting my head back, forcing me to meet his gaze.

"Do you want me to stop?"

His eyes burn with something dark. Something primal.

"Fuck no." I manage to put a whole sentence together.

"Good girl." He nips at my jaw and I melt at the richness of his deep voice.

His other hand slides beneath the thin lace of my panties, and the moment his fingers brush against my swollen, aching heat, his breath stutters.

"Goddamn, baby," he rasps, his voice wrecked with arousal, like the feel of me is choking him. "You're fucking dripping."

I whimper as he drags his fingers through my slickness, teasing, testing, spreading me open with slow, torturous strokes.

He circles my clit, his touch featherlight at first, then firmer, a slow, devastating rhythm that has me gasping, my nails digging into his shoulders.

"Tell me you missed me, Trouble." His voice is low, rough, coaxing.

I can barely think, barely breathe, too lost in the steady pulse of pleasure building between my legs.

He knows exactly how to touch me.

How to drive me insane with nothing but his fingers and his voice.

"Damien—"

His fingers press deeper. "Tell me, Elena." His voice tightens, thick with need. "Because I was fucking dying without you."

I shudder, rolling my hips against his hand, chasing friction, chasing pleasure.

His fingers stroke that devastating spot inside me, flicking my clit in fast, precise strokes.

And I shatter.

"Yes." I pant as my head falls back.

A sharp cry rips from my throat, my body locking around his fingers, pleasure crashing over me in violent waves.

He doesn't stop.

Doesn't slow.

He works me through every last pulse, every last tremor, his other hand gripping my hip, holding me steady, grounding me.

The sounds of the city fade beneath the thunder of my pulse, the high-pitched whimpers spilling from my lips, the rough, wrecked curses Damien whispers against my skin.

"That's it, baby," he breathes, biting my jaw, licking over the sting before kissing his way back to my lips. "Fucking beautiful when you come."

I clench around his fingers as the pleasure slowly ebbs, my body trembling, too sensitive, too desperate for more.

He grins against my mouth, withdrawing his fingers.

And then—he sucks them clean.

Groaning.

Tasting me.

His tongue swirls over his knuckles, lapping up every last drop.

The sight alone has me clenching around nothing, my thighs squeezing him instinctively.

He hums in satisfaction.

His lips brush mine in featherlight kisses, teasing, coaxing. "Tell me what you want, Elena."

His voice is softer now, rough but sincere, his hands gripping my thighs, holding me steady.

"Because there's no fucking way I could deny you anything."

I don't hesitate. I can't. Not anymore.

But deep inside, where the scars still linger, something small and fragile shivers—because the first time I let someone in, he left me bleeding.

I built a life where the relationships are controlled. Where I say when, how and who.

I push the thought away, swallowing the fear before it can take root. Because this is different.

Damien is different.

"You."

His entire body tightens.

I kiss him, slow and deep, pressing myself flush against him, feeling every hard inch of him, the heat, the need.

"Just you, Damien." Another kiss. A promise. "All night."

"Fuck me," I whisper it like a prayer.

He groans, his forehead falling against mine.

"Break me," I whisper.

His fingers clench against my thighs.

"Own me."

A deep, guttural sound rumbles from his chest.

And then—he moves.

He lifts me from the railing, gripping my thighs as I wrap around him, his lips never leaving mine.

The penthouse is dark, lit only by the skyline, but he doesn't need the light.

He knows exactly where he's going.

And once he gets me there—he's going to ruin me.

He already has.

Because the second I sat down next to him that night—I was his.

And I never want him to let me go.

Chapter 30
Damien

I barely make it through the threshold before I have her against the wall, my mouth devouring hers, my hands gripping every inch of soft, warm skin I can reach.

She's just as desperate—pulling at me, tugging me closer, her nails scraping along my scalp, her breathless moans fueling the fire already raging through me.

I can't stop touching her.

I don't want to stop.

I need her. Right fucking now.

My hands slide under her thighs, lifting her effortlessly as she wraps around me, pressing herself closer, grinding against my cock like she's just as wrecked as I am.

I break the kiss just long enough to move us, my steps purposeful, controlled.

My bedroom may as well be a mile away. Too far. Too long to wait.

I can't hold off another fucking second.

She gasps when her back meets the cold marble of the kitchen counter, her body arching at the contrast of heat and chill.

Her legs are already spreading for me, resting over my shoulders as she props herself up on her elbows, watching me with those blown-wide hazel eyes.

She's panting, her chest rising and falling in quick, shallow breaths, her body already chasing the pleasure she knows is coming.

And fuck, I'm desperate to give it to her.

I grip her thighs, my fingers pressing into her skin, sliding higher, my thumbs brushing over the damp lace of her panties.

"Look at you, baby," I murmur, dragging my mouth along the inside of her thigh, watching her shudder beneath me.

"So fucking desperate."

Her lips part, a soundless plea spilling from her as she grips the counter, her hips tilting toward me, seeking more. Needing more.

I don't make her wait.

I hook my fingers into the delicate lace and tug it aside, exposing her to me, her slick glistening in the dim light of the kitchen.

A low growl rumbles from my chest as I lean in, my breath teasing against her sensitive skin.

Then, my tongue is on her.

A sharp, choked cry rips from her throat, her back bowing dramatically, her nails raking through my hair, tugging, anchoring herself as I devour her.

And fuck—she tastes even better than my fingers only a moment ago.

I groan into her, my tongue working her clit, licking, flicking, circling as her thighs tremble, her hips grinding up against my face.

She sounds so fucking perfect.

Her moans, the breathless way she gasps my name, the way she falls apart for me.

I don't stop. I won't stop.

Not until she's screaming.

Not until she knows she belongs to me.

My tongue works her clit, slow and teasing before I flick it faster, circling, sucking, giving her exactly what she needs before pulling back just enough to make her whimper.

"That's it, Trouble."

I murmur against her soaked skin, my breath hot against her pussy.

"Let me hear how bad you fucking need me."

She gasps, her fingers tightening in my hair, tugging, demanding, but I'm in control here.

I slide two fingers inside her, curling them just right, feeling her walls clamp around me, greedy, desperate.

"Goddamn, Elena," I groan, flicking my tongue against her swollen clit.

"This pussy was made for my mouth."

A sharp cry escapes her, her thighs trembling on either side of my head as she writhes, completely at my mercy.

I keep going, my fingers working in perfect rhythm with my mouth—thrusting, stretching, pressing against that perfect spot inside her, sending her higher and higher.

"You taste so fucking good," I rasp, sliding my tongue lower, dragging it up through her slit before sucking her clit back between my lips.

"I could live between these thighs and die a happy fucking man."

She gasps, her body arching, her moans turning into desperate little whimpers, and I know—she's right there, dangling on the edge.

"Come for me, baby," I growl, my fingers moving faster, my mouth relentless.

"Let me feel you drench my fucking face."

She cries out, her entire body shattering as she comes, her thighs clenching around me, her nails digging into my scalp.

She's soaking, her body shaking, and I groan against her as I lap it all up, every last fucking drop.

She's still trembling when I sit up, wiping my chin with the back of my hand, staring down at her completely wrecked, blissed-out expression.

"Jesus Christ, Damien," she pants, her voice breathless, her chest heaving.

I smirk, then scoop her into my arms, cradling her against my chest.

She lets out a soft laugh, her arms wrapping around my neck as I carry her through the penthouse like a fucking prize I just won.

I kick the bedroom door shut behind us and toss her onto the center of my bed.

She bounces once, laughing, her hair spilling across my

pillows as she props herself up on her elbows, still trying to catch her breath.

"You're acting like a wild animal," she teases, her lips curving in a wicked smile as I rip her panties from her body and toss them to the floor.

I grin, shoving my pants down in one motion, letting them drop to the floor as my cock springs free, hard, thick, and aching for her.

"That's because you make me one," I admit, crawling onto the bed, caging her beneath me.

Her smile softens as her legs wrap around my waist, locking me in place.

I brace myself on my forearms, lowering my body so I can feel every inch of her beneath me, our bodies flush, her heat searing against me.

I stroke my fingers through her hair, pushing it away from her face, my heart pounding at the way she's looking at me—like maybe this is more than just lust. Like maybe this is real.

"Damien," she whispers, her hands sliding up my chest, resting over my heart.

I drop my forehead to hers, my breath ragged as I try to slow myself down, to savor this moment, to make it more than just fucking.

"You have no idea how much I want you," I murmur against her lips.

She tilts her head, brushing the tip of her nose against mine.

"I think I do," she whispers.

I close the space between us, kissing her deeply, pouring everything I can't say into the way my lips move against hers, the way my hands grip her waist, holding her like she might slip away if I let go.

She sighs into my mouth, her fingers tangling in my hair, pulling me closer, deepening the kiss, her body pressing into mine.

And I know—

I'm so fucking gone for this woman.

She's underneath me, bare and breathtaking, her body soft and pliant against mine, her skin still flushed from the way I've already worshipped her tonight. The scent of her lingers on my lips, the taste of her still thick on my tongue, but it's not enough. It'll never be enough.

I breathe her in, willing myself to take this slow, to drag out every second of having her like this. My hand moves on instinct, reaching for the drawer beside the bed, my fingers brushing over the condoms inside.

She stops me. "No, Damien."

Her hands wrap around my wrist—gentle but firm—her touch sending a slow shockwave through me.

My brows pull together, my breath uneven. "What's wrong?"

Elena doesn't answer right away. Instead, she pulls me back down, her legs parting beneath me, her body arching to meet mine.

Her hand slides between us, wrapping around my dick and I release a sigh. Closing my eyes, I feel her touch on me.

"I'm on birth control." She guides my fingers to her mouth, parting her lips and sucking me in. Her tongue moves around my fingers, between them, tasting herself on me.

And fuck, it makes my cock pulse in her hand.

She squeezes and slides her hand up my shaft, gripping the head of my dick, massaging me.

"We both know we're clean."

Her eyes find mine in the dim light—steady and deliberate.

"No barriers," she whispers. "I don't want anything between us, Damien."

The world tilts. She keeps working my cock. My hips thrust into her touch and I'm fucking wasting away in her hands.

My pulse slams in my throat, my entire body tight with restraint. She's looking at me like this is a choice—one she's already made.

Never in my fucking life have I fucked a bare pussy.

I could never take the chance. But with her—

"Elena," I pant her name as she strokes me. I could come from this alone, the thought of sliding my dick along the warmth of her pussy.

Its enough to nearly make me explode into her palm.

"This isn't the contract, Wolfie."

Her grin is pure sex, and fuck if I don't think about sticking my cock between those wet lips and fucking her until I pour down her throat.

She runs her tongue along my mouth. "This is just us, baby."

Her legs tighten around me, and her hand never stops

gliding up and down my length, squeezing me and twisting as she goes.

She's giving me everything.

And fuck—I'm going to take it.

"Let me feel you, Damien."

A guttural growl rumbles from my chest as I capture her lips, devouring her with the kind of hunger I can't hold back anymore. My hands slide down her body, gripping her hips as I position myself, the head of my cock teasing her entrance—slick and hot—every muscle in my body pulled so tight I might fucking break.

"Are you sur—" I try to ask her one last time, one last moment of control, but she doesn't let me. She shifts, tilting her hips, giving me her answer.

And I snap.

I thrust into her—deep and claiming—sinking inside in one slow, torturous push.

A strangled gasp leaves her lips, her fingers clawing at my back, nails sinking into my skin as I stretch her, fill her completely.

And I feel it. Every slick, scorching inch of her wrapped around me—gripping me so fucking tight it nearly rips my sanity apart.

"Elena, Jesus fucking Christ," I groan, pressing my forehead to hers, my breath ragged, my body trembling with the effort to keep from slamming into her like a desperate man.

Because that's what I am.

Desperate.

Completely undone.

I rock into her slowly, savoring the heat of her, the way

she clings to me, legs wrapped tight around my waist, hands fisting in my hair.

I cup her face, forcing her to look at me, needing her to see exactly what she's done to me.

"You feel that?" I whisper, thrusting deeper, making her moan, making her tremble. "That's me. And you. Just us."

She whimpers, her lips parting, her nails dragging down my back. "Damien—"

I swallow her plea with my mouth, kissing her like I want to drown in her.

Because I do.

Because for the first time in my life, I feel something I never have before.

Something dangerous.

Something that feels a hell of a lot like mine.

Elena is all around me, her body a furnace of silk and fire, her nails sinking into my shoulders, her lips parting with gasps that drive me fucking insane.

Holding both wrists above her head, I pull back just enough to watch her, to see every inch of her unravel beneath me—bare and willing and all fucking mine.

"Look at you, baby," I rasp, thrusting deeper—slow and deliberate.

A choked moan spills from her lips, her head tilting back against the pillows, her spine arching, offering herself up like a goddamn sacrifice.

I take it, my mouth trailing over her throat, down to the swells of her breasts. I suck a hardened peak into my mouth, biting just enough to make her gasp before soothing the sting with my tongue.

"More," she breathes, her hips rolling up, chasing the friction, her body moving with mine like we were made for this, like we've been waiting for this moment our whole fucking lives.

I smirk against her skin, dragging my tongue to her other breast, my teeth grazing her nipple before I lift my head and meet her gaze.

"More?" I murmur, grinding into her, letting her feel every thick, pulsing inch of me stretching her. "How much more, baby? Tell me."

Her hazel eyes, glassy with pleasure, lock onto mine. "Don't hold back."

A deep, growl escapes me—something raw and primal—because fuck, she has no idea what she's asking for.

I grip the back of her thigh, hitching her leg higher over my hip, opening her up wider, burying myself so deep she cries out.

"Damien—"

"That's it," I groan, watching her fall apart beneath me, her body clenching around me, her breathy whimpers turning to desperate pleas. "Our night is just beginning, Trouble."

I drive into her harder, faster, our bodies colliding in a rhythm that's all hunger and heat. I drop my forehead to hers, swallowing every moan, every gasp, kissing her like I need her to breathe.

"Fuck, you feel so good," I pant, sucking at her lower lip before releasing her wrists and pulling away to watch her. To memorize every flushed, blissed-out inch of her.

"So tight, baby. So fucking perfect."

She clings to me, her fingers digging into my back, her nails scraping, marking, claiming me in a way that makes me fucking wild.

"Damien, I—"

Her breath stutters, her body tenses, and I know—she's close.

I slide a hand between us, my fingers finding her clit—rubbing tight, fast circles—pushing her right to the edge.

"Come for me, Elena."

Her entire body locks up, and then she's falling, crashing around me with a cry that's all pleasure, all surrender.

Her walls clamp down on me—pulsing, milking me—and it shoves me right over with her.

I bury my face against her neck, groaning as my release slams through me, pleasure detonating in every nerve, my hips stuttering as I spill into her—filling her up, branding her in a way that's fucking irreversible.

For a long moment, all I can do is breathe.

Heavy. Shattered. Wrecked.

I press my forehead to hers, my palm cupping her cheek, my thumb brushing over her kiss-swollen lips.

"You okay, Trouble?" I murmur, my voice rough.

A slow, sated smile curves her lips. "More than okay."

I smirk, rolling us so she's sprawled across my chest, tangled in me, her body still humming from what we just did. My cum dripping from her tight pussy and I don't care.

I don't want to move a fucking inch away from her right now.

I'll clean her in a moment. Revere her like the fucking goddess she is. But not yet.

Right now, I just want to stay in this bliss, with her.

"Good." I kiss her temple, my arms locking tight around her. "Because I'm not done with you yet."

She giggles, soft and breathless, before tilting her head, pressing a lazy kiss to my throat.

"I'm never going to be done with you, Trouble."

Chapter 31

Damien

I must be the luckiest bastard in the world.

For the second time in my life, I wake up to the most perfect dream—a dream where Elena's warm, sinful mouth is wrapped around my cock, working me into a state of bliss that has my entire body taut with pleasure.

But this time... it feels different.

Because last night, we didn't just fuck. We didn't just give in to all the pent-up desire we've been dancing around since the moment we met.

We made love.

And now, as the first light of dawn begins filtering through the curtains, my mind is hazy, floating between the remnants of sleep and the intoxicating pleasure coursing through my veins.

The dream is so vivid—her tongue flicking over the sensitive tip of my cock, her lips stretching around me as she takes me deeper, her hand twisting in perfect rhythm with each languid stroke.

I groan, my hips shifting, my fingers tangling in the silk of her hair.

So fucking real.

A slow, wet slide, the perfect amount of pressure, the hollowing of her cheeks as she sucks me like she needs it just as much as I do.

"Fuck, Elena," I rasp, my breath ragged, my body bowing up toward the heat of her mouth.

Then—

The sharp, intrusive blare of my phone shatters the moment.

That goddamn thing has the worst fucking timing.

A frustrated growl rumbles in my chest, but the second I shift, my mind clears just enough to register something crucial.

This isn't a dream.

Elena's mouth is on me.

My eyes snap open, my breath catching at the sight of her beneath the sheets, her dark hair spilling over my thighs, her lips wrapped around my cock as she watches me with that wicked, knowing glint in her hazel eyes.

My head tips back against the pillows, a ragged curse spilling from my lips as I fist the sheets.

"Christ, baby."

She hums around me, the vibration shooting straight to my spine, making me jerk.

The phone rings again, vibrating against the nightstand, and I swear to fucking God, I'm seconds away from smashing the damn thing.

Elena pulls off me with a soft pop, her lips swollen, her smile lazy as she glances at the offending device. "You gonna get that?"

"Not a fucking chance."

Elena releases me, straddling my hips, her warm, naked body stretching over me as she reaches for the phone. My hands instinctively find her waist, but my attention is locked on the way her breasts brush against my chest, her smooth skin gliding over mine.

"Tsk, tsk." She clicks her tongue. "What a naughty CEO you are."

One of those perfect, fucking gorgeous breasts is so close to my mouth that I reach up, my tongue flicking out to catch her nipple—only for her to pull back at the last second, grinning like she enjoys torturing me.

"Fortune favors the bold, Mr. Wolfe," she purrs, her voice dripping with amusement as she swipes her finger across the screen and hands me the phone.

Fuck.

I grit my teeth, my cock still throbbing from the loss of her mouth, and force myself to answer. "This is Wolfe."

Before I can even process whatever the hell Marcus is rambling about, Elena shifts lower, her lips wrapping around me again, her tongue swirling in slow, torturous circles.

My stomach clenches.

A sharp inhale is all I manage before she takes me deeper, her hand gripping the base, stroking in perfect sync with her mouth.

Marcus keeps talking, rattling on about an update from the land-use attorneys regarding the commissioner's email, but fuck if I can focus.

Elena's eyes flick up, mischief dancing in their depths, and when she hums around my cock, my head hits the pillow, a ragged exhale escaping me.

I thread my fingers through her hair, my grip tightening just enough to guide her—to tell her without words just how good she's ruining me.

"Yes."

The word is barely a breath.

She moans softly, the vibrations shooting straight through me.

"Yeah."

Again, the word is meant for her.

Not for Marcus. Not for the fucking land survey. Not for any of the bullshit waiting outside this room.

Just for her.

And she knows it.

Her pace quickens, her tongue flicking along the sensitive underside before taking me deep, her throat flexing as she swallows around me.

My entire body is tense, heat pooling low in my spine, coiling tighter with every stroke of her mouth, every swirl of her tongue.

Marcus is still talking, oblivious, his voice a distant hum in my ear as Elena's fingers tighten around my base, working me in a way that has my vision blurring.

I clench the sheets, trying like hell to keep my voice

steady. "Understood," I grind out, my free hand gripping her hair, guiding her faster, deeper.

I'm seconds away from losing it.

And then she hollows her cheeks, sucking me hard as her nails rake lightly down my thigh, her other hand squeezing my balls.

Gone.

Dead and fucking buried.

I snap.

With a strangled growl, I shove the phone into the pillow, cutting off whatever the fuck Marcus was saying as my hips jerk up, spilling deep into her throat.

Elena moans around me, swallowing every last drop like it's her favorite fucking treat.

My chest heaves, my fingers flexing in her hair as she slowly licks up every bit of me, her tongue flicking one last time over my sensitive tip before she pulls off with a satisfied hum.

She grins.

Smug. Satisfied. Triumphant.

She fucking lives for this. For ruining me.

And I let her.

But not without a little punishment of my own.

I hook my hands under her thighs, lifting her effortlessly, shifting her up my body until she's straddling my face, her glistening pussy inches from my mouth, her creamy thighs bracketing my head.

She gasps, her hands gripping the headboard to steady herself, already knowing what's coming.

I inhale deeply, running my nose up the slick heat of her cunt, taking my time as she shudders above me.

Then, with one hand, I reach blindly for my phone.

I press speaker.

"Yeah, I'm still here," I say, voice smooth, controlled.

Elena tenses. I can feel the shock ripple through her, but I don't give her time to react.

My tongue slides up her wet slit in a long, deliberate stroke, swirling around her clit before sucking it into my mouth.

She chokes back a moan, her thighs trembling.

Marcus' voice crackles through the speaker, oblivious. "Right, so as I was saying, the commissioner's office claims the survey issue is being re-reviewed. They're trying to determine whether this falls under an environmental protection clause or if we need to petition for a special variance."

I hum against Elena's clit, the vibrations making her shudder.

She bites her fist, muffling the moan threatening to escape.

I smirk against her, my hands gripping her ass, guiding her closer, urging her to ride my mouth.

"Told them we already obtained those clearances," Marcus continues. "But it looks like someone's pushing for an independent review. We might need to—"

I flick my tongue faster, circling her clit before dipping lower, tasting her, fucking her with my tongue, stroking deep as her hips start to move.

Her grip on the headboard tightens, her breath ragged,

thighs flexing around my head as I devour her like she's my fucking last meal.

She's trying so hard to stay quiet.

I won't let her.

Not when she just spent the last ten minutes sucking my soul out through my cock while I was on the phone.

Payback's a bitch, baby.

"Damien?" Marcus prompts, waiting for a response.

I pull away just enough to answer, letting my breath skim over Elena's soaked pussy.

"We'll file an injunction if we have to," I say evenly, watching her pulse throb, watching her face contort in pure, tortured pleasure as she fights to stay composed. "And get our attorneys on the line with the commissioner's office today."

Elena's eyes widen, murder and desperation flickering in her gaze.

Because as soon as I finish that sentence, I dive back in—licking her slow and deep, swirling my tongue over her swollen clit before sucking her hard.

Her body bucks, her spine arching.

She's so fucking close.

I feel her tighten, her slick heat pulsing against my mouth, and fuck, I love knowing I can bring her to the edge with just my tongue.

Marcus keeps talking, but I don't hear a fucking word.

All I hear is her.

Her hitched breaths.

Her strangled gasps.

The wet, filthy sounds of me fucking her with my mouth.

Her thighs squeeze around me, and her fingers are digging into my hair—pulling, tugging, her hips grinding down.

She's trying to hold out, but I don't let her.

I seal my lips over her clit, suck hard, flicking my tongue over it in rapid strokes.

She shatters around me, and it's the most beautiful fucking thing in the world.

Her body trembles, her silent scream caught in her throat as she drenches my tongue.

I groan into her, lapping up everything she gives me, holding her against my mouth, working her through it, not stopping until she's twitching, gasping, her body going limp against me.

Slowly, I ease her down, pressing soft, lingering kisses against her trembling inner thighs.

She collapses against my chest, still breathless, her heart pounding.

I reach for my phone, grabbing it from where it landed on the mattress, and press it back to my ear.

Marcus is still fucking going, and I smirk against the silky strands of her hair.

"I'll be in the office soon," I say, my voice low and gruff, before adding, "Right after I finish my breakfast."

Elena groans, swatting my chest as I hang up.

I grin against her, gripping her ass possessively, pulling her closer.

"That was so fucking mean," she mutters, still catching her breath.

I chuckle, pressing a kiss to her hip. "And you fucking loved it."

She doesn't argue.

Because we both know the truth.

I shift, rolling her onto her back, caging her beneath me as I kiss my way up her body.

"Now shut up," I murmur against her lips, "because I'm going back for seconds."

Chapter 32
Elena

Damien left about twenty minutes ago, but my body still hums with the aftershocks of our night and morning together.

God, that man loves to eat my pussy.

He made me come twice more on his tongue before giving me a proper fucking—my hands gripping the headboard, his fist tangled in my hair, the other branding my hip as he drove into me from behind.

He pushed my torso down, lifted my hips higher, and thrust deep until I shattered around him, screaming his name into the dark satin sheets.

Even after, he lingered. Tempted.

I tried to keep him in bed, my fingers teasing across his chest, my lips brushing his jaw, coaxing him into another round.

But he only smirked against my mouth, shaking his head as he whispered, "Nothing but fucking trouble."

And then, because he couldn't help himself, he swirled

his tongue around my nipple, pressed one last open-mouthed kiss against my pussy, and groaned as he tore himself away.

"Fuck me, Elena," he muttered on his way out, half to me, half to himself. "This is going to be the longest fucking day of my life."

He mumbled as he disappeared down the hallway.

I've been lying in his bed ever since, wrapped in the warmth of his scent, the sheets still tangled around my body as I lazily scroll through my phone.

I'm not really seeing anything, my mind going back to last night—to every touch and kiss. The warmth of his arms around me and how it feels to completely disappear in his embrace.

A message pops up.

DAMIEN: Have dinner with me tonight?

A slow, satisfied smile spreads across my lips because as soon as I see his name on my screen—see his small question—it drops like lead in my stomach. And I finally admit what I've been refusing to acknowledge.

I've fallen in love with Damien.

Last night, we threw out the rules that separated us from what we want. Every barrier was broken through, and I gave myself to him in a way I have never given myself to anyone.

Not just physically.

But emotionally.

But as my thumbs hover over the screen, ready to type back my answer, that heavy lead settles into dread.

There is one more barrier I haven't removed yet. And I need to before things turn terrible.

I need to tell Damien about Adrian.

My pulse hikes, my heart thumping against my chest.

I didn't keep it from him to be hurtful. At first, it was because I needed to follow Ledger protocols. I didn't know Damien like I do now.

But when Lucian didn't get back to me, I went to the one person I can count on—myself.

I should have trusted Damien with it, but everything I've experienced my whole life has taught me otherwise. To not trust. To handle things on my own.

And that's exactly what I did.

My fingers tighten around my phone, determination settling in my chest.

Tonight.

I'll tell him everything tonight.

ELENA: It's a date.

Damien's going to react.

And I have no idea how.

A slow breath pushes past my lips, but before I can let myself dwell, another message comes through.

My phone vibrates in my palm, the notification lighting up the screen.

UNKNOWN: See you in 15 minutes.

My stomach plummets.

My pulse skyrockets, my skin turning ice cold as realization slams into me.

Shit.

Today.

Adrian.

I lost track of everything still hanging over my head—so caught up in Damien, in his hands, his mouth, his body, his words, his everything—that I forgot.

I forgot about the meeting written on the back of the photos Adrian left for me.

And now, it's too late to prepare.

He'll dangle those photos over my head, threaten to release them, drag my name through the mud, smear me in front of the Calloways, damage Damien's merger, and set off a scandal that will ruin us both.

Well, I won't let that happen.

Throwing off the sheets, I storm back to my room, my movements swift and purposeful. I grab the first clothes I see—dark jeans, dark shirt.

I don't have time for a shower, so I yank a baseball cap over my hair and throw the dresser drawer open. The yellow folder glares at me as I snatch it up and head for the elevator.

The coffee shop is only a few blocks away from Damien's penthouse, but every step feels heavier than the last, thick with tension.

I force my breathing to stay even, my shoulders squared, my chin up as I push through the door and scan the room.

He's already here in the back corner.

Casual. Comfortable. Smirking like he owns the world. Like he's already won.

The sight of him makes my stomach churn, but I push it down. I refuse to let him see even a flicker of hesitation.

I stride to his table and drop the folder between us with a controlled, deliberate movement.

"I'm not doing this," I say, my voice cool and measured.

Adrian doesn't even flinch. His smirk deepens as he flips the folder open, letting his fingers skim the grainy black-and-white security stills.

The photos make my skin crawl.

From the outside, they could look intimate. But I know the truth.

And so does he.

"You sure about that, sweetheart?" His voice is thick with amusement as he taps the folder—a threat, a promise.

I clench my fists, forcing my face to remain neutral.

"All those pictures prove," I say, my tone like ice, "is that you're a scared little piece of shit who let your girlfriend be gang-raped."

He exhales, slow and easy, like he's shaking off a minor inconvenience.

"Doesn't matter," he says with a small shrug. "People believe what they want to believe. And with a little push..." He taps the folder again, his gaze gleaming with sick satisfaction. "This will be a scandal. Ruin your precious little fiancé. Ruin you."

My heart pounds, but I won't let him see an ounce of my fear.

"You ready to give him up, Elena?"

I lean in, my voice dropping to a quiet, razor-sharp edge.

"I'd rather burn my own life to the ground before I let you hold a match to it."

His eyes darken, but the smirk stays.

"I won't betray Damien."

The words leave my lips without hesitation because they're true.

Without another word, I turn on my heel and walk away.

"You think he'll still want you once he finds out what you've done?" Adrian calls after me, several patrons turning to watch as I leave.

I should have fucking told Damien the moment Adrian confronted me at the tennis courts. Should have trusted him. But I was scared.

I retreated—like I always do. Like I've done my whole life.

Because I've always been alone.

But I don't feel alone anymore.

Damien is different.

He wouldn't judge me for my past. Wouldn't look at me and see something broken, something dirty. He cares about me.

And I know, without a doubt, that he's falling for me—just like I've already fallen for him.

And I won't let Adrian destroy that.

My pulse pounds with every step, my lungs suddenly too tight, the air too thin. I need to get out of here. Get away. Get to Damien.

There's still time to fix this.

There's still time.

I pull up the contact for the Blackstone car service and order a ride to Damien's office.

They must have my name on caller ID because they call me by name as they confirm the ride. "Of course, Ms. Moreau. We'll have your driver waiting for you."

I turn the corner to save myself a block, my steps hard against the pavement.

I should call Damien. Let him know I'm coming.

But chills run down my spine when I hear another pair of footsteps behind me.

Steady. Measured.

Following me. And getting closer. My grip tightens on my phone.

The moment I hear the footsteps quicken behind me, I know I don't have time to think.

I just bolt.

My heart slams against my ribs, my pulse roaring in my ears as my feet pound against the pavement. I don't waste time looking over my shoulder—I already know it's him. Adrian's heavy footfalls hammer behind me, fast and determined.

The late-morning air rips past me, my breath coming sharp and ragged as I push harder. A block and a half. That's all I need. Just one more turn, and I'll be in sight of the Blackstone.

But then my hat flies off, my long hair spilling free, whipping behind me like a fucking flag. And that's all it takes.

A sharp yank at my scalp sends me reeling backward, my neck snapping with the force.

A gasp catches in my lungs, but it's cut off as Adrian shoves me against the brick wall by my throat.

The impact rattles through my body, my back scraping against the rough surface. One of his hands clamps over my mouth. The other grips my wrist, pinning it hard against the wall.

He flattens his frame against me, his knee between my legs, trapping me between him and the wall.

"You're making this harder than it needs to be, Elena," Adrian hisses, his breath hot and sour against my ear. I pull the short hair near the nape of his neck, and he lets go of my mouth to get control of my other hand.

I glare at him, my pulse hammering, but I refuse to let him see fear.

"Let. Me. Go."

He chuckles darkly, panting heavily as he slams my other wrist against the wall. "I tried to give you an easy way out. Tried to let you be smart about this, but no—you want to be difficult."

I twist against his hold, my body coiled with tension, but he doesn't let go.

"You're going to work with me on this," he growls, his fingers tightening like a vise around my wrist. "Just like we used to."

"Fuck you," I spit, struggling against his grip.

His lips curl. "Oh, sweetheart. You don't understand what's at stake here."

He slams into me harder, his knee digging deeper between my legs, pinning me against the rough brick wall.

"My business partners need this deal to fall through," he snaps, his voice low and venomous. "And you're going to help me make that happen. Or I swear to God, I'll make sure you go down with me."

I glare at him, my breathing hard, my skin burning where he grips me.

He leans in, his voice like gravel. "I don't care what you say."

Fury ignites in my veins, a slow burn turning into an inferno. My strength is wearing down, but I don't let up.

I thrash and push. I try to scratch and claw, but I can't.

His jaw clenches, and he growls against my neck. Revulsion rolls down my body in chills as I realize he has an erection and he's grinding against me as I struggle.

"Get the fuck off me!" I buck and elbow, finding renewed motivation to get away from him.

"God, you still feel so fucking good," he grunts. "I hope you enjoyed fucking him because it ends today, sweetheart."

The words slice through me, but I don't let him see it.

I get as much momentum as I can and ram my skull into his face. The crunch of his nose breaking is nearly as satisfying as the howl he yells.

He releases one of my wrists on instinct to cover his nose.

I use my newly freed hand and rake my nails down his cheek with every ounce of strength I have.

He roars, jerking back, but his grip on my wrist only tightens, bruising into my skin.

"Bitch," he spits, fury twisting his features as he back-hands me with all the strength he can muster at this close proximity.

White-hot pain explodes across my cheek, the crack of it ringing in my ears.

For a moment, everything tilts. My vision sparks.

The metallic taste of blood fills my mouth, but I don't have time to dwell on it.

I swing my knee up—hard—and it lands exactly where I want it.

Adrian chokes on a strangled sound, doubling over as agony takes over.

I shove past him and run.

Every nerve in my body screams, my cheek throbbing, my lungs burning, but I don't stop. I sprint toward the Blackstone, the towering glass structure a beacon of safety in the distance.

The town car is already waiting at the curb, the same driver from the other day standing beside it. I slow to a brisk walk.

I know I'm not fooling anyone.

He smiles, polite and professional, but the moment he takes me in, his expression shifts—concern bleeding into his features.

"Everything okay, Ms. Moreau?" His voice is cautious, his gaze flicking past me.

I don't look back to confirm Adrian is there. But at least I know he's not stupid enough to push anything with a witness present.

"Yes. Fine, thank you," I say, my voice steadier than I feel. "Wolfe Industries, please."

He nods and opens the door for me.

The moment I slide into the back seat, I exhale a shuddering breath, my body sagging against the cool leather.

Reaching for a tissue from the console, I blot at my lip, pulling it away to see a small trace of blood.

Shit.

I dig into my back pocket for my phone, needing to use the camera to check the damage—but it's gone.

A new kind of dread unfurls in my stomach, and my hands start shaking as the adrenaline begins to crash.

It must have fallen out when I ran from Adrian.

I have no way to call Damien. No way to call Lucian.

Swallowing hard, I force myself to breathe. I just need to get to Wolfe Industries. Once I'm there—once I'm with Damien—I'll be fine.

But as I glance out the window, my blood runs cold.

Adrian is still there, standing on the sidewalk, hands in his pockets, watching me.

I don't look away. I won't show him that he's won anything in this.

Instead, I lift my chin, every line of my body screaming defiance as the car pulls away, putting distance between us.

But I know this isn't over.

I just hope I can get to Damien before it's too late.

Chapter 33
Damien

The day started out fucking perfect.

I lean back in my chair, rereading the last text Elena sent me, letting the words sink in like a slow burn.

"It's a date."

My thumb taps against the side of my phone as I look at her reply.

Tonight. Dinner at the penthouse. Just the two of us.

I smirk, running a hand through my hair, my body thrumming with something I haven't felt in a long time: anticipation.

The end of our contract is looming, only days away, but for the first time since this arrangement started, I know exactly what I want.

I want her.

Not as a business arrangement. Not as a pretend fiancée. But as mine.

I don't give a fuck about the terms we started with. I

don't care about the lines we agreed to keep in place because every single one of them has blurred into nothing.

Elena belongs with me.

Tonight, I'll tell her.

Maybe it's too soon. Maybe I should be careful, ease into it, play it safe.

But I don't want to.

I'll go as slow as she wants, but I want her in my home, in my bed. In my life.

Permanently.

A glance at the clock tells me I have ten minutes before Calloway arrives. The sixty-fifth-floor conference room is already filling with lawyers, their low conversations a steady hum as they prepare for the final stages of the merger.

Two days. That's all it will take to sign everything, to finalize every detail.

By tomorrow night, it'll be done.

Everything I've built, everything I've worked toward, will expand in ways I never thought possible.

Marcus steps inside, his face a mask of something cold, unreadable.

The shift in the air is immediate. The steady rhythm of my pulse falters.

I know that look. Something's wrong.

I straighten in my chair, the good mood that had been lingering just moments ago slipping through my fingers like sand.

"Everyone out." My voice is steady, with a sharp edge beneath it.

Marcus's eyes sweep the room in confirmation.

We've been friends for so long, we can communicate without words at this point. Whatever this is, it's fucking bad.

The lawyers gather their files, making their exit.

The last one barely clears the doorway before Marcus moves, striding toward the conference table. His fingers fly across the keyboard as he connects his laptop to the screen on the wall.

A sinking feeling coils in my gut.

This isn't good.

This isn't something minor. This isn't just another corporate fire to put out.

This is something worse.

"You're fucking killing me, Marc." I nearly growl the words, my jaw tight. "What is it?"

Marcus exhales, his voice low and measured, controlled in a way that only makes the unease gnawing at my ribs tighten.

"I found something. You're not gonna like it."

The words hang between us like a live wire, pulsing with tension as Marcus's computer connects to the screen.

"I'm sorry, Damien."

I can't look at him—I don't need to. Whatever he found, he already knows it's going to gut me.

The television lights up, and I freeze.

The entire fucking world stops spinning as my mind processes what I'm looking at.

"What is this?" I ask Marcus, but I can't look away.

"It's a deleted account. One of our guys recovered it."

Old social media pictures flood the screen.

At first, I don't recognize her. She looks different—younger. Her hair is shorter, streaked with blonde highlights. Her smile is freer, brighter. Untouched by the weight of the world she carries now.

But it's her.

It's Elena.

My stomach knots as my eyes track to the person standing beside her. Too close. Too fucking familiar with that smug fucking face.

Mother fucking Adrian.

I go still, my breath locking in my chest. The air feels thick, heavy, pressing against me like a vise. Marcus says nothing, watching me carefully.

"Keep going," I grind out.

The images shift. More of them.

Elena and Adrian. Together.

Not just knowing each other—lovers.

Kissing. Embracing. Wrapped around each other in ways that make my blood boil.

"This can't fucking be possible."

I pull his laptop to me, taking it over and moving faster through the files, begging to see proof these have been doctored. Fakes. Digital images created on a computer to drive a fucking spike through me.

One of the files is a social media post several years old. A video.

My world darkens as soon as I open it.

The setting is a beach, waves crashing in the background. Could be the fucking Hamptons. Could be the exact place we were this weekend, where she pretended she didn't fucking know him.

My jaw clenches as I hit play.

Adrian's smirking into the camera, sunglasses perched on his nose, his arms wrapped around her. One hand holding her breast over her bikini. Like she belongs there.

"Partners in crime," he says, grinning.

Elena laughs, shaking her head. Then she looks back at him, her eyes shining.

"Forever," she chimes in.

And then—he kisses her.

Right there. In the open. In front of the whole fucking world. And it hits me like a dagger twisting in my gut.

His lips move against hers, his tongue sweeping into her mouth. The same mouth I kissed this morning.

The same mouth I made mine.

I slam my fist into the table.

Marcus doesn't flinch, but the screen flickers as the impact shakes the laptop.

Pain crashes into me like a freight train.

She fucking played me.

My hands curl into fists as I stare at the screen, my pulse thundering so hard I can hear it in my ears.

Everything between us—all of it. The push and pull, the fights, the stolen moments, the way she trembled for me, the way she fucking melted for me—

None of it was fucking real.

A harsh, ragged breath rips from my lungs, and my chest feels like it's cracking open.

Adrian.

She was his.

She still is.

Every moment they interacted at the Calloway's Hamptons retreat rushes through me.

When she looked flustered just before the yacht. Fuck—he was goddamn staring at her on the fucking boat.

Practically waving a sign in front of my face that says: I FUCKED HER FIRST.

His cock-sucking hands on her as they danced. I knew it looked too familiar.

Because it was. Because he probably knows every inch of her like I do.

But what is their fucking angle? What do they get out of this?

Adrian was clearly trying to sabotage the merger. Is there another buyer waiting to come in after? Take the sale at a cheaper rate when Calloway is fucking desperate, and Adrian gets a fucking kickback?

And what does Elena get out of it?

My ten million fucking dollars, for one.

Our contract never said my merger needed to succeed. Only that she needed to spend the two weeks pretending to love me. To be my fucking pretend partner in life. And if she sold herself perfectly, she'd be a rich woman.

They're playing us at both ends. Calloway and me.

I can't fucking look at that screen another second.

The chair flies away from me when I kick it back, walking over to the windows that overlook the city. It's dead silent out there. The noise of the city is blocked by the thick glass while the storm is right here in this conference room.

In my fucking mind.

My hands rest on my hips to keep me from punching the windows.

The fucking Blackstone stands tall in the distance, and I know she's in my fucking penthouse right this goddamn second.

All I can think of is Genevieve. Walking into my house, hearing her with him. Seeing them.

I feel the rage within me rise, my face burning as my anger becomes something palpable.

"There's something else." Marcus's voice is just as grave now as it was a moment ago.

Of course there's something else.

"You know that trace I had on Adrian's cell?"

I close my eyes, pinching the bridge of my nose. I feel like I already know what he's going to say, and I don't know that I'll survive it.

"He was near the Blackstone this morning."

I swear to fucking God.

"There's another video, Damien." I hear Marcus slide the laptop across the polished wood table. The soft clicking of keys blares around the room.

I don't want to fucking look at it because my goddamn heart is breaking apart in my chest.

"Damien." Marcus's voice is a warning.

Finally, I turn my head, my eyes dead as I take in the scene unfolding.

Coldness creeps back over the empty cavity that I freely let Elena warm up. Like a pathetic fucking moron.

It's a café I know well. Only two blocks away from my penthouse. I stop there all the fucking time.

The timestamp in the corner of the screen nearly makes me implode. The final tendrils of my dead fucking heart snap, leaving nothing within me.

It's less than an hour after I left her in my bed.

Adrian is sitting in the corner, and it's clear he recognizes someone.

Elena walks up to the table and gives him something. The pathetic ball cap she's wearing is a ridiculous disguise.

It's almost insulting.

She leaves, and he follows her.

The recording ends. Just like every fucking feeling I developed for her since that night she walked into my restaurant.

Another manipulating woman I dove headfirst into.

My jaw clenches so tight it aches, but I barely feel it through the rush of white-hot rage flooding my system.

The betrayal is suffocating.

I was going to tell her tonight. I was going to give her everything. I was going to tell her I fucking fell in love with her.

And the whole time, she's been in on this. From the very beginning.

Adrian.

Elena.

Two names I'll carve into my mind, branding them with the promise that they will pay.

For every second I spent believing in her.

For every night I lay awake, thinking about her.

For every fucking moment she made me feel like she was mine.

I turn from the window, my entire body coiled so tight I feel like I might snap.

Marcus watches me carefully, his expression unreadable. "What do you want to do?"

My chest rises and falls, my breath slow and controlled despite the inferno raging inside me.

"I'm going to find out what she gave him."

I meet his gaze, my voice dark, lethal.

"Then I'm going to bury them both."

The entire way to Damien's office, I nearly picked the skin around my nail until it bled. The elevator ride to the seventieth floor is taking a century as I watch the monitor count each floor.

Sixty-fifth, sixty-sixth, sixty-seventh, sixty-eighth, sixty-ninth—

Until finally, the elevator doors open with a gentle ding.

The receptionist desk is being supervised by a new woman. Much older than Vanessa, with a very stern expression.

"Excuse me, I need to see Dam—Mr. Wolfe. It's urgent."

She looks me up and down, her prune lips never extending into anything warm. It's right now that I realize what I must look like—jeans and a dark shirt, windblown hair, and a bruise likely forming on my cheek.

"Mr. Wolfe is unavailable."

My heart is hammering in my chest, and my face is

burning from the anxiety of feeling like I'm too late to fix this.

"I'm his fiancée. Elena." My face must drip with desperation because after a pause, she exhales, typing something into her computer.

"There is no fiancée on record for Mr. Wolfe's personal contacts. I'll have to ask you to leave." She looks just to the side of me and nods to someone in the distance.

I glance behind me, and my stomach vaults. It's a fucking security guard.

"Please, if you could just call—" I reach for my purse, forgetting I didn't bring anything to the coffee shop with me. After the encounter with Adrian, I just got into the town car and headed here. I have nothing. No phone. No identification. And no fucking hope, apparently.

"Escort this woman from the building," she instructs the guard, turning back to her computer. I hate this fucking woman.

I know she's just doing her job. But I'm so fucking close and still a goddamn mile away.

My mind swims with a million thoughts.

Down the corridor, I can see Damien's office door is open.

Does that mean he's not in there? Or maybe he is, and he'll hear me.

If I start yelling, it would likely result in my being handcuffed, and this security guard is getting more antsy by the second.

Tears begin to sting my eyes, not knowing what else to do.

I don't even know Damien's number to try and call him. But there is one number I know.

As soon as the thought rushes into my mind, it pushes everything else out.

My breathing is ragged as I push back the tears that want to fall. I cough to clear the vise that is closing around my throat.

"Could I just use your phone? I lost mine, and I have no way to call anyone." My shoulders drop in defeat, and I know I look pathetic. "Please."

The tears come back. My chin quivers, and I feel fucking helpless.

The receptionist just stares back at me, her mouth set in a thin line, a crease between her eyes.

I don't look away, and I clasp my hands in front of me to try and stop myself from bolting toward Damien's open office door.

Just when I think she's going to tell the guard to take me—

"Make it quick."

She turns a black phone to me, and I pick up the receiver. My trembling fingers pause before I begin dialing the number.

It's a phone number every Ledger Companion has to memorize. A number I've never had to use before, and I work to compose myself.

Eve and I were at The Ledger when a girl called in a Code Red-One before. Several years ago. They brought her back on a stretcher. She was in a coma for a week.

I take a steadying breath.

It's the line of last resort.

The line we call when we need an emergency bailout. When something has gone very wrong. When we're in danger.

The line stops ringing. No one says anything. They aren't supposed to, but I know someone is listening, and I close my eyes tight.

"This is Companion 7446." I swallow hard. "Code Red-One. Location is 929 Wolfe Avenue. Penthouse."

The woman furrows her brow, but I hang up the phone and walk to the elevator.

One foot and then the next, I push my shoulders back and walk away.

The security guard's boots thump just behind me as he follows, his presence a looming wall of dread that sinks to the pit of my stomach like a stone.

As I step back into the elevator and turn, facing the city skyline, I send a prayer up to the universe.

To anything that could be listening.

Please.

Please fucking help me save this.

Chapter 35
Damien

"**I**s the trace still up on Adrian's phone?" I barely recognize my voice.

There is a pause, and I immediately know they lost him.

This day just keeps getting better and fucking better.

"He turned his phone off about an hour ago. Just after the ping came up near the Blackstone."

So, what? Where did they go from there?

My penthouse? Did she take him up to my fucking home? To let him fuck her everywhere I just did last night? This morning?

My blood is nearly boiling, and I can't stop my haggard breathing.

Marcus is still talking, his voice steady, rational—trying to keep me grounded, but there's no steadying me now.

"Damien, listen to me. Maybe it doesn't look like what you think."

I turn to him, my glare sharp, cutting. He knows as well

as I do—it's all right here. The pictures, the fucking video, the evidence staring me in the face.

I rake a hand through my hair, trying to shove down the rage clawing up my throat. My chest feels tight, my skin hot with the kind of fury I haven't tasted in a long, long time.

"You can see it with your own goddamn eyes, Marcus," I bite out. "She's been fucking him. Or working with him to fuck me over. Either way, this wasn't an accident."

Marcus exhales, rubbing his jaw, his expression unreadable. "Then call her."

I scoff. "What?"

"Ask her yourself." His voice is even, calculated. "Call her. Maybe there's another explanation."

I don't believe there's another explanation. What else could there be?

But I need to hear her say it. I need to hear her lie to me one last time before I tear her world apart.

My jaw tightens as I pull my phone from my pocket, my thumb hovering over her name.

I press dial and put the call on speakerphone.

The line rings once. Twice. Three times.

The longer it rings, the harder my pulse hammers in my chest. Every second she doesn't pick up, the deeper the knife twists.

She knows. She fucking knows, and she's a goddamn coward.

Just when I think the call is about to roll to voicemail— it's answered.

A sharp inhale, then—"Damien."

I go completely, violently still.

Every cell in my body freezes, and black forms around the edges of my vision.

Motherfucking Adrian Kingston answered her phone.

His breath is heavy, a little uneven, like he's been interrupted—like he's busy.

I look at the screen again, praying for a miracle that I accidentally dialed the wrong number.

But it's hers.

My blood runs cold. My fingers tighten around the phone. "Where is she?"

"Now's not a good time," he adds, exhaling what sounds too damn much like a groan.

A cold, slicing silence fills the room, and something in me fractures as I hear what's happening on the other end of the line.

The same fucking thing she and I did this morning. My insides are in knots, on the verge of implosion.

Adrian chuckles softly, low and knowing. "Oh—that's it, sweetheart. Right there."

A sound filters through the speaker. Soft. Wet. A muffled giggle.

The ground tilts beneath me.

I can't breathe.

I can't fucking see through the rage that explodes in my chest.

Adrian sighs, dragging out the sound, his voice slow, taunting. "She's talented, you know? Always had a way with her mouth."

My hands curl into fists, my pulse thundering in my ears.

"You're lying," I grind out, my voice deadly, trembling with fury.

"Am I?" There's a smirk in his tone, something viciously smug. "You want to deny it, baby?"

Another fucking choked giggle. She won't fucking answer because her mouth is stuffed with his cock. My stomach churns.

I hear Marcus inhale sharply beside me, but I can't even look at him. All I can hear is her.

My Elena.

No... not anymore. She never was.

Adrian lets out a low, satisfied sigh. "She's so fucking good at her job, isn't she?"

Something inside me breaks apart, shatters, and burns.

My jaw clenches so hard my teeth might crack. My chest is a live wire of fury, rage, and something deeper—something worse.

I grit out, slow and lethal, "I swear to God, you're going to fucking die for this."

Adrian just laughs. The sound is cruel, dripping with mockery.

"Careful, Wolfe," he muses, his voice light, entertained. "She's just doing what she does best. Entertaining powerful men. Wasn't that the whole arrangement you hired her for?"

The world tilts.

I feel like I might snap apart at the seams.

For half a second, I hesitate.

My grip tightens around the phone, my breath dragging in, ragged, uneven. There's a whisper of something beneath the fury—something hollow, aching, desperate to find a reason, any reason, to believe this isn't what it looks like.

But then Adrian laughs again, smug and victorious before he groans loudly, and that whisper dies.

I see red.

"Go to hell."

"Already there," he murmurs. "And your girl?" He chuckles. "Actually, she never stopped being my girl. She's on her knees right in front of me."

Everything explodes when he disconnects the call.

With a growl ripped straight from my soul, I pick up the crystal decanter of whiskey next to me and throw it across the room, shattering it on impact.

My breath is ragged, my vision blurred at the edges. My muscles coil so tightly I think I might combust, might punch through the walls, might tear this entire fucking building to the ground.

Marcus doesn't say a word.

Because there's nothing to say.

Elena is a fucking snake.

And Adrian?

I'm going to end him.

The room feels like it's collapsing inward, the weight of everything suffocating as the reality of this mess tightens around me like a noose.

I barely register the sound of my phone vibrating against the table until Marcus glances up from his laptop, his expression grim.

"Calloway."

Shit.

I swipe to answer, already bracing for impact. "Richard—"

"You arrogant son of a bitch!" His voice is a crack of thunder, livid, shaking with barely restrained fury. "What the hell have you done?"

Every muscle in my body tenses. "What are you talking about?"

"What am I talking about?" He barks out a harsh, humorless laugh. "You tell me, Wolfe! Because your entire goddamn deal just got leaked to the press. Every single fucking detail—the merger, the financials, the development plans, the legal filings. All of it."

My pulse slams into my ribs.

No.

That's not possible.

I push off the table, pacing now, my jaw locked so tight it aches. "That's impossible."

"Oh, is it?" Calloway bites out. "Then maybe you should check the New York Times, because that's exactly where it is. Front. Fucking. Page."

I whip my head toward Marcus, who's already moving, pulling up his phone, his face set in grim lines.

"Every goddamn executive board member is calling me," Calloway continues, his voice a lethal growl. "The press is salivating over this. Do you have any idea how catastrophic this is?"

I do.

I fucking do.

Confidentiality is the backbone of a merger this size. Any

breach—especially one this massive—would destroy everything.

This isn't just an inconvenience.

It's a fucking nuclear bomb.

I shove a hand through my hair, gripping the back of my neck. "We didn't authorize this. We have no leaks internally—"

Calloway scoffs, the sound biting through me like a blade. "No leaks?" His voice is pure disbelief. "Then tell me, how the fuck did the New York Times get a copy of the commissioner's email?"

The words slam into me, knocking the air from my lungs.

"What?"

"Oh, don't play dumb, Wolfe." His voice is laced with disgust. "The email, the soil surveys—the ones you conveniently didn't tell me about. The same ones that put half the development sites in question and could tank this entire fucking deal. You sat on that information. And now the entire world knows about it before I did."

Fuck.

My grip tightens, fingers digging into my scalp as I pace, my mind scrambling.

That email came in the night of the ballgame. Marcus and I were still working through the details. We hadn't told Calloway yet because we were handling it.

And now...

Someone leaked it.

And it makes me look exactly like the corrupt piece of shit Adrian painted me to be.

Calloway exhales sharply, his patience shredded. "You kept critical information from me, and now it's out in the open. What the fuck am I supposed to think?"

"This wasn't us," I grit out, barely keeping my temper in check. "We wouldn't leak our own deal."

Calloway scoffs again, the sound cutting. "That's exactly what a desperate man would do, wouldn't he? Someone trying to get ahead of a problem before it collapses under him."

Jesus Christ.

Adrian played this perfectly.

He knew about the soil surveys before Calloway did.

Because Elena knew.

Because she was right next to me when Marcus showed me the email. When I couldn't focus on anything except how close her body was to mine.

I thought she was working on a way to think ahead if the Calloways brought it up during the ballgame. She was actually thinking of how she and Adrian would use it to their fucking advantage.

The sharp sting in my chest intensifies.

That's how they're working this.

Elena was never just a pawn. She's the primary fucking weapon.

I grit my teeth, barely keeping my rage from spilling over. "This was an attack," I bite out. "Someone wants this merger dead."

"And I'm supposed to believe it wasn't you?" Calloway's voice is cold, laced with unshakable distrust. "Jesus, Damien. Adrian was right."

The words hit harder than they should.

Because hearing them makes it fucking real.

He believes Adrian over me.

Calloway lets out a slow, heavy breath, like he's already written me off. "You have until nine a.m. tomorrow," he says, his voice devoid of the warmth it once held. "To fix this. To find out who's behind it and prove you had nothing to do with it."

The line goes dead.

I stare at my phone, my pulse pounding, my fury boiling over into something lethal.

Marcus doesn't say anything—just turns his phone around, the New York Times article lighting up the screen.

I barely skim it.

I don't need to.

I already know what it says.

Merger of the Decade Collapses: Wolfe & Calloway's Deal on the Verge of Ruin Amidst Leaks and Scandal.

Everything I've built.

Everything I've worked for.

Everything I trusted in Elena.

All of it—fucking destroyed.

I lift my head, my vision red. "Find them."

Marcus doesn't hesitate. "Already on it."

I punch my phone too fucking hard. The security office at the Blackstone answers in a second.

"Mr. Wolfe."

"I have a security breach and need to lock down my penthouse. No one goes in." I bark it out and hear someone on the other end typing rapidly on a computer keyboard.

"The code has gone out, Mr. Wolfe."

"Good."

"Shall we secure your fiancée, Mr. Wolfe?"

What?

It's like a fucking ice bath has just been poured over my head.

She's at my fucking penthouse.

With Adrian.

I put my phone to my chest and lock eyes with Marcus. "They're at the fucking Blackstone," I grit out between clenched teeth, putting the phone back to my ear. "No, say nothing. Do nothing. I'm on my way."

I don't want the building security to alert them. I want their fucking heads on a platter and the satisfaction of pummeling Adrian Kingston's pathetic face with my own hands.

"Call me if anyone leaves."

My legs are already moving toward the conference room door as I end the call.

"You shouldn't drive like this, Damien," Marcus calls out after me, knowing damn well there is nothing that will stop me.

Chapter 36

Elena

As soon as I step back into Damien's penthouse, I move with a single-minded purpose.

I nearly jog to my bedroom, grabbing my iPad from the bathroom counter, my fingers flying across the screen as I pull up the Find My iPhone app.

My breath holds as I wait for the location to register.

"You've got to be fucking kidding me."

I laugh—a bitter, disbelieving sound that bubbles up from my chest.

Of course.

The blinking dot is at a location I know far too well.

Adrian's fucking brownstone.

The same goddamn brownstone he lived in when I was with him.

Spoiled little rich boy. Living in one of his family's many properties, still playing at being powerful when the only real thing he has is his family fortune.

My fingers tighten around the device as I hit the button to report the phone stolen.

It'll lock down immediately, preventing any access.

A sharp breath pushes through my lips as I lean against the counter, my mind racing.

I pray to fucking God Adrian hasn't been able to unlock it. He could wreak havoc by accessing The Ledger app, my contacts.

Damien.

My chest tightens, but I have a job to do. Shaking my head and focusing, I pull up my messages. My fingers move fast, typing out a quick text to Eve.

> ELENA: I'm okay.

I hesitate, then add:

> ELENA: Don't call. I'll explain soon.

She's going to hear about the Code Red-One.

Hell, everyone will.

When a companion calls for an extraction, it sets off alarms across the entire company. It's rare—almost unheard of—but when it happens, the protocol is ironclad.

The moment that code is called in, the entire Black Ledger network mobilizes.

The only priority? Get the companion out.

Eve will know I'm safe now, that I'll be out soon. But it doesn't stop the unease curling in my stomach.

I've likely only got minutes until The Ledger security

gets here, so I hastily throw a few key items in my carry bag. It's already half-packed with clothes I didn't wear at the Hamptons, and I don't waste time emptying it.

I toss my iPad on top and shove my purse inside.

Zipping it up, I set it near the elevator door.

My hands are shaking, and my mouth is like the desert.

A strand of thoughts, one after the other, races through my mind.

Once I'm back at The Ledger, we'll fix this.

Someone can help me with Adrian, and I can explain everything to Damien.

He'll understand.

He loves me. I know he does.

My shaking legs carry me to the kitchen. I grab a bottle of water from the refrigerator. My half-eaten cheesecake still takes up space on one of the shelves.

The memory of Damien, the piano, eating that cheese-cake—it makes my chest tighten.

Why the fuck didn't I just come clean about Adrian right away?

Unscrewing the cap, I gulp a third of the water, wincing when my lip burns like it's been split open again.

Touching two fingers to my mouth, I pull away, seeing blood again.

That fucking asshole. I hope Lucian beats his ass to a pulp when he hears Adrian assaulted me.

I blot my lip a few times, clearing the small leak of blood until I see no more, then place the cool water bottle against my hot, swelling lip.

The elevator doors slide open, and before I can even

process the sound, Damien storms through them like a force of nature. His fury crackles in the air, thick and suffocating, like the atmosphere before a lightning strike.

My stomach drops.

"Dam—" I barely have time to set the water bottle down before his voice slams into me, sharp and unforgiving.

"Where the fuck is he?"

I flinch. What?

"Damien—"

"Is he still here?" His voice is a growl, his steps heavy as he stalks toward me, his eyes like burning steel. "Did you think I wouldn't fucking find out? That I wouldn't put it all together?"

I stumble back, my pulse hammering in my ears. This isn't happening.

His chest is rising and falling fast, hands flexing at his sides, like he's trying to restrain himself, like he's barely keeping himself from putting his fist through the nearest wall.

"Damien, what are you talking about?" I breathe, my voice uneven, my mind racing.

His laugh is low, humorless. Dangerous.

"Don't fucking lie to me," he bites out, closing the distance between us in three slow, measured steps. His anger is controlled—too controlled. Like he's hanging on by a thread.

"I saw the pictures, Elena," he spits my name like it's poison. "I fucking heard you."

My breath catches. Oh my God.

No. No, no, no.

This isn't happening.

"You told me everything about these next two weeks would be a lie."

He sniffs, and even that is filled with resentment. "I guess that was the only truth that came out of your mouth this whole time."

I try to speak, try to force out something—anything—that will slow him down, make him listen. "Damien, please, just let me—"

"Explain?" he snaps. His eyes are dark, sharp. Unrelenting. "Explain what? That you've been playing me since the fucking beginning? That you and Adrian had this whole thing mapped out before I even set eyes on you?"

My panic spikes. This is all getting away from me.

He's spiraling, his rage blinding him, twisting everything until he can't see the truth.

I shake my head, my throat tightening. "That's not what happened—"

"Are you fucking proud of yourself?" His voice lowers to something almost guttural, something raw and aching beneath the rage. "Did you two laugh about it afterward? Did he fuck you in celebration after you signed the contract? Or did you wait to fuck him here in my goddamn home?"

His words cut through me, sharp and deep, making me physically recoil.

"Stop it." I'm surprised by the strength in my tone, despite the claws of my panic choking me. My vision blurring. "That's not—"

"Did you like hearing him taunt me when he answered my call?" he demands suddenly, and I freeze.

Oh God.

I don't dare look back because if I do, I know I'll shatter.

His voice is low and controlled when he finally speaks.

"Let them go."

The last thing I see is Damien.

His face—hard, unforgiving. His eyes—a storm.

Then he's gone.

The elevator descends without a sound.

I press my lips together, swallowing the sob that threatens to break free because I know—I just lost the first man I've fallen in love with.

Chapter 37

Damien

The whiskey burns its way down my throat—smooth and unforgiving. The glass is heavy in my grip, the amber liquid catching the dim glow of the penthouse.

I shouldn't be drinking.

Shouldn't be thinking about Elena.

But I am.

The way she looked at me before she left. The haunted look in her eyes. The sting of her slap.

Liar. Traitor. Whore.

I grit my teeth, my jaw tightening as I tip the glass back again, letting the alcohol drown out the fucking mess in my head. I should be thinking about the merger, about my next move.

But all I can think about is her.

The way she felt under my hands.

The way she tasted.

The way she looked at me like I was the only man who could touch her. Like she trusted me. Wanted me.

God, it felt so fucking real.

And now she's gone.

A muscle ticks in my jaw as I grip the edge of the counter, my knuckles going white. She played me. I should have known better. This is exactly why I don't do relationships.

Why the list of people I trust has about three names on it.

For the second time today, the penthouse doors explode open, slamming against the walls hard enough to rattle the fucking chandelier.

The hit comes fast and brutal.

Lucian's fist connects, snapping my head to the side— the sharp crack of bone against bone ringing in my ears.

I barely feel it. Because I want this fight.

I want somewhere to put the fucking pain.

I slam into him, grappling, my fist driving into his ribs. Lucian grunts, but he doesn't slow down. He catches my collar, twisting as he shoves me back.

My spine hits the wall with a thud, drywall cracking beneath the force.

Lucian's hand fists my shirt, his eyes dark. Livid.

"What the fuck did you do to my employee?" he snarls, his voice low and deadly.

I snarl right back.

"Your employee?" I shove against him, dislodging his grip, throwing him back just enough to swing again. My fist catches his jaw, but he barely flinches.

"She's a fucking liar. A traitor. A gold-digging slut who played us all."

Lucian's fist collides with my ribs, stealing my breath.

"Watch your fucking mouth about her."

He swings again.

I meet him halfway.

Fists fly.

Glass shatters.

The rage is animalistic, raw, spiraling out of control—neither of us backing down.

The elevator doors slide open, and I hear the familiar voice of my friend ring out across the chaos.

"Jesus Christ—break it up!" Marcus growls, James right behind him.

Arms pull at me, wrenching me backward as Lucian is hauled away.

We're both breathing hard. Seething.

James holds a hand to Lucian's chest, keeping him at bay. "Did you fucking hit her?" Lucian spits out, rage in his eyes.

Marcus has me pinned against the wall, his forearm pressed against my throat, fisting my torn shirt.

"Fuck you, Lucian." I spit back at the same time before I answer his stupid fucking accusation. "I would never."

Lucian wipes blood from his mouth, spits onto my floor like he doesn't give a shit. "Yeah, that's not what my guys said it looked like."

We are two seconds from tearing each other apart again.

"Are you fucking working with them too?" My voice is hoarse, my chest heaving as I push against Marcus. My vision tunnels in on Lucian, still fucking furious. "You, Elena, and Adrian?"

Lucian stills.

Then he laughs.

A low, dark, menacing sound that slides under my skin like a blade.

"You stupid fucking asshole." He shakes his head, spitting more blood onto the floor. "You mean the guy who set her up to be gang-raped when she was eighteen?"

Silence explodes across the room, and I swear to God the entire building shifts.

Marcus and James both go rigid.

Something inside me goes cold, freezing me in place.

Lucian's eyes are full of disgust. Fury still vibrates through his frame, but it's colder now. Controlled.

He takes a step forward, his voice dropping into something even more lethal.

"The only involvement I want with that prick is to watch the light leave his eyes when I fucking strangle him to death."

His words sink deep, settling in a place that makes my stomach twist, my pulse hammer.

"What the fuck happened with my contract, Wolfe?"

"Damien," Marcus cuts in. "We were wrong, Damien." His hold on me tightens. His voice breaks, raw with conviction.

"We were so fucking wrong."

The tension in the room doesn't break. It doesn't dissipate.

It tightens, winding like a noose, constricting everything in its grip.

Marcus still has me pinned against the wall, his grip unrelenting, his forearm pressing into my chest.

He's breathing hard, his jaw clenched so tight it looks like his teeth might crack.

I stare at my old friend like the explanation will be right there in his eyes.

Lucian hasn't moved either. His fists remain at his sides, still coiled, still ready—like a predator calculating its next strike.

James lingers just in front of Lucian. His posture rigid, his normally cool composure shattered. His eyes burn with something dangerously close to fury—at me.

Their stares weigh down on me like lead, suffocating in a way the fight wasn't.

The adrenaline is still there, thrumming beneath my skin.

But it no longer has an outlet.

Lucian exhales sharply, dragging a hand through his already-mussed hair, like even he's barely keeping himself in check.

His voice is rough when he finally speaks.

"Sit the fuck down."

He doesn't wait for compliance, pulling a barstool out harshly—like I'm nothing more than an irritation.

I don't move at first.

Because I can't.

My muscles are still locked, my breath coming sharp and

uneven, my mind trying to make sense of the last five minutes.

Marcus stays close by, still not trusting that I won't launch myself at Lucian. James walks over broken glass back to the elevator and picks up Marcus's laptop bag from the floor.

Lucian pours four glasses of whiskey, setting them down with deliberate force, the crystal ringing against the marble counter.

He slides one toward me.

Lucian throws his liquor back in one go and rolls his shoulders. Dragging in a slow, measured breath, he keeps his steely eyes firm on me as he speaks.

"She was an orphan."

"I know that." I interject.

"Shut the fuck up and listen, Wolfe."

Lucian bites back, pouring another whiskey and pushing mine closer to me.

I finally gulp it down and slam the crystal glass onto the counter.

"Elena St. James." He pauses. "Not her real name. But they didn't know who she was. All the unidentified kids are named after the orphanage. The only name she had to claim when she left its walls behind."

It suddenly strikes me why she knew so much about the orphanage. Claiming she volunteered there. Margo's contributions.

Because that was fucking real.

Lucian keeps going, oblivious to the revelation hitting me like a freight train.

"She lived there until she had to leave on her eighteenth birthday. Got a job at a strip club, living with a few of the other girls. She met Adrian there. He was her first real relationship. A connection she thought was something solid. Something secure."

I already fucking hate this.

That video of the two of them on the beach—she couldn't have been any older than eighteen, nineteen. Already having to fucking survive by herself, and she crosses paths with a snake.

"Adrian made a deal with some guys who were a bigger deal than he anticipated. They wanted Elena as part of it. He thought he could outsmart them. He fucked up, and they came to collect."

Lucian pauses, the weight of the next part already bearing down upon the room.

"Five of them."

Jesus.

"She never even fucking knew. Just walked into that club one night, expecting the usual—a VIP dance—and suddenly, her whole world was gone."

Lucian's voice is calm. Too calm.

But beneath it, there's something sharp. Something lethal.

"She told me Adrian found her bleeding on the bathroom floor of the club. Told her to clean up. She smelled like a whore."

I flinch at this part.

My own voice—calling her the same fucking thing— slams into my chest, stealing the air from my lungs.

I have to brace myself against the counter.

"She went to the hospital. Filed a police report. But what did that matter? The men who took her had connections. She had nothing. No one. A stripper reporting a sex crime? Who the fuck would care? So she did the only thing she could."

Lucian leans forward, bracing his hands on the counter—a mirror of my stance.

"She changed her name. Started over. Some old guy gave her a job at a bakery. She put herself through school." His gaze flickers up, locking onto mine with something that burns. "Eventually, she joined The Ledger."

A bitter taste crawls up the back of my throat.

Every breath feels too shallow. Too fucking insufficient.

Five.

Something tightens in my chest, and I rub my sternum, trying to stop the images my imagination is conjuring up.

Elena fighting for her life. Those men—taking her. Breaking her.

Her body—broken and bleeding on a floor. Makeup streaming down her face.

She probably couldn't call out for help. Her voice too hoarse.

Then that fucking waste of life—Adrian. Finding her. Leaving her.

I grit my teeth so hard I think I'll hear them crack.

"I'll fucking kill them."

I don't even realize I said it out loud until Lucian's lips curl into a slow, dark smile.

A predator's smile.

The kind that means the killing's already been done.

"You're a few years too late for that, buddy."

His voice is calm. Almost indifferent.

But the look in his eyes is anything but.

Lucian found them. All of them.

Tracked them down one by one. Stacked their bodies in the middle of that club where they took everything from her.

Tied the owner to a chair and doused the whole fucking place in gasoline.

Then listened to him scream as he threw a match and watched it burn.

Walked out. Never looked back.

His voice remains steady, void of regret. "I wanted to kill Adrian next."

He exhales slowly, fingers tapping once against the counter.

"But Elena begged me not to."

The words knock the wind out of me.

Lucian wanted Adrian dead. So do I. So would any man with a shred of fucking decency.

But Elena stopped him.

Lucian doesn't stop for anyone.

He can see the question brewing in my mind. Why?

"Said it would come back on her." His jaw flexes. "His family had money. She just wanted to move on."

The bitter taste in my mouth worsens.

She was eighteen when it happened. Barely out of that orphanage. Barely had a chance to build anything for herself before it was ripped away.

And I was fucking blind. Selfish.

I picture the way she looked at me this afternoon—the betrayal in her eyes. The way her voice cracked when she tried to defend herself.

I called her a liar. A manipulator. A whore.

I threw her out.

The world tilts again as Lucian keeps talking.

"You need to know, Wolfe—Elena called me the second Adrian approached her," he says, his voice quieter now. "That's protocol. That's what she's supposed to do."

Lucian drags a hand down his face, looking wrecked in a way I've never seen before.

Because this was personal.

Because Elena isn't just some contract to him.

She's one of his girls.

She's his responsibility.

"So if you want to be pissed at someone, Wolfe," he says finally, meeting my gaze, "you can hate me. I already hate myself because I wasn't there when she needed me."

His words land like a punch to the gut.

Lucian isn't making excuses. He's not dodging blame. He's owning it.

Because he wasn't there.

And I?

I was.

I was right fucking there. And I failed her too.

"Another Ledger girl was taken by her contract. I had to find her before it was too late. I—" Lucian swallows hard. "I should have called someone else in to help Elena. I shouldn't have fucking waited until she felt like she was in danger. She called in for us to bail her out of here because it wasn't safe anymore."

The breath in my chest stills.

"Why didn't she come to me if she wasn't safe? I would have fucking done anything to protect her."

"She did."

Marcus finally speaks, and my head snaps to him.

"What?"

"She did come to you."

He blinks slowly, looking exhausted.

"Your security threw her out of the fucking building," James adds.

He's fuming at the entire situation.

I finally sit down on the barstool.

My mind is rushing with a million thoughts, but it's like I can't hear a single one.

"It's why we came over here."

Marcus opens his laptop bag, pulling out his computer. "Watch. Everything."

The series of events guts me.

Elena leaves the cafe, fire in her eyes.

Adrian follows her, and I watch her call someone.

"She called the car service to bring her to the office," Marcus fills in, his tone grim. It's clear he's looked into every minute of what happened—just like I asked him to do.

Adrian chases her, and we all tense when he slams her into the wall by her hair.

Her phone clatters across the sidewalk, away from her, and I feel like I'm going to vomit.

She fights back.

When he slaps her, my entire world turns red.

"I'm going to kill that fucking asshole," Lucian grits out, and I agree with the sentiment.

Elena knees him, runs away—and I stare at her phone, still on the sidewalk.

I know what happens before I watch it.

The pit in my stomach plummets deeper.

Adrian picks it up and chases after her again.

Marcus clicks another video. The Blackstone valet.

The driver greets her, notices Adrian, and helps her into the car before pulling away.

That smug fucking bastard watches as the car drives right past him.

Another video is opened. Wolfe Industries lobby.

Elena nearly runs inside. The seventieth-floor reception.

The guard calls her over, and the shattered look of defeat on her beautiful face when she is handed the phone—

"She called in a Code Red-One," Lucian adds, his voice quieter now. "Gave your penthouse address. That's a companion's last resort. It means they're in danger and need an immediate extract."

Everything clicks into place.

And I want to throw myself off this building.

She never betrayed me.

She was trying to protect me.

"What was in the envelope she gave to Adrian?"

Lucian snorts an angry laugh through his nose. "That asshole sent her pictures of her rape from the strip club. He was going to blackmail her when she refused to help him."

My throat closes, and black dots form on the edges of my vision.

My own words, screamed at her earlier, haunt me.

I saw the pictures, Elena.

"I'm going to be sick."

I can't sit here anymore.

The stool scrapes across the floor as I stand up—too fast.

The air in the penthouse feels thick. Suffocating.

I press my fingers against my temples, trying to fight off the nausea rolling through me.

But it's there—deep and gnawing.

In my mind, I replay every second with her this afternoon.

What I said to her.

Each word slicing into her.

The look in her eyes.

Fuck.

That might be the worst part.

I was too angry to see it then, but replaying it now, I see the fresh cut on her lip.

Her red cheek.

The way she grimaced when I grabbed her.

It wasn't guilt.

It was fear.

It was pain.

Because Adrian had already bruised that same fucking wrist—

Then I did too.

He treated her like a whore.

And I called her one.

My grip tightens around the edge of the counter, my knuckles going white.

I failed her.

Lucian failed her.

This whole fucking world has done nothing but fail her.

And for the first time, I understand.

Why she keeps people at a distance.

Why she doesn't ask for help.

Why she built herself into a woman who doesn't need saving.

Because the only person who hasn't let her down—is herself.

My voice is hoarse when I finally speak.

"Where is she?"

Lucian exhales sharply, dragging a hand through his hair.

The rage simmering beneath his skin has lessened, but it's still there.

Still directed at me.

"I don't know." His voice is clipped. "Her best friend knows but isn't talking."

He levels me with a look that fucking burns.

"She needs time, Wolfe."

He reaches into his pocket and tosses something onto the counter.

"And you'll fucking give it to her."

The small metal-and-diamond ring pings as it bounces —like it's nothing more than a trinket.

Lucian doesn't even glance at it.

Then he's gone.

The silence claws at me.

I close my eyes as reality crashes over me like a freight train.

She's cutting ties with me.

And she doesn't even want to be near me to do it.

And why the fuck would she?

I was a monster to her.

My throat tightens, something raw and unfamiliar lodging in my chest.

I don't realize I'm still staring at the ring until James speaks, his voice bitter.

"Anyone could look at her and see she fell in love with you."

A muscle in my jaw twitches.

James scoffs. "And you fell in love with her too."

The words gut me.

Because they're true.

I fell.

I fell so fucking hard.

She did too.

And I ripped her apart.

"You fell in love with her and then thought the worst of her."

James shakes his head, his disappointment cutting deeper than any of Lucian's fists.

He turns toward the door, Marcus following.

Neither of them say another word as they leave me alone.

They don't need to.

Because James is fucking right.

I sink onto the barstool, staring at the ring like it holds all the answers.

My chest feels like it's caving in.

Like I'm the one suffocating now.

Because I was so fucking wrong.

And now—

I have no clue how to fix it.

Chapter 38

Damien

The conference room on the seventieth floor is silent.

The kind of silence that crackles with the weight of what's coming.

Marcus sits next to me, his arms crossed, his expression unreadable. He hasn't said a word in the last five minutes—just watching me. Waiting.

He knows I'm barely keeping it together.

I know it too.

I scrub a hand down my face, feeling the sting of the split in my lip where Lucian's fist connected last night. The bruises on my cheek and ribs throb in dull, steady pulses, but they're nothing compared to the wreckage inside me.

I look like shit.

I feel worse.

Not because of Lucian. Not because of the fucking merger hanging in the balance.

Because of her.

Because I didn't protect her.

Because I wasn't there when she needed me.

Because I threw her to the fucking wolves when she was already bleeding.

I close my eyes for a second, trying to shake the image from my mind.

I glance at the clock. 8:59 a.m.

Calloway will be here any second, and I need to focus.

Adrian leaked the merger details. I just don't know how the fuck he got them.

I can't accuse him without proof.

I can't lose my temper.

I need to be in control.

My lawyers filter into the room, their presence a steady reminder that this isn't just personal—it's business.

A business I built.

A business I refuse to let that pissant motherfucker take from me.

The door swings open, and at 9:00 a.m. on the dot, Richard Calloway walks in, his presence sucking the air from the room.

He's flanked by his own legal team.

And by Adrian.

I don't take my eyes off him.

Not as he strolls in like he owns the place.

Not as he pulls out his chair, settling into it with an arrogance that makes my fingers twitch with the need to wrap around his fucking throat.

Not as I catch the fresh claw marks down his cheek—courtesy of Elena.

A flicker of satisfaction coils in my gut.

But it's not good enough.

The sting of that mark is nowhere near enough to pay the blood debt he owes.

Adrian Kingston doesn't realize it yet, but he's not going to make it out of this alive.

Still, he's smug.

Smug because he thinks he's won.

And maybe he has.

Because while he sits there grinning, Elena is gone.

And I have no one to blame but myself.

Calloway doesn't waste time.

He plants his hands on the table, his glare locked onto me like I personally set his goddamn house on fire.

"So, what the fuck happened?"

Before I can take a breath to answer, the conference room doors burst open.

It sounds like a cannon firing as Elena strides into the room, sucking the air from my lungs with each step.

Heels clicking on the polished floor, she holds a folder in the crook of her arm, her hazel eyes lit on fire and locked on Calloway.

Behind her, several security guards sprint toward the conference room, followed by the new receptionist who replaced Vanessa.

I hold out my hand, standing. They stop.

She doesn't even glance at me.

Doesn't spare me a single fucking look.

Her cheek is bruised, and I see the cut on her lip concealed partially with red lipstick.

My fingers twitch, aching to reach out and caress her. To pull her into my arms.

To get her far the fuck away from Adrian.

I inhale sharply.

"Elena—"

It's barely a whisper. More like a plea.

But she ignores it.

Because she doesn't need me to save her.

She's here to burn down the man who hurt her, and she's not going to let anyone—even me—get in the way of that.

Her focus is locked on Richard Calloway, her chin high, her expression calm and lethal all at once.

"Before you throw away billions," she says, her voice smooth and even but razor-sharp, "I thought you'd like to know what your nephew's been up to."

A suffocating silence swallows the room.

Every eye snaps to Adrian.

His entire body stiffens.

But he tries to mask it, his smug mask slipping for just a second before he forces it back into place.

The moment Calloway picks up the documents, his expression hardens into something lethal.

His grip tightens, fingers curling around the edges of the pages as his sharp gaze scans the damning evidence.

"What the hell is this?"

His voice is low, edged with fury.

Adrian shifts beside him, stiffening.

A brief flicker of panic crosses his face before he schools

it into something more neutral, feigning confusion like the snake he is.

Elena doesn't give him a chance to speak.

She flips open the folder, spreading a mess of incriminating financial records across the polished surface of the table.

"I had the misfortune of knowing Adrian years ago."

Her voice is smooth, measured, but underneath it, I hear the venom.

"Back then, he was running a scheme—skimming money off the top of deals. Looks like he never stopped."

Calloway's jaw tightens.

His brows furrow as he flips through the evidence, his breathing sharp, shoulders tensing with each new page.

Elena tilts her head, watching him absorb the information like she already knows exactly what he'll find.

"Only difference is, now he's using your company's assets to do it on a much larger scale."

Adrian shoots up from his seat, his face flushing red with anger.

"Where the hell did you get this?"

His voice is wild, unhinged, defensive.

"She's lying—this is bullshit!"

Elena finally turns to him.

Smiling.

A slow, razor-sharp smirk that's nothing but a death sentence in silk.

"I tracked my phone you stole to the same brownstone you lived at all those years ago."

She shakes her head like she can't believe how fucking stupid he is.

"Same hide-a-key. Same password. Same arrogance."

She leans forward, her voice mocking, dripping with amusement.

"You always thought you were the smartest guy in the room. Turns out, you're just the easiest to rob."

Then she tilts her head slightly, like she's just remembered something interesting.

"Though, I was a bit surprised to see Vanessa in your bed."

A slow-moving ice storm creeps through my veins.

Marcus's head snaps to me at the exact same time my entire body goes numb.

"Yeah, she was really surprised to see me too."

Elena's voice is light, almost conversational, but there is venom laced beneath it.

"She must have broken—what—a dozen or more NDA agreements feeding you Wolfe Industry secrets. I don't think she's going to be backing up your defense anytime soon."

It wasn't just Vanessa feeding Adrian information.

It was her on the phone yesterday.

The woman in the background.

The one I thought was Elena.

The one I thought was sucking Adrian's cock while he taunted me.

A slow, acidic wave of realization churns in my stomach.

I was wrong.

So fucking wrong.

My throat tightens, pure fucking revulsion climbing up my spine like a disease.

Adrian's fury morphs into something animalistic, his hands curling into fists as he lunges forward, ready to spit his denials—

But Elena moves first.

She reaches into her purse and pulls out a USB drive.

Before he can open his filthy fucking mouth, she tosses it onto the table, her voice calm. Steady.

"Before you say anything too incriminating . . ."

Adrian stills.

The color drains from his face.

He's terrified.

Of what she has on him.

Of what she could throw at him next.

Elena straightens, turning to Calloway—and her next words hit the entire room like a wrecking ball.

"I'm pressing charges against your nephew for assaulting me yesterday in broad daylight. It's all there if you want to see a hint of the vile relative you have."

Calloway sucks in a sharp breath, his skin going white as a fucking sheet as he takes the USB in his hands.

"The police will be here any moment."

"Adrian." Calloway gasps, his eyes wide in disbelief. "Is that true?"

"How could you ask me that?" Adrian tries to defend himself but it's like sinking in quicksand. The more he moves, talks, the faster he goes down. "How do you think she could even get all this in what–an hour today? Two tops?"

"My phone is still in his pocket." Elena says cooly, keeping her gaze fixed on Calloway. "I've been tracking it."

Calloway looks at Adrian expectantly. Adrian just scoffs.

"Empty your pockets." Calloway stands and I'm seconds away from jumping over that table and handling him myself.

"Uncle–"

"Do it!" Calloways voice booms just as the conference room doors slam open again.

Uniformed officers flood the space, their boots echoing against the floor, handcuffs clinking in the heavy silence.

"Adrian Kingston, you're charged with assault and are being placed under arrest."

Adrian's panic is instant.

His gaze whips to his uncle, eyes wide. Pleading.

"Uncle—wait, you're not seriously gonna let them—"

The officers close in, restraining him, pulling his arms behind his back.

He thrashes. Curses. Struggles.

Trying to shake them off, but he's got no fucking way out.

Calloway doesn't even look at him.

His voice is cold. Final.

"Take him."

Adrian erupts.

Screaming. Thrashing. Cursing Elena. Cursing me.

Wolfe security rushes in.

The new receptionist demands answers, but she's drowned out by Adrian's frantic shouts.

And through all of it, Elena turns on her heel and walks away.

Her chin is lifted.

Her shoulders squared.

She doesn't falter.

She doesn't fucking look back.

She never looked at me once, and I feel like I'm fucking drowning.

Freezing and stranded, living on the dark side of the moon without her light to give me warmth.

"Elena!"

I shove forward, pushing against the throng of attorneys, security guards, police officers. Employees are gathered, trying to look in and see what the commotion is.

I can't see through the chaos, but I catch a glimpse of her just as she reaches the elevator.

She presses the button, and the doors open immediately.

"Elena, wait!"

She turns.

Her body facing forward, expression unreadable.

And the doors close.

Marcus's grip clamps down on my arm, holding me back.

"Wolfe."

Rage explodes through me.

"What the fuck are you doing?"

I snarl, shoving at him.

Marcus is stone-faced. Calm.

Too fucking calm for what just happened.

"Now is not the time, Damien."

His voice is firm.

A warning.

I don't get the chance to respond because Adrian fucking loses it.

The officers slam him down on the conference table.

The sound echoes around the room.

They zip-tie his wrists and ankles, his screams turning into wild, incoherent threats.

His pockets are emptied and Calloway looks at the small bag of white powder until two cell phones thud onto the table.

One of them lights up. The picture on the lockscreen nearly does me under.

It was on the helicopter. Me at the controls. The sunrise peeking over the horizon.

Four of them lift him up together, carrying him straight through the doors.

His body thrashes like a rabid animal.

His voice echoes off the walls—

"FUCK YOU! FUCK ALL OF YOU! SHE'S A FUCKING WHORE!"

I pull my phone from my pocket.

Press the name.

Put it to my ear and wait for the answer.

"It's Lucian."

"Adrian just got picked up for assault."

There's a pause.

"I'll make it slow."

The call ends and regret hits me like a freight train.

For the first time in years, I don't know what to do.

Behind me, the room settles, the chaos dissipating into a tense, weighted silence.

Calloway leans forward and picks up Elena's phone from the pile of Adrian's discarded belongings. His expression dark and unreadable.

Marcus exhales sharply, rubbing his temple. Then he moves toward our attorneys, speaking in low, controlled tones.

They're likely strategizing a press conference—

Figuring out how to minimize the fallout.

How to contain the damage of an arrest inside Wolfe Industries.

But I don't give a single fuck about any of it.

Not the merger.

Not the media.

Not the fucking empire I built.

Because all I can think about is Elena walking away.

Not even looking at me.

My pulse thunders, my chest tightening with something unbearable.

A long, excruciating beat passes before Calloway stands and joins me by the widows.

His voice is cool. Calculated.

Laced with disappointment. "She saved your ass, Wolfe."

I swallow hard, my jaw locking.

I know it.

Marcus knows it.

Everyone in this fucking room knows it.

Elena walked in here today and handed me my salvation—

After I kicked her out of my life just yesterday.

She could have just pressed her charges against Adrian, but she wanted to destroy him.

Make sure his family knew what a piece of shit he was. That it was him tanking the deal. Leaking the merger information to the press.

Calloway flips her phone over in his hand, his movements deliberate.

His sharp gaze lifts, pinning me in place.

And his next words land like a goddamn hammer to my ribs.

"She wasn't wearing her engagement ring."

My stomach plummets.

I slide my hand into my pocket.

My fingers toying with the ring there.

The diamond I slipped on her finger to sell a lie—

Somehow, it became real.

It became a dream I wanted.

And now it's become a fucking nightmare.

I don't say a word.

Because there's nothing to say.

The weight of my own failure presses down on me like a collapsing building.

I don't have to see my own reflection to know I look defeated.

Because I am.

Calloway exhales slowly, handing her phone over to me, before he says the only thing that matters.

"Now . . . what the hell are you gonna do to fix it?"

I don't fucking know.

Chapter 39

Elena

Three days of hell.

That's how long it's been since I walked out of Wolfe Industries.

Since I left Damien standing there, not even looking back.

Since I shattered into a million pieces and convinced myself I could just sweep them up and move on.

Three days of forcing myself to keep going.

Three days of crying myself to sleep, hating myself for still missing him.

For still loving him.

But today is the end of it.

This morning, I told Lucian I was done—done with The Ledger, done with Damien, done with all of it.

He didn't argue, just told me my bonus was still being paid in full.

A part of me wanted to tell him to take that ten million

dollars and shove it straight up Damien's perfect, arrogant ass.

But I didn't. Because I need it.

I need it to start over. To finally build the life I've worked so goddamn hard for.

So I do what I have to do.

I step out of my apartment and into one of The Ledger's town cars, watching the city blur past the window as I brace myself for one last visit to Lucian's office—one final step to officially close this chapter of my life.

The driver, Felix, an older man I've known for years, glances at me in the mirror, offering a familiar grin.

"We're gonna miss you, Elena," he says as he pulls into traffic. "Not many can say they left The Ledger on their own terms."

I force a small smile, staring out at the streets passing by.

"Yeah... I'll miss you too. But I'm looking forward to what's next."

At least, that's what I tell myself.

Eve texts me the entire way, and I'm glad for it. She takes my mind off things, makes me smile, makes the car ride pass in a blur.

The drive is smooth, with no traffic. But when we slow down, something feels off.

I glance up—expecting to see the sleek, dark building that houses The Ledger's headquarters.

Instead, my heart plummets, because we're stopped in front of my bakery.

The one I lost.

I can't breathe.

My dream is sitting right in front of me, and I have no idea why we're here.

My fingers tighten around the door handle.

"What is this?" My voice is barely a whisper.

The driver shifts in his seat, looking at me through the mirror. "Lucian says to just hear him out."

Fucking Lucian. I'm going to kill him.

My stomach twists.

I don't want to go inside.

I can't go inside.

But something in me won't let me walk away either.

I take a slow breath, my heart pounding, and before I can talk myself out of it, I push the door open and step out.

The bell above the door chimes as I step inside.

And I freeze.

The scent of fresh flowers—roses, peonies, lilies, every kind imaginable—hits me all at once, overwhelming and intoxicating.

The entire front of the shop is covered in bouquets, towering arrangements, and delicate clusters of wildflowers spilling across the counters, the display cases, the small seating area I once imagined filling with customers.

It's ridiculous.

Over-the-top.

So goddamn Damien.

My throat tightens, emotions slamming into me all at once—shock, confusion, anger. But underneath it all, there's a sliver of something dangerous.

Something stupidly hopeful.

In the center of it all is Damien Wolfe.

Tall. Immaculate. Beautiful in that dark, devastating way that should be illegal.

He stands in the middle of the space, looking every bit the man I spent the last two weeks falling for—but there's something different in his eyes.

A rawness. A desperation.

Like a man standing on the edge of a cliff, ready to jump if I tell him to.

I swallow hard, forcing my voice to be steady, cold.

"What the hell are you doing here?"

Damien doesn't move.

For a long second, he just looks at me—really looks at me, like he's committing every detail to memory.

"I needed to see you." His voice is hoarse, like it's been dragged over broken glass.

I exhale sharply, shaking my head.

"You don't get to do this, Damien." I gesture around at the ridiculous display of flowers. "You don't get to show up with grand gestures and expect everything to just—" I choke on the word, my chest tightening. "—fix itself."

"I know." His voice is quiet. Earnest.

But I don't want to hear it.

I don't want him to apologize, because that means I have to relive it.

The anger. The betrayal. The way he looked at me like I was nothing—like I was exactly what the world had always tried to reduce me to.

I turn toward the door, ready to leave.

"Wait." His voice catches, and something in it makes me stop. "Just five minutes."

I squeeze my eyes shut, my nails biting into my palms.

I shouldn't. I really, really shouldn't.

But the second I stopped heading toward the door, I knew I would stay if he asked me to.

When I turn around, his expression guts me.

Like a man who has already lost but still has one last prayer left to whisper.

"Five minutes," I say, my voice flat. "And then I walk."

His chest rises and falls, and he nods once.

"Okay, thank you."

Damien exhales, running a hand through his hair. For a man who is always so perfectly composed, he looks wrecked.

"Elena," he starts, voice low, rough, like he's been choking on this for days. "I was wrong. About everything."

I lift my chin, crossing my arms over my chest, bracing myself for whatever version of the truth he's about to feed me.

"You didn't just call me a liar, Damien." My voice is steady, but my hands are shaking as I hold myself. "You threw me out. You humiliated me. You—" I exhale sharply, shaking my head. "You didn't even listen."

That last part comes out as a whisper, my sorrow threatening to choke me.

"I know." He steps forward—just the slightest movement, like he wants to reach for me—but I take a step back, my body going rigid before I can stop it.

It's instinct. Reflex.

But the second I do it, something flickers across his face.

Something that guts him like I just drove a knife straight through his ribs.

He swallows hard, his hands sliding into his pockets, like he's physically stopping himself from touching me. From closing the distance between us.

"I know," he says again, his voice quieter now, like the weight of it is crushing him. "And I hate myself for it."

I shake my head. Firm. Resolute. Even though inside? I'm seconds from shattering.

"I don't need your self-loathing, Damien," I whisper.

"Then what do you need?" His voice breaks, his chest rising and falling unsteadily. "Tell me how to fix this. Tell me how to—"

"You can't." The words slice through the air like a blade. Final. Absolute.

His jaw locks, like he was bracing for it, but it still hits him hard.

"Don't say that."

I can't do this.

I can't stand here and listen to him apologize, watch him look at me like he's drowning and I'm the only thing that can save him.

I need to breathe. I need to get out of this moment before it pulls me under.

So I shift, forcing my focus away from him. Away from the desperate, haunted look in his eyes.

Instead, I gesture around us, my voice sharp.

"Why here, Damien?" I demand. "Why bring me to the one place I lost? The one thing that was taken from me?"

Something changes in his face.

A flicker of something else. Determination. Resolve.

"Because it's yours, Elena."

My breath catches.

"No." I shake my head slowly, not daring to believe what he's saying. "It's not. Someone else bought it."

His gaze holds mine, steady and unyielding.

"No, baby. It's yours."

A sharp exhale pushes through my lips.

"How?" My voice is barely above a whisper.

Damien steps closer, his hands still in his pockets, like he's terrified of making another wrong move.

"Because the second I found out someone took it from you, I bought it back." His throat works around the words, his voice heavy. Careful. "And now I'm giving it to you."

My knees almost give out.

I shake my head again, disbelief crashing into me like a tidal wave.

"Why?" The question tears from my throat, raw and vulnerable before I can stop it. "Why would you do this?"

His gaze burns into me, his answer immediate.

"Because I love you."

My heart fucking stops.

The words hang between us, suspended in the charged air, crashing over me with the force of a goddamn storm.

I can't move. I can't breathe.

My heart slams painfully against my ribs, my mind fighting against the truth he just laid bare.

Because if I let myself believe it...

If I let myself feel it...

It'll destroy what little is left of me.

"Don't," I whisper, my voice barely holding steady. "Don't say that."

His throat works, his jaw clenching like the words are tearing him apart on the way out.

"It's the truth, Elena." His voice is gravel and desperation, thick with emotion. "And I should've said it sooner."

I shake my head, teetering on the edge, my fingers curling into fists at my sides.

"You called me a liar." My voice is soft, but the words cut. "You called me a whore."

His face contorts with agony, like each syllable is a fresh wound opening inside him.

"I know," he says, hoarse, wrecked. "I fucking know, Elena. I didn't believe in you." His confession is quiet, haunted. "I didn't protect you. I didn't listen." He swallows hard, shaking his head. "And the worst of it?"

A ragged breath shudders from his lungs.

"I abandoned you."

My whole body goes rigid.

He steps forward—slowly, cautiously—watching me like I might shatter at any second.

"You asked me to listen, and I didn't." His voice is low, thick with regret. "You begged me to hear you, and I turned my back on you." He drags a shaking hand down his face, like he hasn't slept since that day. "I left you, Elena. I let you down. I did exactly what the rest of the world has done to you your whole fucking life."

A sharp inhale rips through me, my control cracking,

splintering, and I hate him for knowing that. For seeing me so clearly.

For breaking past every wall I've tried to hold in place.

"I am so fucking sorry." His voice catches, and my eyes finally snap open, my breath locking in my throat. "And I love you, Elena."

He's wrecked.

His strong frame, usually so unyielding, looks like it's barely holding together. Like he's barely keeping himself from falling apart completely.

I swallow hard, my heart pounding.

"And if I have to spend the rest of my life proving it to you, I fucking will."

The air feels too thick, too heavy, pressing in on me from all sides.

I need to get out of here.

I need to breathe.

"Just take the bakery, Elena." His voice is gentle, but there's a raw urgency beneath it. "It's yours. No strings. No expectations."

My stomach clenches, a lump forming in my throat.

"You never have to see me again," he continues, forcing the words out like they're physically hurting him. "I'll walk out that door, and if that's what you want—if that's what you need—I won't come back."

My breath catches, my fingers trembling at my sides.

"But if you give me one more chance," he says, his voice aching, pleading, "if you let me prove to you that I will never leave you again—I swear to God, Elena, I will fight for you."

A sob lodges in my throat, my vision blurring.

"I will be there, every single day. Every moment. I will believe in you. I will stand beside you. I will be everything you need me to be."

He swallows hard, his voice hoarse. "Just don't shut me out."

Everything inside me trembles, the world tilting, my control shattering into a thousand fucking pieces.

I've spent my whole life surviving.

Building walls.

Keeping people at a distance because when you let them in, they always leave.

But Damien is standing here, giving me a choice.

He's offering me everything.

His love. His loyalty. His promise.

And I don't know if I have it in me to walk away.

The space between us feels like a loaded gun.

My chest rises and falls in shallow, unsteady breaths, my body vibrating with the effort to keep standing, to hold on to the last fraying strands of my resolve.

Damien sees it.

Of course he does.

He's always been able to read me, to know what I'm thinking before I even say it. He knows I'm standing on the edge, that one more push will send me falling.

But he's not rushing me.

Not pushing.

Not demanding.

Instead, he moves carefully, like I'm something fragile. Breakable.

And fuck him—because I am.

Slowly, deliberately, he closes the distance between us, step by agonizing step, giving me every opportunity to run.

I don't.

I should.

But my feet don't move. My body betrays me, rooted in place, my lungs barely pulling in air as he stops just close enough that I can feel his heat.

Not touching. Not yet.

Just waiting.

"You don't have to say anything." His voice is quiet, raw, aching with emotion. "You don't have to forgive me right now. You don't even have to decide anything tonight."

I squeeze my eyes shut, my fingers curling into fists, my nails digging into my palms as my entire world tilts beneath me.

"But I need you to know something," he murmurs, his voice so soft, so reverent, like a confession he's never said aloud before.

I can't look at him.

I can't.

Because if I do, I will break.

I will fucking shatter.

"The first time I saw you," he breathes, "you weren't even looking at me."

A ragged inhale rips through me, my chest burning.

"You were standing at the hostess stand in Ember & Ash," he continues, his voice dipping into something low, something devastatingly intimate.

My lips part, my breath hitching, my stomach twisting itself into knots.

"And I swear to God, Elena," his voice breaks, and when I finally force myself to lift my eyes to his, what I see in them—the wrecked, unguarded emotion written all over his face—destroys me.

"I knew right then—right fucking then—that if you weren't in my world, nothing I built in it would ever mean a goddamn thing."

The last piece of my resistance shatters into dust.

A choked sob breaks free, my hands shaking, my chest splitting open, and before I can fall—

Damien catches me.

His arms wrap around me, pulling me flush against him, and I don't fight it.

I let go. I let go of it all.

And he's right there to hold me together.

Chapter 40

Elena breaks apart in my arms, and I hold her like my fucking life depends on it.

Because it does.

I bury my face in her hair, my arms wrapped so tightly around her that I don't know if I'm keeping her from falling apart or if she's the only thing keeping me from doing the same.

Her fingers clutch at my shirt, gripping me, anchoring herself. Broken sobs spill against my throat, and each one cuts me deeper than the last.

"I was so scared," she chokes out. "I was so—"

"I know, baby." My voice is wrecked as I cup the back of her head, pressing my lips to her temple. "I know. I'm so fucking sorry."

I sway us gently, whispering soft, broken words against her hair, against her skin, breathing her in, absorbing her pain.

I did this. I caused this.

And I will spend the rest of my life making it right.

Minutes pass. Maybe hours. Time doesn't fucking exist when she's in my arms, when she's trembling against me.

But slowly—so slowly—her body stops shaking. Her sobs quiet. Her breathing evens.

I hold her tighter, pressing my lips into her hair, whispering against her scalp. "I've got you." Another kiss. "I'll always have you."

She doesn't pull away.

I shift slightly, angling her face to me, brushing a kiss to her temple. "I love you, Elena." A kiss to her cheek. "I'll never hurt you like that again." A kiss to the delicate line of her jaw. "You're everything to me."

Her breath catches, her fingers curling into the fabric of my suit, holding on like I'm the only thing keeping her tethered to the ground.

I cup her face, wiping away the last of her tears with my thumbs. Her lips are parted, her hazel eyes swimming with emotion, and fuck, I need to taste her. To feel her. To remind both of us that we're still here, still together.

I tilt her chin up.

Our mouths meet in the barest brush of lips—hesitant, aching—a kiss that feels like a prayer.

But then she sighs, and that sound—fuck, that sound—undoes me.

The dam breaks.

I groan, pulling her flush against me, my fingers tangling in her hair as I kiss her deeply, hungrily. She answers with a whimper, her arms winding around my neck as she presses into me, her body molding to mine.

The soft, slow desperation between us ignites into something scorching, something feral. Teeth, tongues, the slide of mouths that have been apart for too long.

She's fire. She's home. She's mine.

And this time, I'm never letting her go.

She pulls back just enough to catch her breath, her forehead pressed against mine, her fingers still tangled in my hair. Her lips are swollen, her breathing unsteady, but it's the way she looks at me that wrecks me completely.

Like I'm the only man in the world. Like I'm hers.

Her thumb brushes along my jaw, tracing the stubble there, and her voice is barely above a whisper when she speaks.

"I love you too, Damien."

I swear to fucking God, the words nearly drop me to my knees.

She swallows, her eyes searching mine, as if making sure I understand the weight of what she's saying.

"I think I've loved you since that first night. Since I sat down next to you, and you looked at me like I was something worth wanting." A shaky breath escapes her, but she doesn't stop. "And every moment after that— every glance, every touch, every time you looked at me like I was the only thing that mattered—I just fell even harder."

I cup her face, my chest tightening with something fierce, something unbreakable. "You are the only thing that matters."

A tear slips down her cheek, but this one isn't from pain. It's something else. Something raw and real.

She lets out a soft, breathless laugh, shaking her head. "I love you so much, I feel fucking ridiculous."

I don't let her say another word.

I kiss her again, deep and consuming, pouring everything I feel into her—every ounce of love, every promise, every fucking shred of devotion I have left to give.

She melts into me, kissing me back just as fiercely, just as desperately, and I know, right then and there—this is it.

This is forever.

I brush my thumb across her cheek, drinking in every detail of her face—the flush of emotion still warming her skin, the slight part of her lips, the way her eyes soften as she looks at me.

"Come back with me," I murmur. "Come home."

Her breath catches.

Not my home. Ours.

The weight of it lingers between us, unspoken but felt in every charged second that passes. It should feel fast. Two weeks. That's all we've had. But fuck, when has time ever dictated what's right? When has anything about us ever followed the rules?

"Okay." She says it so softly, but it drops within me like an anchor.

Her lips twitch, and I recognize the faintest hint of a smile breaking through. "Besides," she says, voice laced with something teasing, something lighter than the storm we've just weathered, "my driver pulled away, so I need a ride anyway."

I huff out a laugh, shaking my head, unable to stop

myself from brushing my lips over hers again—just a quick, teasing taste. "Nothing but trouble."

She hums, pressing her hands to my chest. "And you love it."

"Fucking right, I do."

I lace our fingers together, leading her toward the door, the weight that's sat on my chest for days finally easing as we step outside and toward the waiting limo.

Elena slides into the limo first, the dim interior lighting casting a soft glow over her as she settles onto the leather seat.

I climb in after her, barely getting the door shut before she moves.

The second the latch clicks, she grabs my tie and yanks me toward her, closing the space between us in an instant.

A startled breath leaves me—more of a growl than anything—before her lips crash against mine, all heat and desperation, taking exactly what she wants.

Me.

I barely have time to process it before instinct takes over —before my hands are in her hair, tilting her head just the way I know she likes. Before I'm groaning against her mouth and letting her fucking devour me.

Everything fucking ignites.

This kiss isn't like the one at the bakery.

This is need. This is hunger. This is possession.

Her fingers slide into my hair, her body pressing against mine, and I'm done fucking waiting.

My hands find her thighs, spreading her wide as I drag her onto my lap.

She gasps into my mouth, and I use it to my advantage —sliding my tongue against hers, swallowing every sound she makes.

Her dress slides up her thighs, her body rocking against me, and I groan into her lips.

"Fuck, Elena."

"Damien—"

I can't take it anymore.

I flip us, laying her flat against the leather seat, my hands gripping her knees and spreading her apart.

"I've dreamed about this." My voice is dark, wrecked. "Twice, to be honest."

Her breath hitches. "Only twice?"

I silence her when I rip her panties from her body. "And tonight, I'm making it a fucking reality."

I drag my lips down her body, over the curve of her thigh, down to the place that's soaking wet for me.

"If you keep that up, at this rate, I'll be walking around with no panties on."

I groan at the thought of her pretty pussy on display for me and have to actually squeeze my hard cock to alleviate some of the fucking pain.

"That's fine with me."

I speak the words against her cunt a second before my mouth is on her, claiming what's mine.

She cries out, her back arching, her nails digging into my scalp as my tongue slides through her.

I flick her clit, lapping at her like she's the only thing keeping me alive.

She thrashes, her heels digging into my back, her hips rocking against my mouth.

"Damien, please—"

I slide two fingers into her, curling them against that sweet, soft spot that makes her fall apart for me.

And fuck—she does.

Her entire body tenses, her breath catching, her pussy squeezing my fingers like a vice.

And then she falls apart. Her gasps and moans are loud, wrecked, and perfect.

I lap up every drop, savoring her, worshipping her.

And when she finally comes down, when her body stops trembling, when her breath steadies, she pushes me back.

"I need you, Damien," she whispers, climbing onto my lap, straddling me.

Her dress slides down her arms, pooling at her waist—and fuck—her tits spill free, bouncing as she unbuckles my pants.

In seconds, she's gripping my cock, lining me up, and then she's sinking down on me.

My head falls back, my hands digging into her hips as she takes me to the hilt.

"Christ, baby." I groan, gritting my teeth. "You feel like fucking heaven."

Her nails scrape down my chest, her walls clenching around me.

"Show me how much you missed me," she whispers, rolling her hips.

And fuck—I do.

I grip her thighs, thrusting up into her, my mouth dragging over her collarbone, her breasts, her throat.

Her moans fill the car, her body rocking against mine, and I know I will never fucking let her go again.

I grip her hips, guiding her movements, meeting her thrust for thrust as pleasure builds—sharp and blinding—between us.

Her name leaves my lips in a hoarse growl, her nails dig into my shoulders, and then—fuck—we're coming together.

She trembles in my arms, her body pulsing around me, and I hold her through it, pressing open-mouthed kisses against her neck, her jaw, anywhere I can reach as we come down from the high.

She's still straddling me, our bodies slick with sweat, our breath tangled in the space between us.

The world outside doesn't exist.

Just us. Just this.

Just the quiet after the storm, where everything feels whole again.

I reach into my jacket pocket, pulling out the small blue box protecting her diamond ring.

She stills, watching intently as I slide it back onto her finger, my gaze locking onto hers.

She blinks, her lips parting, a teasing smile playing at her mouth. "You told me this was just on loan."

A low chuckle rumbles through my chest as I tighten my grip on her hips. Mischievous little thing. "I lied."

Her brows lift, amusement flickering through her expression.

"As soon as I left that meeting with Lucian, I went straight into the jewelry store and bought it." I run my thumb over the band, the sight of it on her hand filling me with something fierce and unwavering. "The second I saw it, I knew how beautiful it would look on your finger."

She exhales, something unreadable flickering through her gaze before she bites her bottom lip, her smile growing.

"You're not going to ask me?"

I smirk, my hands tightening on her hips, keeping her firmly in place.

"Asking implies you have a choice to say no."

I lean in, my lips brushing against hers, my voice a low growl of possession and devotion all at once.

"We can go as slow as you need, baby but my mind is already made up." I place a tender kiss on her knuckles before I wrap my arms tight around her waist.

"You're mine, Elena. And I'm yours."

"Forever."

Her breath catches, her fingers tightening against my chest as she kisses me like she fucking means it.

Her kiss is fire and salvation, a promise sealed between us. Every shattered piece, every broken fragment, mended in this moment, reforged into something unbreakable.

This isn't just our reunion.

It's our beginning.

The start of something greater than anything I've built, anything I've claimed, anything I've fought for.

Because this—her, us, together—this is my legacy.

And I'll spend the rest of my life proving it.

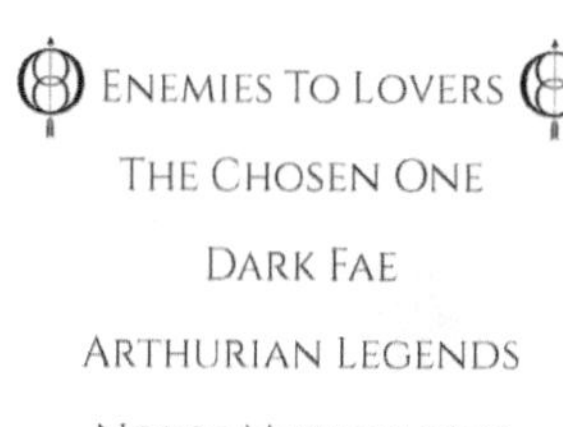